KERRY BARRETT was a bookworm from a very early age and did a degree in English Literature, then trained as a journalist, writing about everything from pub grub to *EastEnders*. Her first novel, *Bewitched, Bothered and Bewildered*, took six years to finish and was mostly written in longhand on her commute to work, giving her a very good reason to buy beautiful notebooks. Kerry lives in London with her husband and two sons, and Noel Streatfeild's *Ballet Shoes* is still her favourite novel.

Also by Kerry Barrett

The Forgotten Girl

A Step in Time

The Girl in the Picture

Kerry Barrett

ONE PLACE. MANY STORIES

HQ
An imprint of HarperCollins*Publishers* Ltd
1 London Bridge Street
London SE1 9GF

This paperback edition 2018

18 19 20 21 22 LSC 10 9 8 7 6 5 4 3 2 1
First published in Great Britain by
HQ, an imprint of HarperCollins*Publishers* Ltd 2017
Printed and bound in the United States of America by LSC Communications

ISBN: 978-0-00-831259-6

I owe one big thank you to my lovely friend Becky Knowles. One day, as we strolled round an exhibition of Pre-Raphaelite paintings, she wondered aloud what it would have been like to have been a female artist at the time, and inadvertently gave birth to Violet Hargreaves.

I'd also like to thank my editor Victoria Oundjian for her help and support, and wish her lots of luck in her new role. And, as always, thanks to the team at HQ Digital, my family, friends and all my readers.

Chapter 1

Present day
Ella

'It's perfect,' Ben said. 'It's the perfect house for us.'

I smiled at the excitement in his voice.

'What's it like?' I asked. I was in bed because I was getting over a sickness bug but suddenly I felt much better. I sat up against the headboard and looked out of the window into the grey London street. It was threatening to rain and the sky was dark even though it was still the afternoon.

'I'll send you some pictures,' Ben said. 'You'll love it. Sea view, of course, quiet but not isolated …' He paused. 'And …' He made an odd noise that I thought was supposed to be a trumpet fanfare.

'What?' I said, giggling. 'What else does it have?'

Ben was triumphant. 'Only a room in the attic.'

'No,' I said in delight. 'No way. So it could be a study?'

'Yes way,' sad Ben. 'See? It's made for us.'

I glanced over at my laptop, balanced on the edge of my dressing table that doubled as a desk, which in turn was squeezed into the corner of our bedroom. We'd been happy here in this poky terraced house. Our boys had been born here. It was safe here. But this was a new adventure for us, no matter how terrifying I found the thought. And just imagine the luxury of having space to write. I looked at my notes for my next book, which were scattered over the floor, and smiled to myself.

'What do the boys think?' I asked.

'They're asleep,' Ben said. 'It's pissing down with rain and we're all in the car. I rang the estate agent and he's on his way, so I'll wake the boys up in a minute.'

'Ring me back when he arrives,' I said. 'FaceTime me, in fact. I want to see the house when you do.'

'Okay,' Ben said. 'Shouldn't be long.'

I ended the call and leaned back against my pillow. I was definitely beginning to feel much better now and I'd not thrown up for a few hours, but I was glad I'd not gone down to Sussex with Ben because I was still a bit queasy.

I picked up my glass of water from the bedside table and held it against my hot forehead while I thought about the house. It had been back in the spring when we'd spotted it, on a spontaneous weekend away. Ben had a job interview at a football club in Brighton. Not just any job interview. THE job interview. His dream role as chief physio for a professional sports team – the job he'd been working towards since he qualified. Great money, amazing opportunities.

The boys and I had gone along with him at the last minute and while Ben was at the interview, I'd wandered the narrow lanes of Brighton with Stanley in his buggy and Oscar scooting along beside me. I had marvelled at the happy families I saw around me and how my mood had lifted when I saw the sea, twinkling in the sunshine at the end of each road I passed. That day I felt like anything was possible, like I should grab every chance of happiness because I knew so well how fleeting it could be.

The next day – after Ben had been offered the job – we'd driven to a secluded beach, a little way along the coast, and sat on the shingle as the boys ran backwards and forwards to the surf.

'I love it here,' I said, shifting so I could lie down with my head resting on Ben's thigh and looking up at the low cliffs that edged the beach. I could see the tops of the village houses that overlooked the sea and, on the cliff top, a slightly skew-whiff To Let sign.

'I wish we could live here,' I said, pointing at the sign. 'Up there. Let's rent that house.'

Ben squinted at me through the spring sunshine. 'Yeah, right,' he said. 'Isn't that a bit spontaneous for you?'

I smiled. He was right. I'd never been one for taking risks. I was a planner. A checker. A researcher. I'd never done anything on a whim in my entire life. But suddenly I realized I was serious.

'I nearly died when Stanley was born,' I said, sitting up and looking at him. 'And so did Stanley.'

Ben looked like he was going to be sick. 'I know, Ella,' he said gently. 'I know. But you didn't – and Stan is here and he's perfect.'

We both looked at the edge of the sea where Stanley, who was now a sturdy almost-three-year-old, was digging a hole and watching it fill with water.

'He's perfect,' Ben said again.

I took his hand, desperate to get him to understand what I was trying to say. 'I know you know this,' I said. 'But because of what happened to my mum I've always been frightened to do anything too risky – I've always just gone for the safe option.'

Ben was beginning to look worried. 'Ella,' he said. 'What is this? Where's it come from?'

'Listen,' I said. 'Just listen. We've lived in the same house for ten years. I don't go on the tube in rush hour. I wouldn't hire jet skis on our honeymoon. I'm a tax accountant for heaven's sake. I don't take any risks. Ever. And suddenly I see that it's crazy to live that way. Because if life has taught me anything it's that even when you're trying to stay safe, bad things happen. I did everything right, when I was pregnant. No booze, no soft cheese – I even stopped having my high-lights done although that's clearly ridiculous. And despite all that, I almost died. Oscar almost lost his mum, just like I lost mine. And you almost lost your wife. And our little Stanley.'

'So what? Three years later, you're suddenly a risk taker?' Ben said.

I grimaced. 'No,' I said. 'Still no jet skis. But I can see that some risks are worth taking.' I pointed up at the house on the cliff. 'Like this one.'

'Really?' Ben said. I could see he was excited and trying not to show it in case I changed my mind. 'Wouldn't you miss London?'

I thought about it. 'No,' I said, slowly. 'I don't think I would. Brighton's buzzy enough for when we need a bit of city life, and the rest of the time I'd be happy somewhere where the pace of life is more relaxed.'

I paused. 'Can we afford for me to give up work?'

'I reckon so,' Ben said. 'My new job pays well, and …'

'I've got my writing,' I finished for him. Alongside my

deathly dull career in tax accountancy, I wrote novels. They were about a private investigator called Tessa Gilroy who did all the exciting, dangerous things I was too frightened to do in my own life. My first one had been a small hit – enough to create a bit of a buzz. My second sold fairly well. And that was it. Since I'd had Stan, I'd barely written anything at all. My deadlines had passed and my editor was getting tetchy.

'Maybe a change of scenery would help,' I said, suddenly feeling less desperate when it came to my writing. 'Maybe leaving work, and leaving London, is just what I need to unblock this writer.'

That was the beginning.

Ben started his job at the football club, commuting down to Sussex every day until we moved, and I handed in my notice at work. Well, it was less a formal handing in of my notice and more a walking out of a meeting, but the result was the same. I was swapping the dull world of tax accountancy for writing. I hoped.

My phone rang again, jolting me out of my memories.

'Ready?' Ben said, smiling at me from the screen.

'I'm nervous,' I said. 'What if we hate it?'

'Then we'll find something else,' said Ben. 'No biggie.'

I heard him talking to another man, I guessed the estate agent, and I chuckled as the boys' tousled heads darted by.

It wasn't the best view, of course, on my phone's tiny screen, but as Ben walked round the house I could see enough to know it was, indeed, perfect. The rooms were big; there was a huge kitchen, a nice garden that led down to the beach where we'd sat all those months before, and a lounge with a stunning view of the sea.

'Show me upstairs,' I said, eager to see the attic room.

But the signal was patchy and though I could hear Ben as he climbed the stairs I couldn't see him any more.

'Three big bedrooms and a smaller one,' Ben told me. 'A slightly old-fashioned bathroom with a very fetching peach suite …'

I made a face, but we were renting – I wasn't prepared to risk selling our London place until we knew we were settled in Sussex – so I knew I couldn't be too fussy about the décor.

'… and upstairs the attic is a bare, white-painted room with built-in cupboards, huge windows overlooking the sea, and stripped floorboards,' Ben said. 'It's perfect for your study.'

I couldn't speak for a minute – couldn't believe everything was working out so beautifully.

'Really?' I said. 'My attic study?'

'Really,' said Ben.

'Do the boys like it?'

'They want to get a dog,' Ben said.

I laughed with delight. 'Of course we'll get a dog,' I said.

'They've already chosen their bedrooms and they've both run round the garden so many times that they're bound to be asleep as soon as we're back in the car.'

'Then do it,' I said. 'Sign whatever you have to sign. Let's do it.'

'Don't you want to see the house yourself?' Ben said carefully. 'Check out schools. Make sure things are the way you want them?'

Once I would have, but not now. Now I just wanted to move on with our new life.

'Do you want to talk to your dad?'

'No.' I was adamant that wasn't a good idea because I knew he'd definitely try to talk us out of it. I'd not told him anything about our move yet. He didn't even know I'd handed in my notice at work – as far as he was aware, Ben was going to stick with commuting and I'd carry on exactly as I'd been doing up until now.

I got my cautious approach to life from my dad and I spent my whole time trying very hard not to do anything he wouldn't approve of. I'd never had a teenage rebellion, sneaked into a pub under age, or stayed out five minutes past my curfew. I'd chosen my law degree according to his advice – he was a solicitor – and then followed his recommendations for my career.

This move was the nearest I'd ever got to rebelling and I knew Dad would be horrified about me giving up my safe job, about Oscar changing schools, and us renting out our house. And even though moving to Sussex would mean we lived much nearer him, I thought that the less he knew of our plans, the better.

'We could come down again next weekend,' Ben was saying. 'When you're feeling well?'

'No,' I said, making my mind up on the spot. 'I don't want to risk losing the house. We were lucky enough that it's been empty this long, let's not tempt fate. Sign.'

'Sure?' Ben said.

'I'm sure.'

'Brilliant,' he said, and I heard the excitement in his voice again, along with something else – relief perhaps. He would be pleased to leave London.

'Ella?'

'Yes?'

'I've been really happy,' he said softly. 'Really happy. In London, with you, and the boys. But this is going to be even better. I promise. It's a leap of faith, and I know it's scary and I know it's all a bit spontaneous, but if we're all together it'll be fine.'

I felt the sudden threat of tears. 'Yes,' I said.

'We're strong, you and me,' Ben said. 'And Oscar and Stan. This is the right thing for us to do.'

'I know,' I said. 'We're going to be very happy there.'

Chapter 2

From then I barely had time to draw breath, which was lucky really. If I'd had time to think about what we were doing I'd have changed my mind, because the truth was I was absolutely terrified about the move.

On paper, the house was perfect and I trusted Ben's judgement. And it wasn't as if I hadn't been involved, I told myself, when all my worries about how I'd not even seen our new home surfaced. I'd spotted it first. I'd seen it on FaceTime and on the estate agent's website. I'd been part of the decision-making from the start.

So, I concentrated on the fact that we'd found a tenant for our London house with almost indecent haste. I worked out whether our battered sofa would fit in the new lounge, and if the boys would need new beds, and I dreamed of having my own study, a haven, tucked away in the attic room.

The one fly in the ointment was Dad. I had to tell him we were moving of course. So one day, a week or so before we finally went and just before I finished work, I took a half-day and drove down to Kent to see him and my step-mum, Barb.

'I thought we could go for a late lunch at the pub,' I said when I arrived, thinking that if I told Dad the news in public, it might go better. I breathed a sigh of relief when Barb and Dad agreed, so we all strolled along the road towards their local. Truth be told, I had no idea how Dad would react because I'd never done anything he didn't agree with before.

'He might be fine,' Ben had said. 'I think you're overthinking this. He just wants you to be happy.'

But I wasn't sure. I was scared my whole relationship with my dad was conditional on me doing what he wanted me to do. I knew he would be nervous about the risk we were taking, and he'd expect me to listen to his concerns, and then announce he was right and change my mind. But I wasn't going to do that this time – and that's why I was so worried.

I'd grown up, with Dad, in Tunbridge Wells. Dad didn't live in the same house any more because he and Barb – who I loved to bits – had moved when they got married, soon after I started university. It wasn't far from where we'd lived when I was a kid, but far enough, if you see what I mean.

'So how's Ben's job going?' Dad asked, as we settled down at our table.

'Good,' I said. 'Really good.'

'Dreadful commute,' Dad said.

'Awful,' I agreed. 'And that's why we've made a decision.'

Dad and Barb looked at me as I took a breath and explained what we were doing.

'It's a lovely house,' I said. 'And we're just renting, though Ben says the landlord mentioned he'd be willing to sell if we like it.'

Barb smiled at me.

'It sounds wonderful,' she said. 'But won't it mean you commuting instead?'

There was a pause.

'Well,' I said. 'Actually.'

Dad took his glasses off and rubbed the bridge of his nose and I felt my confidence beginning to desert me.

'Actually?' he prompted.

'Actually, I've handed in my notice,' I said. I picked up my sparkling water and swigged it, wishing it was gin.

Barb and Dad looked at each other.

'That's a big decision,' Barb said carefully.

'It is,' I said. 'But we're confident it's the right thing to do. Ben's salary is good enough for us to live on, and I've got my writing.'

Dad nodded as though he'd reached a decision. 'You'd be best taking a sabbatical,' he said. 'What did they say when you asked about that? If they said no, you've probably got cause to get them to reconsider. I can speak to Pete at my old firm, if you like? He's the expert on employment law ...'

'Dad,' I said. 'I didn't ask about a sabbatical, because I don't want to take a sabbatical. I'm leaving my job and I'm going to write full-time. It's all planned.'

Dad looked at me for a moment. 'No, Ella,' he said. 'It's too risky. What if Ben's job doesn't work out? Or the boys don't settle? Have you checked out the school for Oscar? He's a bright little lad and he needs proper stimulation. And don't even think about selling your house in London. Once you leave London you can never go back, you know. Not with house prices the way they are.'

'Dad,' I said again. 'It's fine. We know what we're doing.'

'I'll phone Pete, now,' Dad said. 'Now where did I put that blasted mobile phone?'

'Dad,' I said, sharply this time. 'Stop it.'

Dad winced. 'Keep your voice down, Ella,' he said. 'What's wrong?'

I shook my head. 'I knew this is how you'd act,' I said. 'I knew you wouldn't want me to give up work, or for us to move house.'

'I just worry,' Dad said.

I felt a glimmer of sympathy for him. Of course he worried. But I wasn't his little girl any more and we didn't have to cling to each other as though we were drowning, like we'd done when I was growing up.

'Don't,' I said, more harshly than I'd intended. 'Don't worry. I'm fine. Ben's fine. The boys are fine.'

Barb put her hand over Dad's as though urging him to leave things there, but Dad being Dad didn't get the message.

'I think I should phone Pete,' he said. 'Just in case.'

I pushed my chair back from the table and stood up. 'Do not pick up your phone,' I said. 'Don't you dare.'

Dad and Barb both looked stunned, which wasn't surprising. I'd never raised my voice to Dad before. I'd never even disagreed with his choice of takeaway on movie night.

'Ella,' Dad said. 'I think you're over-reacting a bit.'

But that made me even more determined to put my point across.

'I'm not over-reacting,' I said. 'I want you to understand what's happening here. I'm leaving my job, and we are moving to Sussex. Which, by the way, means we will be nearer to you than we are now. I thought you'd be pleased about that.'

My voice was getting shriller and I felt close to tears, but as Dad stared at me, shocked into silence, I continued. 'I know it's risky, but we have decided it's a risk worth taking. Because, Dad, you know better than anyone that things can go wrong in the blink of an eye. You know that.'

Dad nodded, still saying nothing.

'So it's happening. And I knew you wouldn't approve. And I'm sorry if this makes me difficult. Or if me doing something that you don't like means you don't want me in your life any more. But it's happening.'

'Ella …' Dad began. 'Ella, I don't understand.'

'Oh you understand,' I said, all my worries about the move and about telling him spilling over. My voice was laden with venom as I leaned over the table towards him. 'You understand. I've always been a good girl and done what you wanted me to do, haven't I?'

Dad still looked bewildered and later – when I went over and over the conversation (if you could call it a conversation when it was really only me talking) in my head – I saw the genuine confusion in his face, the hurt in his eyes, and it broke my heart. But at the time, all I thought of was that I'd been proved right.

'For the first time in my whole life, I'm doing what I want to do,' I said. 'And it's not what you want me to do but I'm going to do it anyway.' I picked up my bag. 'And you can't send me away this time – because I'm going.'

Ignoring Dad's shocked expression and Barb's comforting hand on his arm, I threw my coat over my shoulder and marched out of the pub, and down the road to my car, where I sat for a while, sobbing quietly into my hands. I wasn't sure what had just happened and I had a horrible feeling that I'd got everything wrong.

Chapter 3

I drove home from Kent in a bit of a daze, ignoring my phone as it lit up with missed calls from Dad. And I carried on screening our landline and my mobile – avoiding any calls from him and Barb – for the next few days while we packed up our house and said goodbye to our friends in London.

'Phone him,' Ben said as I was getting dressed ready for my last day in the office. I ignored him.

'I won't be late,' I said. 'I'm not going to stay for drinks or anything like that.'

I looked at my reflection in the mirror. Hair neatly twisted up and out of the way, smart suit, sensible shoes.

'I'm going to throw this outfit away,' I said. 'And I'm going to cut my hair.'

'Good for you,' Ben said. He was still in bed because he'd got the day off to finish packing, sitting up drinking a cup of tea and reading a biography of a footballer I'd never heard of. 'Phone your dad from the hairdresser's.'

I scowled at him. 'I'll phone him when we're settled,' I said. 'Invite him down for a weekend. It will be fine.'

But I wasn't sure it would be.

As we pulled up outside the house on moving day, I felt

my nerves bubbling away in my stomach. I knew what the house looked like, of course, but seeing it in real life, up close instead of peering at its roof from down on the beach, made it all seem – suddenly – like a very big decision for Ben to have made on my behalf. All of Dad's warnings about the risk we were taking, and having no safety net were weighing heavily on my mind.

It wasn't a pretty house, I thought, as I pulled the car on to our new drive. It squatted at the end of the lane, at right angles to the other houses, with its back to the sea. It was the back view we'd seen all those months ago from the beach – and the back view was a lot prettier than the front, I now realized. It was built from reddish brick, and it had three storeys and white-painted gables. It had a higgledy-piggledy extension on the side and mismatched windows.

It was about as far away as it was possible to be from the chocolate-box cottage everyone imagined when we said we were moving to Sussex. But Ben was adamant that it was completely right – even the fact that it had stayed empty from the time we'd spotted the to-let board from the beach until the time we'd been ready to move was a sign, he claimed. I heard him telling friends that it was exactly the house we'd have designed for ourselves if we'd had the chance. I hoped he was right and that Dad was wrong. My spontaneity seemed to have abandoned me now we were actually starting our new lives.

I pulled up the handbrake and Ben grinned at me. I smiled back. His enthusiasm was infectious and despite my worries, deep down I did feel like this was a new start for us. I peered out of the car window at our new home. The house had probably been quite grand once, but now it looked slightly forgotten and in need of TLC. Maybe we'd give the house a new lease of life, I thought. I'd even wondered whether, if we bought it, we could add a conservatory on the back where we could sit and look at the sea.

Ben grabbed my hand as I went to undo my seatbelt.

'It's not too late to change your mind,' he said in a murmur so the boys wouldn't hear. 'We can turn round now and go back to London if you want.'

I felt a wave of nerves again. Now I'd given up work, Ben was going to be shouldering the financial burdens of the family. So far it had been fine, but there was a lot of pressure on him at the football club. They had a lot of very valuable players and the legs Ben was looking after were worth millions – or so he kept telling me. This was his big break and he had to make it work.

Meanwhile, after months and months of not writing anything, I'd told my editor, Lila, I was going to start. But I was regretting that a bit now because I had no ideas, even less motivation, and Lila was breathing down my neck desperate for words. I was worried Ben was putting too much pressure on himself and putting too much faith in the house. What if I couldn't write any more? What if Ben's job didn't work out? Was it all a terrible mistake, just like Dad had warned me it could be?

I took a breath. 'Of course I don't want to go back to London,' I said, as much to myself as to him, squeezing his hand. 'This is absolutely the right thing for us to do.'

Ben looked at me for a second, then he squeezed my hand back. 'So let's move in,' he said.

I leaned over to unstrap Stan's car seat. 'Everything's going to work out perfectly,' I said firmly.

'In this perfect house, with this perfect family?' Ben said, chuckling with what I thought was relief. Or maybe he was just as nervous as I was? 'How could it not?'

He helped Stan clamber out of the car and then grabbed him for a cuddle. 'What do you think, little man?' he said. 'What do you think of your new home?'

Stan whacked him on the head with a wooden Thomas the Tank Engine. 'Nice,' he said. 'This is a nice house.'

Oscar yanked my hand. 'Come. ON. Come on, Mummy.'

He dragged me out of the car and up the path.

'Hurryuphurryuphurryup,' he breathed as he pulled me along. I laughed in delight and threw the car key to Ben so he could lock up.

Stan wriggled out of Ben's hug and raced to join his brother and me. I felt Ben's eyes on us as he beeped the car doors and followed. We had to make this work, I thought. But he was right. How could it not?

'The door should be open,' Ben called.

Oscar grabbed the handle and it opened. 'Mummy, Mummy,' he gasped as we all fell through the front door. 'Look at the staircase.'

'Staircase, Mummy,' Stan echoed.

'Mummy, can we get a dog? Daddy said we could get a dog. So can we?'

I let myself be dragged around the house, laughing, as the boys and Ben fell over themselves to be the first to show me things.

'Look, Mummy, there's a fridge,' said Oscar proudly as I admired the large, if slightly dated, kitchen.

Sunlight streamed through the windows, which were gleaming. The whole house was sparkling clean, actually. Ben said the estate agent – Mike – had arranged for it to be done as it had been empty for a while. It all shone in the sunshine and the house was filled with light but strangely all I felt was dark.

Ben was so proud as he showed me round; I could see he really loved the house. And me? Well, I felt a bit funny. Like it wasn't really ours. Probably I just had to get used to it; that was all. Get all our belongings in there. Settle down. It just all seemed a bit temporary and that made me nervous.

'It's wonderful,' I said, squeezing his arm. Suddenly desperate to get out of there, I muttered something about seeing the garden, and walked out of the French doors on to the lawn.

Listening to the boys' excited voices as they tore round the house, I wandered down to the end of the garden, breathing deeply, glad to be out of the house.

There was a line of trees at the end of the lawn, and behind them a rocky path led down to the narrow, stony beach where the waves crashed on to the shingle.

'Amazing,' I said out loud. It was incredible. I thought of our London house, with its tiny garden where the boys roamed like caged tigers. Here they could run. Burn off their energy in safety. Swim in the sea. Collect shells. It would be idyllic, I told myself. A perfect childhood in the perfect house.

Thinking of the house again made me shudder. I turned away from the sea and walked back across the grass towards the back door, but I couldn't quite bring myself to go inside. Instead I dropped down on to the lawn and sat, cross-legged, looking back at the house.

From the back it wasn't so ugly. It was all painted white – in stark contrast to the red brick front – so it dazzled in the bright sunshine and looked less thrown together. I was being silly, I thought sternly. It would be lovely living close to the sea and the light was beautiful. Maybe it would inspire me to write.

The sun went behind a cloud and I gazed up at the top of the house, trying to work out which windows belonged to the room that would be my new study.

There were two large windows on the top floor on this side, which I knew would bring light flooding into the room, and one smaller window. I suddenly felt excited about things again, so I decided to go upstairs and check out the room – Ben had been so enthusiastic and I wondered – hoped – if some of his glee would rub off on me and perhaps kick my writer's block into touch. But as I got to my feet, a movement at the top of the house caught my eye.

I glanced up and blinked. It looked like there was someone up there, framed in the attic window. I couldn't see them clearly but it certainly looked like a figure.

My mouth went dry. 'Ben,' I squawked, hoping it was him up there. 'Ben.'

Ben appeared at the French windows from the lounge. I looked at him then looked back up at the window. There was nothing there. I'd been imagining it.

'What's the matter?' he said. 'What's wrong?'

I forced a smile. 'I thought I saw someone upstairs,' I said. 'I'm seeing things now – I must be tired. Where are the boys?'

Ben stepped into the garden, blinking in the bright sunlight. 'They're in the kitchen,' he said. 'Where did you see someone?'

I pointed to the window, and as I did, the sun came out from behind the cloud and reflected off the glass, dazzling me. 'Must have been a trick of the light,' I said, squinting.

'Must have been because there's no one there.' Ben nudged me gently. 'Come inside and have a cup of tea – I've unpacked the kettle. We're all tired and you could do with a break.'

Chapter 4

I let Ben guide me back to the house, telling myself it had been a trick of the light. There was that thing, wasn't there, where your mind makes people out of abstract shapes? It must have been that.

While Ben made tea I chatted mindlessly with the boys, reminding them about the beach, and wondering if they'd like to go for a paddle in the sea tomorrow. The house seemed too big and echoey without our furniture – where were those removal men?

I looked round. Rationally I knew this house was as ideal for our family as the garden was. It was just so different from our old place, and suddenly the leap we'd taken seemed way too big for us to cope with.

'Shall we explore some more?' I said, desperately trying to muster up some enthusiasm. The boys jumped at the chance and raced off upstairs. Ben and I followed more sedately. I was keen to get into the studio, but also nervous about what I might find; I was still unsure whether I'd seen someone at the window.

As the boys and Ben discussed which room Oscar wanted

and which room would be best for Stan, I took a deep breath and climbed the stairs to the attic.

It was empty – obviously – and it was also perfect. I grimaced a little unfairly at Ben being right about that, too. It was a big room, sloping with the eaves of the house to the front and with two huge windows to the back – the window where I thought I'd seen the figure standing was on the left. It had bare floorboards, painted white. The walls were also white, emulsion over brick, or over the old wallpaper in parts. It was cool and airy.

I wrapped my hands round my mug of tea and wandered to the window. The view was breathtaking and the light was incredible. It seemed to me like an artist's studio and I wondered if a former resident had painted up here. Surely someone had? I could think of no other use for the room. It wasn't a bedroom, or a guest room. The staircase to get up to the room was narrow and the door was small. I doubted you'd get a bed up there unless you took it up in pieces and built it in the room.

I looked down at the lawn where I'd sat earlier and glanced round to see if anything in the empty room could have given the appearance of a person. There was nothing.

Perching on the window ledge, as I always did back in London, I examined the studio with a critical eye. It wasn't threatening or scary. It was just a big, empty room. A big, empty, absolutely lovely room. What I'd said had been right: the figure must have just been a trick of the light. The sunshine was so bright in the garden, it could have reflected off the old glass in the window …

My thoughts trailed off as I realized something. From

downstairs, I'd seen two large windows and one small. Up here, there were only two large windows. That was weird.

Putting my empty mug on the windowsill, I went out into the hall. As far as I could tell there was nothing at the far end. No extra room, or door. The hairs on the back of my neck prickled. This was a strange place.

Tingling with curiosity – and feeling a little bit unsettled – I went back downstairs to the bedrooms.

Ben and the boys were in the biggest room, which also looked out over the garden. Stan's face was flushed and Oscar looked cross.

'Mummy,' he said as I walked in. 'I am meant to have this room because I am the biggest but Stan says he has to have it because he wants to watch for pirates on the sea.' His face crumpled. 'But I want to look for pirates too.'

'Bunk beds,' I said. 'We'll get you bunk beds and we can make them look like a ship. Then you can sail off at bedtime and look for pirates together.'

Ben shot me a grateful glance and I smiled at him.

'I've found something funny,' I said, casually. 'Can you come and see?'

Ben and the boys followed me up the narrow, rickety stairs to the attic room. We all stood in a line in the middle of the floor, staring out at the sea.

'Look,' I said. 'When I was in the garden, I could see three windows in this room. There were the two big ones, and a little one – remember?'

Ben nodded, realization showing on his face. 'But up here you can only see two windows,' he said. 'That's mental.'

He went over to one of the windows and pushed up the

sash, but it was fixed so it couldn't open too far. 'I thought I could lean out and see the other window,' he said. 'But I won't fit my head through that gap.'

'My head will fit,' said Oscar.

'No,' Ben and I said together.

Oscar looked put out. 'Maybe the little window is on next door's house,' he said.

Ben ruffled his hair. 'Good idea, pal. But next door isn't attached to our house. It's not like in London.'

I was standing still, staring at the windows, feeling a tiny flutter of something in my stomach. Was that excitement?

'You're loving this,' Ben said, looking at my face. 'One sniff of a mystery and you're in your element.'

He had a point.

'Oh come on,' I said. 'A missing window? Don't pretend you're not interested.'

He smiled at me, not bothering to deny it.

'Maybe there's a hidden room,' I said. 'Maybe it's a portal to Narnia.'

'Or maybe there's a ventilation brick in these old, thick walls.'

I snorted. 'Don't ruin it.'

Ben grinned. 'I think we'd notice if the house was bigger on the outside than the inside,' he said.

'Like the Tardis,' Oscar shouted in glee. Then he frowned. 'But the other way round.'

I started to laugh. 'I don't think you guys are taking this seriously enough,' I said, mock stern. 'This could be something very exciting.'

Ben nodded. 'Okay,' he said. 'I've got this.'

He went over to the wall at the far end of the room and tapped it. Then he tapped it again in a different place, and again and again. I sat down on the floor, with Stan on my lap, and watched.

'What are you doing?' I asked eventually.

Ben looked at me in pity. 'I'm checking to see if the wall sounds hollow,' he explained. 'If it sounds hollow then perhaps there's another room behind here.'

'Does it sound hollow?'

There was a pause.

'I don't know,' he admitted.

I laughed.

'Well then we need to compare it to the other walls,' I said.

And then there was chaos. Stan and Oscar raced around, banging the walls, as Ben and I listened and said, 'hmm'. We had no idea what we were listening for, but it was fun. The boys shouted, and we laughed, and I thought that maybe everything was going to be okay.

Chapter 5

1855
Violet

I almost slipped on the rocks as I struggled down to the beach, even though I'd been that way hundreds of times before. My easel wasn't heavy, but it was cumbersome, and the bag of paints and brushes I was carrying banged against my legs. Eventually, though, I found my perfect spot. It was warm, but the sun wasn't too dazzling and I breathed in the sea air deeply.

Working quickly, I set up my easel and pinned my paper down securely. I arranged my paints on the rock behind me, as I'd planned, pushed a stray lock of hair behind my ear, and picked up my brush. I paused for a second, appreciating the moment; I was completely content. This was how I'd dreamed of working for – oh months, years perhaps. I finally felt like a real painter. My room in the attic was wonderful, of course, and I would always be grateful to Philips, the lad from the village who did all the odd jobs around the house and garden and who'd helped me secretly create my own studio.

I frowned, thinking of Father, who didn't like me to draw. He said it was vulgar. He wanted me to marry and lead a normal life. A normal, boring life, I thought. A mundane life. A life with no purpose.

But out here, breathing in the sea air, I felt like I had a purpose. I was telling a story with my work and it seemed it was what I'd been waiting for. For years all I'd drawn was myself – and various kitchen cats. Endless self-portraits that helped my technique, undoubtedly, but – if I was honest – bored me stupid.

Then, one day, I'd picked up Father's *Times*, and read about a new group of artists known as the Pre-Raphaelite Brotherhood. They painted stories – Bible stories, tales from Shakespeare, all sorts – and they used real-life models to do it. It had been like a light turned on in my mind. Suddenly I knew what I wanted to do – I wanted to be like those artists. Paint like those artists. Live life like those artists.

After that, I devoured any articles on the Pre-Raphaelites in Father's newspaper, and I read the *Illustrated London News*, and even *Punch*, when I could get it, though Father wasn't keen on that one. I saved the issues that mentioned art and kept them hidden away with my drawing equipment.

The Times – and sometimes the other papers, too – were often critical of my heroes, who were determined to shake up the art world. But the more criticism they received, the more I adored them. They were so thrilling and forward-thinking – everything I wanted my life to be like.

I dreamed of living in London and imagined myself debating what makes good art with Dante Gabriel Rossetti – who was impossibly handsome in the pictures I'd seen – or John Millais – who had a kind, friendly face. I had to admit, I was hazy on the details of where these debates would take place – I had an uneasy feeling the painters I so admired spent a lot of time in taverns – but I knew just spending time with those men would make me feel alive.

'Why, Miss Hargreaves,' I imagined Dante or John saying. 'You are truly a force to be reckoned with.'

It wasn't just the men I admired. I had read that Elizabeth Siddal, who modelled for the painters and who was rumoured to be in love with Rossetti, had taken up painting herself. Oh, how I longed to be like her. Sometimes when I was feeling particularly vain, I thought I looked a bit like her, because I had long red hair, like hers.

Some people thought red hair was unlucky, but Lizzie made it look beautiful. She didn't hide it or twist it under her hat like I always had, so I had started wearing my hair loose now, too, when I could. When I was away from Father's disapproving eye. It got in my way and often irritated me but I thought it was all part of my plan – like venturing out to paint on the beach. After all, if Lizzie Siddal could be a painter, then why couldn't I, Violet Hargreaves, do the same?

Lost in my dreams of success, I painted swiftly, my brush flying over the paper. I was just painting the background today. I'd already sketched Philips, draped in a sheet that was strategically pinned to create royal robes and wearing a crown I'd found in my old dressing-up box. He was ankle-deep in a tin tray of water. He had been very willing to pose for me. He was so good to me, and though I was happy he was so amiable I did occasionally wonder if he was harbouring feelings for me that were, perhaps, inappropriate. Father would be furious.

Mind you, Father would be furious if he knew what I was doing now, I thought. He grudgingly allowed me to indulge my love of art as long as I was in the house and out of sight.

I'd never have dared go out to the beach if he hadn't gone up to London for the week.

I daubed white paint on the top of the waves I had painted, and stood for a second, gazing at the sea beyond the easel.

'King Canute turning back the tide?' a voice said behind me.

I jumped, feeling a scarlet blush rise up my neck to my cheeks. I hadn't expected to be interrupted, and I was horrified I had attracted anyone's attention.

'I'm sorry, I didn't mean to startle you.' It was a man, older than me, and handsome with a kind, intelligent face and bright blue eyes. I looked at my feet, not sure what to say. Father's disapproval of my painting stung, so I had never talked of it outside the house.

'It's very good,' the stranger said. 'Is this your own work?'

I nodded. I felt the man's eyes roam over me and I shifted on the sand uncomfortably.

'It's interesting that you're telling a classical story within a real landscape,' he said.

'I'm influenced by the Pre-Raphaelite Brotherhood.'

The man gazed at my painting and nodded slowly. 'Of course,' he said. 'I can see that.'

I gasped. He could tell? Maybe I was doing something right.

'I adore them,' I said, my words falling over each other as I spoke. 'They're wonderful. I want to paint detail like they do. The colours, and the form, of nature ...' I stopped, very aware that I was babbling and barely making sense.

But the man tipped his hat to me and smiled. 'I'm Edwin Forrest,' he said.

Recovering my composure, I bowed my head slightly. 'I'm pleased to make your acquaintance, sir,' I lied, wishing he would leave.

'Forgive me,' said Mr Forrest. 'It is very hot and I've been walking a while. Would you mind if I rested here?' He didn't wait for my answer, but took his hat off and sat on a large rock a little way from me.

I looked at him in horror. I didn't want an audience while I painted. And I certainly didn't want a man – a handsome man – at my shoulder. I was shy and uncomfortable around strangers at the best of times, and unknown men made me very uneasy.

'Please carry on,' Mr Forrest said. 'I'd love to see how you compose your work.'

Feeling self-conscious, but not wanting to argue, I picked up my brush again. I tried to carry on painting the waves, but I couldn't concentrate knowing Mr Forrest was watching. I felt his eyes on me, hot as sunlight, and my hand shook as I dabbed the paint on the paper.

I took a breath. 'I don't wish to be rude, sir,' I said. 'But would you mind continuing on your walk?'

I couldn't believe I'd spoken my mind so bluntly. But I was horribly aware that the time was ticking on and before I knew it, Father would be home and my chance to paint outdoors would be over.

'I'm so sorry, Miss …'

I managed a half-smile. 'Hargreaves. Violet Hargreaves.'

'Miss Hargreaves, please accept my most humble apologies for interrupting you.' Mr Forrest patted the rock next to him. 'I know your time is precious, but I wonder if we could talk a while. I'm very interested in the arts and I think we may be useful to one another.'

He flashed me a dazzling smile and I found myself thinking again how handsome he was. Despite my longing to be painting, I sat down next to him and arranged my skirt around my ankles. It was warm on the beach and I suddenly had an urge to pull off my petticoat and run into the cool sea. I shot a shy glance at my companion, wondering what he would do if I did.

'I have many friends in London who are interested in art,' he was saying.

'Yes?' I said, politely.

Mr Forrest looked out across the sea, as though he were trying to remember something. 'There is John Everett ...' He paused and I couldn't resist jumping in.

'Millais,' I said. 'Do you mean John Everett Millais?'

Mr Forrest gave me another dazzling smile. I felt a bit dizzy and wondered if it was the effect of too much sun.

'Indeed,' he said. 'Are you familiar with his work?'

I was sure my heart stopped, just for a moment. I almost couldn't speak. He knew Millais? My hero? 'Millais?' I gasped. 'Of course I know his work.'

'I know he is always keen to nurture young talent. So, I was wondering, do you have more?' Mr Forrest asked. 'More paintings like this?'

I nodded. I had three that were finished and many more sketches. My head was whirling.

'Could I take them to show John?'

'Show him my paintings?' I stammered.

'I think he'd be very interested,' Mr Forrest said. 'He

and the rest of the Brotherhood are always searching for interesting painters.'

'I know it's hard for women,' I said, feeling like I should be honest from the start. Despite my daydreams, I was painfully aware my options were limited. 'There aren't many female artists.'

'No,' Mr Forrest said, thoughtfully. 'But I believe there are a couple. I read just the other day about one Elizabeth ...'

Once more, I thought I might faint. 'Elizabeth?' I said. 'Lizzie Siddal?'

'Yes, she was a model but I read she's painting now,' said Mr Forrest, telling me nothing I didn't already know, but somehow it had more authority when it came from this man. 'Apparently, she's even got that critic, Ruskin, interested in her work.'

He glanced at me.

'John says she's rather good,' he said, in an offhand manner. Oh how I longed for someone to discuss my work in such a matter-of-fact way. I couldn't believe that this man, this handsome, charming man, was talking about my art in the same breath as he discussed my heroine Lizzie Siddal. I felt like all my dreams were finally coming true, as though all the hours painting alone in my studio, listening with dread for Father's tread on the stairs, were not for nothing. I was not going to let convention stop me telling Mr Forrest exactly how I felt.

With my heart in my mouth, I explained how much I wanted to go to London and become part of the art world. If I could just find a patron, I said, someone who believed in me, and who would take care of the bills while I could paint, then I could go.

Mr Forrest smiled. 'Dear girl,' he said. 'You certainly have the talent. I'm due in London later this month. Perhaps I could take one of your paintings with me then?'

I agreed at once, though I had no idea what Father would think if he found out. Could I possibly do this behind his back?

'Should I speak to your parents?' Mr Forrest said.

'No,' I almost shouted, before I collected myself. 'My mother is dead,' I explained. 'Father is, well, he doesn't think I should paint.'

Mr Forrest nodded in understanding. 'Some older people still think women shouldn't have a voice.' He put his hand close to mine where it lay on the rock. 'I disagree. I think you've got something very special, Miss Hargreaves. Let me mould that.'

I was giddy with joy. I looked out at the sea and allowed myself a little shiver of pleasure. This was it. Finally my life was beginning.

Chapter 6

1855
Frances

Frances was climbing the stairs when she saw him out of the staircase window. He was sitting on a rock with a girl, who couldn't be more than twenty, and who was gazing at him with adoring eyes.

She sighed. They'd only lived here a few weeks. Was it really starting again so soon?

Slowly, she carried on up the stairs into her dressing room. She couldn't see the beach from this window so she couldn't torment herself by watching him. Instead she sat down at her dressing table and examined herself in the mirror. Tilting her head, she looked at the bruising on her neck. It was definitely fading, finally. She pulled her dress down and leaned closer to the mirror. The marks on her collarbone and chest were fading too. She felt a wave of relief that she'd got away with it again.

She let her hand drift down on to her stomach, still flat, and thought of the tiny life flickering inside her. This time would be different. This time she would be careful. She shuddered as she remembered Edwin's face when she told him she was pregnant last time. He'd said nothing then, simply stared at her with no expression in his cold, blue eyes.

But later, when he came home from his club, brandy on his breath and fire in his belly, she knew she'd made a mistake.

The first punch – to the back of her head as she went to leave the room – sent her sprawling across the couch. And when she begged, 'Please, Edwin, the baby …' rage flared in his eyes. He hit her again and as she fell on the floor, he kicked her hard in the stomach. Sobbing, she crawled into the corner of the room and curled into a ball, while Edwin read the paper by the fire and ignored her quiet whimpers.

But when she felt a gush of blood between her legs and, despite her efforts, cried out, he was contrite. Back to his charming self, he carried her upstairs and tucked her into bed, smoothing her forehead and covering her with kisses.

'I'm sorry, my darling,' he whispered. 'We'll try again. I'm sorry, my darling.'

When the doctor came, Edwin was every inch the caring husband. But the doctor wasn't fooled. Edwin left the room, and the doctor looked grim-faced. He lifted her nightgown to feel her tender stomach and saw the livid bruise to her side.

'Does he have a temper, your husband?' he asked, pushing gently on her lower belly. Frances winced but said nothing. Shame flooded her.

'You must be more careful,' the doctor said. 'He's a busy man. An important man. Don't anger him.'

And with that, Frances knew she was alone. Which was why she'd come up with her plan. As soon as she'd realized she was expecting again she knew she had to get away. Edwin had gone from regarding her with a kind of benign disinterest when they were first married to vicious contempt and she knew if he realized she was pregnant – and desperate to be a mother – he'd punish her. As far as she knew he had no strong feelings either way about becoming a father but if he realized motherhood would make Frances happy, he'd take it away from her. Just to be cruel.

She was keeping money aside, squirrelling it away from the housekeeping and hiding it under a loose floorboard she'd found in her dressing room when they moved in. She'd been saving for years, if truth be told. She'd started putting some coins away almost as soon as she and Edwin had married. She knew from the start what sort of man he was, but her father was determined to see them wed and Frances couldn't disagree.

Since her father's death, and since Edwin took over the family law firm started by Frances's grandfather – the one he'd always had his eye on and the one, Frances thought, that had sealed her fate as his bride before he'd even met her – he'd felt no need to keep his true nature hidden any longer.

When they'd moved and she realized her nausea each morning was because she was pregnant again, she'd started working out a proper plan. As much as she wanted this baby fiercely, she felt the same passionate determination that Edwin would never know his son or daughter. She needed to get away – and that was what was driving her now. She thought she'd stay as long as she could, loosening her corset as much as she was able before her condition was obvious, and then she'd act. It was good to have everything in place before she went, because she couldn't afford for anything to go wrong.

After talking to some of the people in the village, she'd decided what to do; though it seemed drastic she wanted to be sure Edwin couldn't – or wouldn't – try to find her. So, she planned to take some clothes to the beach and leave them by the rocks. Maybe throw a hat into the waves and hope it washed up in the right place, or snag a piece of a gown onto a sharp stone. There was a nasty current in the sea, which had claimed the lives of many people over the years – she could easily be washed into the water as others had before. If she were lucky, she'd just become one more sad story of an unfortunate walker.

She planned to hide her suitcase behind the rocks in advance, and after setting the scene carefully, she'd change into simple clothes, the clothes of a maid or a governess, tuck her hair into a hat, and walk to the station. She was unremarkable in looks; she knew that. Plain, her grandmother had always said. Years ago, that made her think she was worthless, but now she thought the fact that no one glanced at her twice could save her life.

Once she was on the train, she'd change again, in case anyone remembered her cloak or hat, simple as they were. And she'd travel as far as she could afford. North, of course – you couldn't go south from Sussex and stay in England, and she couldn't speak French. She hadn't thought much further than that yet. All she cared about was getting away from here.

She went out on to the landing and looked down at the beach once more. Edwin was sitting closer to the girl now, and as she watched, he put his hand over hers. Frances allowed herself a brief fantasy where Edwin ran away with this girl and let her, Frances, be. But she knew that would never happen.

A shaft of sunlight lit up the girl's face and Frances realized she was even younger than she'd thought. Eighteen perhaps.

No older. The same age Frances had been when Edwin had pursued her. Perhaps it was the baby in her belly making her feel this way, but she suddenly felt a wave of fierce maternal protectiveness towards this girl with her loose skirts and messy red hair. She couldn't – wouldn't – let Edwin hurt her as well.

Chapter 7

Present day
Ella

As it turned out, the mere whiff of a mystery was all it took to help me start feeling at home in Sussex. Even a whole twenty-four hours without furniture ('satnav,' said the removal men vaguely when Ben quizzed them about where they'd been) didn't bother me too much, unless you counted the crick in my neck from sleeping on the floor.

While the removal guys unpacked everything, I played in the garden with the boys, mentally checking for hidden dangers. It didn't take me long to find one. At the bottom of our garden was a gate, which led on to a sandy path. The path snaked along the top of the cliff a short way, then plunged steeply down to the beach. I stood and looked with an appraising eye. The fence at the end of our garden was sturdy enough but the wooden gate was shut with only a latch. A latch that could easily be opened by a small, curious boy.

'Padlock,' I said, clapping my hands. 'Come on, boys. Let's go and explore the village.'

Heron Green wasn't a large village, but it was well equipped. We passed one pub and I knew there was another, at the far end near the boys' school. There was a small Tesco, a little bakery with a café area, a newsagent and – thankfully – a hardware shop. Outside there was a selection of brushes and brooms hanging up, and lots of different-sized dustbins.

'Let's try here,' I said to the boys, taking Stan's hand.

Inside it was bright and cheery with well-ordered shelves and several customers browsing. I looked round and decided I'd be much better off going straight to the counter, where an older man stood chatting to a slightly younger man who was buying a huge bag of nails. The older man had greying hair, and he wore a checked shirt with a pair of glasses in the top pocket – even though he had another pair perched on the end of his nose. He reminded me so much of my dad that my heart ached for a moment.

'What can I do for you, sir?' he asked Oscar, leaning over the counter.

I flashed him a smile and watched as my son put on his most serious face.

'We need a padlock for the gate at the bottom of the garden,' he said. 'To stop me and Stan being monkeys and going to the beach without Mummy.'

The man nodded. 'Very sensible,' he said. He reached behind him and took a lock from the shelf. 'This is what you need, young man. It's £9.99.'

He held out his hand and Oscar looked alarmed. 'Mummy does the paying,' he said.

I laughed. 'I certainly do.'

The man rang the purchase into the till, and the younger man, who was still choosing between bags of nails, looked at me.

'Just moved into the cliff house?' he asked.

I nodded, handing the shopkeeper a ten-pound note.

'Think so,' I said. 'It's the house on the cliff, anyway. We just call it number 10.'

He smiled. 'How do you find it?'

'It's great,' I said. 'Perfect.'

The shopkeeper handed me my receipt and gave Oscar the penny change.

'Me too,' said Stan.

The man grinned, opened the till again, and gave him a penny too.

'Fanks,' said Stan in his best North London accent.

'But?' said the younger man, exchanging a look with the shopkeeper.

I turned my attention back to him, blinking in surprise. 'But?'

'It sounded like there was a but coming,' he said. 'Perfect, but …'

I wondered how long these men had lived in the village and if they knew anything about the history of our house.

Leaning in slightly, I said: 'It's a funny house. Odd.'

The younger man, who had a shock of messy dark hair and a nose that looked like it had been broken more than once, nodded. 'You've heard the stories?'

Again I felt that flutter of interest and excitement. 'No,' I said. 'What stories?'

The shopkeeper tutted. 'Don't listen to him,' he said. 'Hal's always been one for a spooky tale.'

'Spooky?' I said in glee. 'Is it haunted? By someone who died tragically?'

Hal looked grave. 'It's not the dead you need to worry about. It's the living.'

41

I chuckled. 'Got that right.'

'I heard there was a murder,' Hal said. 'You've heard those tales, right, Ken?'

The shopkeeper – Ken – nodded. 'It's not true, though,' he said. 'I've lived here since the Seventies and no one's ever been killed since I was here.'

Hal looked thoughtful. 'Could have been before then,' he said. 'Sixties, perhaps? Or in the war?'

'Or it could all be codswallop,' Ken said.

The word made me smile, but I was interested and I wasn't going to let him change the subject.

'Maybe it wasn't a murder,' I said. 'Maybe it was another crime.'

'Robbery,' said Hal with relish. 'Or kidnapping.'

'Pirates,' added Oscar, who was listening intently.

Hal ruffled his hair. 'Definitely pirates,' he said. 'And smuggling.'

'Ooh yes,' I said, thinking of the Daphne du Maurier novels I'd read over and over when I was a teenager. 'Wreckers.'

Ken chuckled, eyeing me with interest. 'I remember now,' he said, nodding. 'My wife says you're a writer.' He looked at Hal. 'She writes books,' he said. 'Crime.'

Astonished at this first-hand experience of village life after years in anonymous London, I could only mutter, 'Well, more like thrillers, really.'

'Good ones?' Hal asked. 'Have I read them?'

'I hope they're good,' I said, embarrassed like I always was when people asked about my writing. 'They sell a bit. Not sure if you'll have read them. I'll bring you a copy and leave it here for you if you like?'

Hal grinned. 'I'll read it, and then I'll tell you if it's good,' he said.

I grinned back. 'Or,' I said, 'you could just say it's good even if you hate it.'

Gathering up the boys and the padlock, I said our good-byes and headed out of the shop.

'How about we see if that bakery sells cakes?' I said. Oscar clapped his hands.

'Excuse me?' I turned at the voice. A woman – who I'd seen in the hardware shop when we went in – was behind us, waving. She was tall and athletic-looking with inky dark hair pulled back into a ponytail and she was – I guessed – about seven months pregnant.

'Oh thank goodness you stopped,' she said waddling over. 'I'm not sure I'd have caught you if you hadn't.'

She had a Manchester accent and a broad smile.

'I'm Priya,' she said, sticking her hand out.

'Ella,' I said, cautiously. I may have moved to Sussex but I was still a Londoner at heart.

'I heard what you said in the shop,' she said, slightly breathless. 'About you writing crime novels?'

'Thrillers,' I said. Polite in case she was a reader, but still cautious. I took Stan's hand.

'Oh God, you probably think I'm a weirdo. I'm not,' she said, laughing. 'I promise.' She took a breath. 'I'm a police officer who's stuck on light duties because of this ...' She pointed to her bump. 'And I'm bored out of my mind. I thought maybe I could help you with research or something.'

I stared at her, not sure what to think.

'And we've not lived here very long either,' she said. 'And

I thought you seemed like someone I should be friends with, so I knew I had to catch you before I lost my nerve and didn't say hello.'

She laughed again, more nervously this time.

'I'm going to start again,' she said. 'Hello, I'm DI Priya Sansom from Sussex Police.'

She stuck her hand out again and I shook it again, smiling properly now.

'Ella Daniels,' I said. 'Writer, mother, former tax accountant. And new to rural friendliness.'

We smiled at each other. I thought Priya was right – she did seem like someone I could be friends with. I was glad she'd approached me.

'Cake, Mummy.' Stan tugged my arm.

'We were going to check out the café,' I said to Priya. 'Fancy a cuppa?'

Chapter 8

Priya was not as far along in her pregnancy as I'd thought.

'Five months,' she said, through a mouthful of coffee cake. 'Twins. Bit of a shock.'

'Got any more?'

She nodded glumly. 'Two,' she said. 'And two stepkids. All girls.'

'Whoa,' I said. 'But congratulations.'

She smiled. 'I'm excited really, but my husband's terrified these ones will be girls too. He's headmaster at Sussex Lodge School – which is all boys. So we can't even use the discount he gets on school fees.'

I giggled. I liked Priya already.

'Tell me about your books,' she said. 'What are you working on now?'

I made a face. 'I'm supposed to be writing my third novel featuring Tessa Gilroy, a maverick private investigator who inadvertently gets caught up in domestic mysteries.'

'Not going well?'

'Not going at all,' I admitted. 'I'm hoping moving down here will help unblock me.'

'Let me help you,' Priya begged. 'I'm so bored.'

'Bored?' I said. 'With four kids and two more on the way?'

She waved her hand as though six children was nothing more than an inconvenience.

'Jas is at university,' she said. 'Millie's in sixth form, but she's at her mum's most of the time anyway, so they're no trouble. Layla is eight and desperate to be like her big sisters, and Amber is five. She's quite the little princess and I think not being the baby any more will do her good.'

'I'm five,' said Oscar.

Priya looked at him. 'Then you will be in Amber's class at school. I'll bring her along next time we meet up and you can play together.'

I was pleased she thought there would be a next time.

'I love my job,' Priya went on. 'And I've got nothing to do. I'm shuffling bits of paper around, because my pregnancy is considered high risk and they won't let me do anything. Please let me help.'

I picked up my cup of tea.

'Back in London,' I said, 'I had a tame retired police officer – his name is Reg and he's an old friend of my dad's. We used to just drink coffee and he'd tell me stories about cases he'd worked on.'

'And it gave you ideas for stories?' Priya said, her face lighting up. 'I can do that. And if you need me to check procedural stuff I can help with that too.'

'That would be brilliant,' I said. 'I was worried about making new contacts down here – and I've been thinking about bringing Tessa to the seaside, so I'd need to get to know the police in Brighton.'

'Where does Tessa normally work?'

'Camden,' I drawled, Laaaaahndahn-style. Priya giggled.

'I've got loads of stories from my time in Manchester,' she said. 'And Brighton's got a dark side too.'

'I don't doubt it.' That made me think about what Hal had said. 'Did you hear what else those guys mentioned?' I asked Priya. 'In the shop?'

'About your books?'

'No, before that – about our house?'

She looked blank. 'Must have missed that bit,' she said. 'I was engrossed in the doorbell selection.'

'Hal said there were stories that there had been a murder in our house,' I said, lowering my voice so the boys didn't hear. 'But Ken said he'd lived here since the Seventies and he'd not heard anything.'

There was a flash of interest in Priya's eyes, which I recognized because I'd seen it in my own face many times.

'I just thought it might be a good place to start,' I carried on. 'For Tessa, I mean.'

Priya gave me an appraising glance. 'For Tessa?'

I grinned.

'And for me.'

Priya picked up her teacup and chinked it against mine. 'I'm on it,' she said. 'Watch this space.'

Chapter 9

1855
Violet

I didn't see Mr Forrest again for nearly a week though I thought about him a lot. In my memories of our meeting on the beach, with his blond hair and the sun behind him, he'd become almost like an angel. A guardian angel who was going to nurture my talent and look after me and help me escape.

Then when I walked into church on Sunday on Father's arm, there he was. Much more real than in my dreams, but just as handsome. I felt giddy with relief that I hadn't dreamt our whole encounter on the beach, because I'd started to fear it had all been in my imagination.

Our pew was closer to the front than Mr Forrest's, and he didn't acknowledge me as we walked past. I stared straight ahead, but throughout the service, all I could think of was him. I felt the warmth of his gaze on the back of my neck and barely heard a word the vicar said.

After the sermon, I noticed Mr Forrest – who was with a woman – stop and talk to the vicar. So I seized my chance.

'Father,' I said, tugging his arm. 'There are the people who have moved into Willow Cottage. We should introduce ourselves.'

I felt a thrill in my solar plexus that could have been nerves or could have been something entirely new, as I led Father over to where Mr Forrest stood.

'Ah,' said Reverend Mapplethorpe. 'These are your new neighbours. Marcus Hargreaves and his daughter, Violet.'

Father shook Mr Forrest's hand vigorously. I bowed my head slightly as I'd done on the beach.

'Edwin Forrest,' said Edwin. 'And my wife, Frances.'

'A pleasure,' said the woman, in a deep, pleasant voice. I looked at her in surprise. I was confused. His wife? I had assumed she was his sister. I'd felt a connection between him and me when we'd met on the beach – a connection that surely wouldn't have been there if he were married. Would it? I felt myself blushing as I worried I had misread the situation.

Mr Forrest was talking. 'Frances has been ill, you see, so we've not had a chance to meet anyone,' he told Father.

I looked at Mrs Forrest. She didn't look ill. She was neatly dressed, with a large skirt and a tidy waist. Her dark hair was tightly pulled into a knot at the nape of her neck.

'Much better, thank you,' she was saying to Father. She didn't smile. I felt a rush of sympathy for vibrant Mr Forrest. To be married to such a dull woman must be difficult.

'Have you been to the beach?' I asked Mr Forrest's wife boldly.

Mrs Forrest looked at me, sharp eyes piercing my face, but Mr Forrest smiled.

'It's very beautiful,' I went on, not sure what I was hoping for her to say. 'A walk on the beach is very good for the constitution, Mrs Forrest.' I stared at Mrs Forrest in defiance, as though daring her to admit she wasn't ill.

'You are very kind,' Mrs Forrest said, lowering her eyes from my gaze. 'I will take a turn as soon as I am able.'

'But not today,' Mr Forrest said, his firm tone suggesting there would be no argument. 'Today you must rest.'

Mrs Forrest simply nodded and Mr Forrest turned to Father.

'I am very fond of the outdoors,' he said as we began to walk out of the churchyard and bade farewell to Reverend Mapplethorpe. Mr Forrest leaned towards Father, as though he were telling him a secret. 'I fancy myself as an artist. Wildlife sketches, mostly. I will enjoy drawing the seabirds here.'

They continued – Father asking surprisingly knowledge-able questions about Mr Forrest's hobby, while I fumed quietly. Father had never shown such interest in my art, or at least not for years, and not without a patronizing pat on my head to accompany his questions.

Mrs Forrest and I walked behind my father and Mr Forrest, not speaking, and as they approached the Forrests' house, the men paused to let us catch up.

'I was just saying to your father that I think I will take your advice and go for a walk on the beach later,' Mr Forrest said. He looked up at the sky. 'Though it's hot now. I feel later would be better – perhaps around five o'clock.'

He looked intently at me and I dropped my gaze. Was it an invitation? I looked up at him through my eyelashes and he gave a tiny, barely noticeable nod. I felt myself begin to blush again and turned away so he wouldn't see.

Father said our goodbyes, then he led the way to the house, and Mr Forrest walked up the path to his cottage. But as I turned to go, Mrs Forrest glanced at her husband's back, then caught my hand. I gasped in surprise but Mrs Forrest didn't let go.

'Miss Hargreaves,' Mrs Forrest said in a low, urgent voice. 'Please, be careful.' Then she turned and walked quickly to the cottage.

I was bewildered. I wondered if the ailment that had afflicted Mrs Forrest was in her head, instead of her body. Perhaps she was hysterical. I'd read of that in Father's *Times*. How difficult things must be for poor Mr Forrest.

I followed Father home, barely listening as he told me how I should wear my skirts fuller like Mrs Forrest, and wear my hair neatly like Mrs Forrest, and speak softly like Mrs Forrest. I could only think about how I would sneak away later to meet Mr Forrest on the beach.

After an unseasonably heavy lunch of roast mutton and treacle tart, Father and I retired to the drawing room. Father read the paper, while I picked out a tune on the piano. I was not a natural musician and I could feel Father's irritation growing as I hit the wrong keys. Eventually, I sat opposite him and read his newspaper out loud until I saw his head droop and his eyes close.

Quietly, I folded the paper and rested it on the arm of his chair, then I crept out of the room and closed the door behind me.

'Mabel,' I called to our housekeeper, as I tried in vain to tease my unruly hair into a roll. 'I left my gloves at church. It's such a beautiful day, I'm going to walk up and retrieve them.' I was surprised at how easily the lie fell from my lips, but not ashamed. So keen to begin my art career was I, that I felt almost anything was justified.

I pulled my hat on, then calmly strolled down the path, shutting the gate behind me. Then I walked towards the church, but as soon as I was out of sight of our house, I ducked down the side of a cottage, hitched up my skirts, and ran along the path to the beach.

I saw him before he saw me. He was sitting on the rocks, a little way from where we'd met before. Out of sight from Father, I noted with relief.

'And his wife,' a disloyal voice in my head added. I pushed the thought away and concentrated on scrambling down the steep path to the sand.

As I reached the beach I paused and smoothed my hair where it poked out from under my hat – in vain, I feared – and caught my breath. Mr Forrest had his back to me, watching the waves, and I studied him for a second, admiring his broad shoulders and the way his hair curled under his hat.

As if he sensed me behind him, Mr Forrest turned, and my heart lifted at his smile.

'Dear Miss Hargreaves,' he said. 'I feared you wouldn't get away.'

I flushed at his informal greeting. 'Father went to sleep,' I admitted.

Mr Forrest smiled again, the corners of his eyes crinkling. 'Then let's make the most of the time we have,' he said. He offered his arm and I took it. I felt very grown up and very young at the same time. We strolled across the sand, by unspoken consent hugging the low cliffs that flanked the beach and ensured we were unseen from above.

Mr Forrest asked questions about my painting and, heady

with the joy of talking about it, I explained – or at least I tried to explain – why I loved it so much.

'It's as though I haven't chosen it,' I said, struggling to find the right words. 'It's like breathing; it's part of me.'

Mr Forrest studied me, and I turned away feeling self-conscious.

'I only wish I had your talent,' he said. 'But what I lack in ability I make up for in passion. I am certain you have a great future ahead of you.'

'In London?' I breathed.

'If you wish,' Mr Forrest said. 'I flatter myself, but I have been told I have a good eye and I know if your work excites me, then it will undoubtedly excite my friends in the PRB.'

He took my hand. His touch was hot like the sun. The only man who'd ever touched me before was Father.

'This is a way out for you, Violet,' he said, gripping my fingers. It was as though he could see into my soul and I suddenly felt raw. Stripped bare. How did he know what I was thinking? Confusion flooded me.

'I must go,' I stammered. 'Father …'

I pulled my hand away abruptly. Mr Forrest didn't object. Instead he tipped his hat.

'Miss Hargreaves,' he said politely. Then he turned and walked away up the beach.

I watched him go, my hand still burning from his touch. I felt an enormous sense of loss.

Chapter 10

Present day
Ella

Those early days in Sussex were chaos. It was a blur of boxes and rearranging furniture, and hanging pictures. The weather was glorious, so the boys spent all their time in the garden, kicking balls, bouncing on their trampoline, and generally running wild. I watched them, amazed at how much energy they had, and relieved that I'd bought the lock for the gate.

It was very different from London. More different than I'd expected it to be, considering how close we were. Because our house was at the end of the lane, there were no cars driving by, and it was so quiet. The first few nights, Ben and I had even struggled to sleep, because we were used to the white noise of passing traffic, not the complete silence of the Sussex countryside.

I was determined to make this work but it was hard going those first days. Ben had been thrown straight into work so I spent a lot of time on my own with the kids, which didn't help. Deep down I was worried we'd made the most awful mistake. What if giving up life in London

– giving up my safe, if dull, job – was a massive, enormous, unfixable error?

I kept thinking about Dad saying I would have been better off taking a sabbatical so I still had a job to go back to and I fought the urge to phone him and wail down the phone that he'd been right all along. I knew as soon as I expressed any doubts at all, he'd say it wasn't too late. That I could go back to accountancy in a heartbeat, that he knew someone who knew someone who could ask about opportunities in his firm and before I knew it, I'd be back behind a desk in the city, on hold to HMRC.

And actually, when I thought about it, that wasn't what I wanted at all. I was just finding it hard to come to terms with such a big change. I'd settle down. And I'd stop missing my dad so much eventually. Wouldn't I?

Ben, on the other hand, was embracing our new life. He was really busy at the football club – the new season hadn't started but he was meeting new players and helping with pre-season training and medicals and fitness tests. I knew he was absolutely loving it so I didn't want to rain on his parade.

I was both itching to get started on writing and terrified that once I began I'd realize I didn't have anything to say. I felt like there was a lot riding on this book – it would be the first one I'd had proper time to write. If it bombed, I couldn't blame my lack of focus or the fact that I was an accountant really. It would be all down to me. For the first time in my life I was a writer. But I didn't want to write. What if I couldn't do it any more? The idea made me shudder.

The removal men had taken all my writing stuff up to the

study, but I hadn't sorted it out yet. I told myself it was because I was busy looking after the boys. And I said the same to Ben when he gently suggested that I switched on my laptop.

'The boys,' I said, vaguely, waving my arm in the direction of the garden. 'We should probably think about getting some childcare.'

Ben grinned. 'I've thought,' he said.

'You have?'

'Margaret,' he said. 'She's Mike's wife.'

'Who's Mike?'

'The estate agent guy who rented this house to us,' Ben reminded me. 'His wife was a teaching assistant at the village school for years, but she's retired now and he said she was looking for some part-time work.'

I was thrilled. 'She sounds perfect,' I said. 'Ring her.'

So Ben did, and Margaret was just as keen as he thought she'd be.

'She's coming round to meet you now,' Ben said, hunting for his car keys – he was off to do another medical on another player. 'She said she'd love to look after the boys.'

'She hasn't met them yet,' I said with a grin as Ben waved goodbye.

But as soon as Margaret arrived, I knew we had to have her. She was just so capable. She sat at the kitchen table and made Stan laugh as I made tea.

She'd brought little packets of Lego figures for Oscar, and a whoopee cushion for Stan, and the boys were already smitten with her. I liked her too.

'It's just afternoons, really,' I explained. 'I can take the boys to school and nursery and I'll pick Stan up at lunchtime and feed him. If you could just come after lunch to watch him, pick Oscar up at 3 p.m. and then give them tea, that would be great. I'll be here – in the study – and Ben works funny hours at the football club so he might be around too. So if you need us, you can shout. Would that suit you?'

'That would suit me very well,' said Margaret. She was in her late fifties, perhaps, with neat blonde hair and a tidy figure in very clean jeans. I gave her a mug of tea and offered her a biscuit.

'How are you settling in?' Margaret asked, her eyes roaming my face. I tried to resist the urge to screw my nose up but I failed.

'It's fine,' I said. 'Wonderful. Ben loves it. And the boys.'

'And you?'

'Not so much,' I admitted. I rubbed the palm of my hand over my hair. 'I'm restless and nervous that we've swapped our life in London – which we loved by the way – for this great unknown.'

'Sometimes it's good to take a leap,' Margaret said.

I nodded. 'It's definitely the right move for Ben. He's got his dream job. As long as I've known him he's wanted to run the physio department in a football club. He's in his element.'

'So you don't want to tell him you don't like it here?'

'I don't dislike it,' I said. 'Honestly, I don't. It's just different, that's all. I've always been really nervous about taking risks or doing anything spontaneous – this move was risky and spontaneous so it's no wonder I'm feeling a bit out of my depth. I don't want to leave. At least, I don't think I do …'

Margaret patted my hand. 'It will get better,' she said. 'Once the boys start school and you're in a routine. And you'll make some friends in the village.'

I nodded, comforted. 'I met a nice woman,' I said. 'Priya.'

'Oh yes,' Margaret said. 'Pregnant?'

I grinned. 'Very pregnant. And I chatted to Ken in the hardware shop.'

'He's our next-door neighbour,' Margaret said. 'Ever so handy when something goes wrong in the house.'

Again I marvelled at how everyone knew everyone else down here. 'His friend Hal was there too,' I went on. 'And he said he'd heard stories about our house.'

Margaret looked at me. 'Stories?' she said. 'What kind of stories?'

'Just about some things that happened here,' I said vaguely, wanting to see what she knew before I told her what I'd heard.

She nodded. 'I've always thought it was a sad house.'

'Sad,' I said. 'Why do you think it's sad?'

Margaret looked embarrassed. 'It's just silly gossip,' she said.

I offered her another biscuit and she shook her head.

'My granddad told me something terrible happened here. I can't remember exactly but I think someone died. Maybe more than one person.'

'A murder?' I said, possibly with a bit too much excitement.

Margaret gave me a sharp look. 'Maybe,' she said. 'Or some sort of tragic accident.'

'Your granddad,' I said more to myself than Margaret. 'So it must have been a long time before the Seventies, then. I could ask at the police station …'

I realized Margaret was staring at me in horror and looking like she was about to leave – obviously she thought I was some sort of murder-obsessed criminal.

'I'm a writer,' I said in a rush. 'I write crime novels.'

'I've never really been one for books,' Margaret said. She looked quite pleased about it. Or perhaps she was just pleased that the village newcomer wasn't about to kill her in cold blood.

I beamed at her. 'Hal and Ken said they'd heard there had been a murder, but we all assumed it was recent. If your granddad knew about it, though, it could have been much earlier. I'd like to find out more about the history of the house. See if there is a mystery here.'

Margaret screwed her forehead up in concentration. 'I wish I could remember more,' she said. 'I think my granddad said no one ever knew what had happened. It must have been a really long time ago, though. Before he was born I think.'

'I'll do some digging,' I said. 'It'll keep me busy.'

'Do you have a lot of work to do?' Margaret said suddenly.

'I do, actually.' I didn't want to think about how I still had a whole novel to write. And maybe I could Google the house, or find out who lived here years ago, and see if there was any record of this crime …

'And is your husband here?' Margaret looked round.

I shook my head. 'Pre-season fitness tests or something,' I said.

'So why don't I take the boys out into the garden and you can have an hour or so getting yourself sorted out,' Margaret said. 'Give you a break, and give me and the boys time to get to know each other.'

Considering I'd spent days avoiding work, I was surprised how pleased I was with the offer. I looked at Margaret in gratitude.

'That would be brilliant,' I said. 'Are you sure you don't mind?'

'Go,' said Margaret. 'Sort.'

Chapter 11

I bounded upstairs. The attic was the huge – the whole top floor of the house, so there was lots of space. It was a million miles away from my desk/dressing table combo in our old house.

I stood at the door and surveyed the room. I would put my desk in between the two large windows. It was an astonishing view and I hoped it would inspire me. The bookshelves were on the opposite wall, either side of the small windows that looked down the lane. On my right was the wall that Ben had knocked on to see if it was hollow – the one with the ventilation window on the outside. I could put some pictures up there, perhaps. And on my left was a built-in cupboard with a door that had been painted shut. I narrowed my eyes as I looked at it. That wouldn't stay shut for long, if I had anything to do with it.

The removal men had left everything in a pile by the door, so I cleared the boxes that were stacked on top of the desk and dragged it to the wall.

I plugged in my computer and the printer, then printed out some photos of the boys, and stuck them to the right-hand wall. As I pinned them up, I knocked the wall once or twice, just to see if it was hollow. But I still couldn't tell.

Knowing I should be thinking about a plot for my next Tessa book, I instead opened the internet and found the census records for England. I thought about Margaret and how old she was and scribbling some dates down on my notepad, I worked out that her grandfather would probably have been born around the turn of the twentieth century.

'Hmm,' I said out loud. 'Did Margaret say it happened before he was even born?'

I typed our address into the search box and was pleased to see there were records going back to 1841.

'Let's start at the very beginning,' I sang under my breath, Julie Andrews style, clicking on the first entry.

At first I was confused as the village was simply listed as one entry without individual addresses. But thanks to the pubs, which had obviously been in the same place for all that time, I worked out the census recorders had started at the opposite end of the village and just worked their way along towards the sea. Our house, therefore, had to be the very final entry. I scrolled down and found it.

Marcus Hargreaves, I read. *Male. 34 years old. Industrialist.*

Below Marcus was a wife, Harriet, listed as thirty years old, and a little girl, Violet. She was just four years old.

'Aww, a little family,' I said. 'Did you have more children, Marcus? This house is built for lots of kids.'

I clicked on the next entry, for 1851.

Marcus Hargreaves, I read again. *Male. 44 years old. Industrialist.*

But beneath Marcus was no mention of Harriet. Instead

just Violet – who was now fourteen – was listed. Beneath her was a woman called Elizabeth Pringle, who was listed as a governess, a housekeeper called Betsy Bolton, and a maid – who was just sixteen – called Mabel Jonas.

'Where's Harriet?' I said, feeling unaccountably sad, but intrigued nevertheless. 'Was she the murder victim?'

I went back to the search results and chose 1861 this time. But now our house was listed as unoccupied. And the same in 1871.

'No one at all,' I said. 'Where are you all?'

I clicked off the census website and found another that showed birth, marriage, and death certificates. But there was nothing online this time. Instead the website suggested checking parish records for the time.

Disappointed, I sat still at my desk for a minute. Then I gave up all pretence of working on my book and instead I picked up my notebook and a pen, and headed downstairs.

Margaret was throwing a ball to the boys in the garden. I went outside and she looked round.

'All done already?' she said. 'That was quick.'

'Not exactly,' I said. 'I just need to pop out – I can take the boys with me but if you don't mind staying, I would get it done quicker ...'

'Go,' she said, without hesitating. 'We're having a great time.'

Pleased to have something to think about other than Dad and the stress of our move, I bounded down the lane towards the village church.

I'd not been inside before, but we'd admired it on our walks to the shops. It was a gorgeous Norman church with old graves in the churchyard and a square bell tower. The heavy wooden door was open, so I ducked inside.

Luckily for me, the vicar was there, pinning a notice to the board in the porch. He smiled at me as I walked in.

'Hello there,' he said.

I introduced myself and explained what I was after. And the vicar – who was much younger than I expected vicars to be and who told me to call him Rich – showed me into a side office where the parish records were kept.

'They're all fascinating,' he said. 'I sometimes look up people at random and trace their family back to see how far they go. Lots of folk have lived here for generations.'

He pulled out the books for me and I settled myself down at the desk.

It wasn't as easy as searching online, but it didn't take me long to find the christening record of little Violet in 1837, and then, in 1842, I found the record of Violet's mother's death. Harriet had died of childbirth fever, the record said.

Not a murder then, I thought. I was disappointed that the mystery wasn't a mystery after all.

'Found what you were looking for?' said Rich, peering over my shoulder.

'I did,' I said. 'But she wasn't murdered. She died in childbirth.'

'The baby died, too,' Rich pointed out. He showed me the line below Harriet's entry. 'A little boy – look.'

'Frederick Hargreaves,' I read out loud. 'Aged two days.' My voice caught in my throat on the last words.

'Oh,' I said. 'Violet was five.'

'Violet?' Rich asked.

'Harriet's daughter,' I said. 'She was five when Harriet died. My mum died when I was five.' I paused. 'And I lost my baby brother too.'

The vicar put his hand on my shoulder. 'I'm sorry to hear that,' he said. 'You said you were a writer?'

I nodded, still looking at the entry in the records.

'Maybe writing this story can help you make sense of your own,' he said.

'Maybe it can,' I said. 'Maybe it can.'

I thanked him and promised to come back another day to do more research. Then, with my head full of this unknown Violet who lost her mum as I'd done, and poor Harriet, I wandered home.

I'd only been back about two minutes, and I was saying hello to the boys and Margaret, when I heard the front door open. Ben walked out into the garden, a bundle cradled in his arms. A little bubble of excitement popped in my tummy as he placed the bundle gently on the grass in front of the boys.

'Careful,' he said to Oscar who was bouncing up and down. 'He's just a baby.'

'Mummy!' shouted Oscar, almost roaring with excitement. 'Mummy! It's a puppy! Come and see!'

I exchanged a look with Margaret.

'Looks like you're staying put then,' she said with a smile.

I nodded. 'Looks like it,' I said.

Chapter 12

1855
Violet

After I'd run away from Mr Forrest on the beach, I went into the house through the kitchen – I didn't want to see Father asleep or awake – and went straight up to the attic. I slumped in the chair and took my hat off. I could hardly bear to look down at the bottom of the cliff, where I'd been so rude to Mr Forrest. Cutting him off, rejecting his kindness.

I flushed again, thinking of how he'd seen right into my soul. How had he known how trapped I felt? How I was looking at him to help me escape? I knew I'd been lucky so far, that Father hadn't married me off to the first man to show an interest. But recently he'd started talking about a man called John Wallace, who worked with him on one of his projects. He mentioned how clever he was and how good with money, and how he ran a tight ship. And I knew – I just knew – that these were qualities Father admired. Qualities he thought would make a good husband.

So far I'd resisted all his efforts for me to meet Mr Wallace, but it wouldn't be long, I thought in misery, before Father invited him down to Sussex, and that would be it.

I knew I ought to speak to my father. I should tell him how I felt, that I wanted to paint and that Mr Forrest seemed to be taking my painting seriously, because for all his talk of taking my work to London, I knew that in reality I could do nothing without Father's approval. But what would he say if I told him? I shuddered at the thought.

On the whole, Father had been supportive of my love of art to begin with. Lots of girls like me took drawing lessons and I had been taught by a mousey-haired woman from the village who'd been very keen on technique. She'd sent me down to the beach to collect things – shells, feathers, a stick – and then made me sketch them over and over using only charcoal. Never any colour.

Despite the repetitive nature of the task, I had loved it. Loved it more than the lessons I got from my succession of elderly governesses who droned on about kings and queens and made me recite poetry. Urgh, just remembering old Mrs Pringle who had a passion for the Reformation and who liked to share it with me, made me want to curl up into a ball and go to sleep. But when I was drawing I felt like I had become who I was supposed to be.

When my lessons were over, I would shut myself in my bedroom and draw some more. First I sketched parts of myself – a foot or a hand. Then I would gaze at myself in the mirror and draw my face again and again, struggling to get my hair right.

I sketched Father then too and he exclaimed in delight that I'd got his expression 'just so' and patted me on the head proudly. He even took me to the Royal Academy most years, laughing as I gazed in speechless wonder at the paintings there.

But as I got older, Father's indulgence of my art waned.

'No more talk of painting, Violet,' he would say if I tried to talk to him. 'It's not becoming for a young woman to be so focused on one thing. You need to extend your skills. Your arithmetic could do with half the attention you give to drawing.'

He would tut if he saw me with paper or pencil and refuse to answer if I asked for another visit to the Royal Academy. So I took to drawing upstairs in my bedroom, moving into the lounge – which had much better light – only when Father was on one of his frequent trips away.

The only people who knew about my work – until Edwin found me on the beach that day – were Mabel, our house-keeper, and Philips, who did everything else around the house and garden. Mabel regarded my drawings with a sense of wonder – briefly.

'Oh look, you've got your father's eyes perfect there,' she said when I showed her a sketch. 'Aren't you clever? Now move out the way while I clean this floor.'

Philips was more interested. He asked me questions about my work and pointed out where things weren't quite right – and when I'd improved. I complained to him about the lack of light in my bedroom and wished aloud that I had a place of my own in which to paint. Then one day, when Father was in Manchester, he'd taken me up the rickety stairs to the attic room, which had once been a home for old furniture, trunks, and linen.

'Look,' he'd declared, standing back to let me enter the room.

I'd gasped in pleasure. He'd moved all the junk out – into the outhouse in the garden he told me later – cleaned the wooden floor, and distempered the walls. A battered old chaise stood in one corner ('Who knew that was up here?' Philips had said with a good-natured grin.) and there was a bowl with a jug next to it.

'I thought this would be a good spot,' he'd said. 'It catches the sun, see?'

I had been overcome with gratitude and excitement. Now I could really work.

That had been nearly two years ago. The attic room remained hidden from Father. I hadn't lied exactly but I'd never told him about it and he'd never asked, obviously just assuming it was still a storage space. Philips continued to help me. He mended the stairs and made them safer for me to run up and down. He even bought paints and brushes for me in Brighton when I asked him to, and proved to be a useful sounding board for my musings about art.

As time went on, Father seemed relieved that I had – as far as he knew – abandoned art. He began to talk about my potential as a wife and I ignored him most of the time. I knew nothing of men. In fact, I knew little of women. I had no friends, only a cousin who I'd lived with for a few years when I was younger. But he'd mostly ignored me, and anyway the family had moved away and I hadn't seen them for years. With Father away so much we rarely had visitors and when we did, it was normally another man just like Father. I would dine with them in silence while they discussed business and then escape to my room when we'd finished eating. The idea of marriage was so odd to me that I disregarded it entirely.

But now – now the vague talk of becoming a good wife had changed to specific mentions of Mr Wallace – I knew I was at a crossroads. I knew that unless I asserted myself, I would be Mrs Wallace within a year, and I wasn't sure I could live that way. But the alternative – the very idea of telling Father how I really felt – was horrifying.

Father and I had always rubbed along quite nicely. I knew I was loved, even if Father was strict. I missed him when he was away, which was often, but I didn't miss my mother any more. Not really. She had died when I was so young that I could barely remember her.

Only once recently had I wished my mother was there. I'd been looking out at the sea from the attic window, when I'd heard laughter from the front of the house, so I'd gone to the opposite side of the room and looked out of the smaller windows there.

Outside Mabel was talking to an older woman who looked just like her, only a bit shorter and more squat, and who had to be her mother. There were two little girls playing in the lane, running up and down with their hair flying behind them – it was their laughter I had heard. A slightly older boy with fair hair like Mabel's leaned against a tree and watched the girls – his sisters, I assumed – with an expression of disdain.

Mabel, who was the oldest of her siblings, I knew, was talking to her mother in what seemed to be an urgent way, waving her hands about as she told her story. The older woman listened, and she took Mabel's hands and held them still as she replied. Then she brushed a stray hair from Mabel's forehead and tucked it up under her cap, talking all the time.

Mabel nodded and threw her arms round her mother as I watched. Her mother extracted herself from Mabel's embrace, kissed her on the cheek then walked off in the direction of the village. The little girls ran after her waving goodbye to Mabel gaily and, after a few seconds, the boy followed, giving Mabel a salute that she returned.

Mabel watched them go, then she adjusted her cap and walked back into the house, smiling.

I had stood at the window wondering what it would be like to have a mother who listened to your woes, who gave advice, and who made sure your hair was neat. Imagining having little sisters who played with you, or a younger brother to torment. I pictured our echoey house full of noise and laughter with children in all the rooms and my mother looking after them all, and I felt a pain in my heart so acute that I had to sit down on the floor for a moment to recover.

'I miss my mother,' I whispered to myself.

I stayed on the floor for a little while, feeling lost and alone. Then I got up, brushed the dust from my skirt, and carried on with my painting.

Chapter 13

Present day
Ella

The puppy was called Dumbledore. Stan had pushed hard for his name to be Batman but when Oscar suggested Dumbledore, the puppy bounced around the lawn and we all agreed he'd chosen his own name.

He was sitting on my lap in the kitchen a few days later when Priya came round. Mike was mending the back door, which was sticking, and we were chatting about not much as he worked.

When the doorbell rang, Dumbledore stirred slightly in my lap. Gently I picked him up – he was still just a little bundle of fluff and too-long ears – and put him in his basket where he burrowed into the blanket and went back to sleep. Then I ran to the front door.

For as long as I'd been writing my thrillers, I'd wanted a massive whiteboard so I could scrawl ideas for my twisty-turny plots and check everything made sense. I pictured it like the incident boards I'd seen in CID offices, only with fictional incidents recorded instead of real-life crimes. So I was absolutely delighted to see Priya in our drive wrestling the very thing I'd imagined out of the boot of her mud-splattered car.

'We're moving offices so we're having a clear-out,' she said. 'Thought you could probably make use of this.'

I was speechless with delight.

'God it's brilliant,' I said. 'Can I give you something for it?'

Priya shook her head. 'Honestly, it was heading for a skip.'

'Cup of tea at least?'

She shook her head again.

'Midwife,' she said, pointing to her bump, which seemed to have got bigger in the few days since I'd last seen her.

'Later?' I asked.

'Definitely,' she said. 'Or, come and see me at work one day this week? I want to know more about this mystery of yours so I can do some digging.'

'Deal,' I said.

Mike helped me carry the board up to the attic, and lent me his drill so I could fix it to the wall. I put it on the far side of the room – on the wall with the extra window, or air vent. I half expected – or hoped perhaps – the drill to go right through and prove the wall was just plywood but it didn't. The wall was definitely brick – the dust drifting down onto the floor proved that. Slightly disappointed that our mysterious window was simply for ventilation after all, I shoved rawl plugs into the holes I'd drilled, and with Mike's help, screwed the board to the wall.

'Not bad,' I said, standing back to admire my work.

'Dead straight,' Mike agreed. 'What are you going to use it for?'

'Plotting,' I said with a grin.

After Mike had gone, I checked on the puppy, then I took a cup of tea, some biscuits, and feeling faintly ridiculous, Stan's old baby monitor so I could hear if Dumbledore woke up, upstairs. My heroine, Tessa Gilroy, was a private investigator. She mostly worked on divorces but occasionally – and usually reluctantly and inadvertently – got involved in something more dangerous. I was well aware my sort of writing was enjoying its moment in the sun right now, and I knew my next book had to be good enough to appeal to readers on its own merits, rather than being just another thriller.

I'd been collecting cuttings about crimes and mysteries, and jotting notes about stories Reg had told me for months, and started sketching out an idea involving a woman being set up for something. Probably a murder, I thought, but the alleged victim would still be alive. I thought the 'murderer' would contact Tessa from prison and ask for her help in proving the victim was still breathing …

I pulled out the whiteboard pens Priya had brought with her and wrote a few ideas on the board, feeling the rusty cogs in my mind beginning to whir. But all the time I was writing, at the back of my mind, was the stuff I'd heard about our house, and the story of the Hargreaves family and poor motherless Violet.

'How's it going?' Ben said as he peeked round the door of the study an hour or so later.

I was hunched over my laptop trying to write a synopsis. I jumped, not expecting Ben to be home.

'I'm going back to the training ground in a minute,' he said. 'I just had to go and pick up some equipment in

Brighton, so I thought I'd pop in and say hello. You look engrossed. Is it going well?'

'Not bad,' I said, reluctant as always to discuss a book while I was still thrashing out the plot.

'I thought you'd like a cup of tea,' Ben said. He came over to my desk, put a mug down next to my coaster, and peered at the screen of my laptop.

Pointedly I moved the mug on to the coaster and shut my screen.

'Don't look,' I said. 'I'm not ready for you to read it yet.'

Ben chuckled. 'What's it about?'

I looked up at him. 'Tessa's working in Sussex,' I said. 'That's all you need to know for now.'

Ben grinned at me. 'So you're writing?'

I nodded then made a face. 'It's words,' I said. 'But I'm not convinced they're quite right yet.'

'It looks better in here,' Ben said. 'Like you've settled in.'

'I have,' I said in satisfaction, looking round at the room. 'But I want to open that cupboard. It would be good to stash some books and stuff in there.'

I pointed at the cupboard nestled under the eaves in the corner of the room. The one with the door painted shut.

'Mike's still downstairs,' Ben said. 'I'll get him to have a look at it if you like?'

'Brilliant,' I said. 'It probably just needs a good yank.'

It took a bit more than that, but Mike got the cupboard open in the end. He gouged out paint from the edge of the door, and wiped the edges with paint stripper and eventually, it opened.

I was downstairs by then, trying to put on some laundry

without Dumbledore jumping into the washing machine. Mike yelled over the bannister, 'Ella! Cupboard's open.'

'Fab,' I said. Scooping up the puppy, I bounded up the stairs. All these steps would definitely help me keep fit. In the attic, Mike was standing at the open cupboard door, shaking his head.

'Think I've just made a whole lot more work for you,' he said.

I looked inside. The cupboard wasn't empty, as I'd expected. Instead its wooden shelves were full of books and papers.

'I can get someone from the office to come and clear all this out if you like,' Mike said.

'Absolutely not,' I said. 'No way. Look at all this stuff. It could belong to someone.'

'Someone who didn't want it,' Mike pointed out.

'Still,' I said. 'We can't just dump it. I'll go through it and see what's here.'

The hairs on the back of my neck were standing up. 'I've heard stories about this house,' I told Mike. 'Stories about a mystery. Maybe this is linked. Perhaps the cupboard was painted shut for a reason.'

Mike gave me a sympathetic look. 'Or perhaps some lazy so-and-so couldn't be bothered to paint it properly,' he said.

But I was undeterred. I reached into the cupboard and took out a stiff cardboard folder, full of paper and tied with cord. 'I'm going to start with this,' I said.

It was a while before I got to go through the folder, but much later, when the boys were bathed and in bed, and Ben had come home again, wolfed down some dinner, then gone out to an evening training session back over in Worthing, I settled down on the sofa, and opened the file.

It was actually something of a disappointment at first. Lots of crumbling, yellowing newspaper pages, mostly.

I took one from the top and read it.

Opinions are divided over the latest works by the self-titled Pre-Raphaelite Brotherhood, I read. *Mr Charles Dickens despises their work and has said the depiction of the Virgin Mary in* Christ in the House of his Parents *by John Everett Millais is 'horrible in her ugliness'. Others are lauding the bold use of colour and realism …*

Long ago, I'd studied art history for A Level and I remembered bits and pieces about the Pre-Raphaelite Brotherhood. Not much though, if I was completely honest, and I seemed to remember not being overly interested in them. I could Google them, though, if I needed to, or better yet speak to my old university friend George, who was now a lecturer in art history at St Andrews.

I leafed through the cuttings, reading occasional articles and laughing at some of the writing. It seemed there was nothing here to suggest a mystery but it was still amazing to read genuine newspapers from so long ago. The papers that were dated all came from 1854 and 1855 – so after Harriet Hargreaves had died, I thought to myself – and I wasn't sure I'd ever even touched anything so old before. Apart from the house itself of course.

At the back of the folder, I found another yellowing page. This one, though, was on different paper. It was soft with age and looked like it had been torn from a sketchbook, and on it was a pencil drawing of a young woman.

The woman in the picture looked to be in her late teens. She was wearing a long dress with a loose skirt, not the stiff crinolines I'd seen in the newspapers, and the fabric was printed with small flowers. Her hair was tied up but it was wavy and snaked down her cheeks as though it wouldn't be contained. She had freckles and clear eyes and her lips were curved upwards in a joyful smile.

I smiled back at the girl – I couldn't help myself. She looked so happy. Then, eager to see what else was in the folder, I went to put the picture to one side. But as I did, I noticed the background to the drawing – the girl was standing in between two long windows, and through the glass I could see the sea. She was in my study. In this house.

More interested now, I picked the picture up again and stared at it. Along the bottom, in beautiful copperplate writing was written: Self-portrait. June 1855.

'Self-portrait of who?' I said to the girl in the picture, working out with the help of my fingers that Violet Hargreaves would have been eighteen in 1855. 'Are you Violet? Is the mystery about you and not your poor dead mother?'

Holding the drawing in one hand, and the folder in another, I climbed the stairs to the attic and stood where the young woman must have stood to draw herself. The view from the windows was the same as it had been in 1855 and I felt another flicker of excitement.

On my whiteboard I'd written Tessa in Sussex and below it, some notes about the murder-that-wasn't-a-murder. But now, spontaneously, I picked up a cloth and wiped off what I'd written.

Along the top of the newly clean board I wrote CLIFF

HOUSE MYSTERY. Then I fixed the self-portrait to the middle of the board with a magnet and wrote underneath: Is this Violet Hargreaves?

I was determined to find out more.

Chapter 14

'So you think this woman has got something to do with the mystery?' asked Ben, looking at the self-portrait on my board.

I shrugged. 'Dunno. But the Hargreaves family definitely lived here in 1851 when the census happened – at least Violet and her father did. The mother was dead by then.'

Ben frowned. 'But her death isn't the mystery?'

'Don't think so. She died having a baby. But by 1861 there was no one living here at all. The family might just have moved but I think it's strange that all that stuff was left behind, and I can't help wondering if this is what Margaret's granddad talked about.'

'Amazing,' said Ben. 'So do you reckon there's a book in this?'

It was my turn to frown. 'Probably not,' I said. 'I should be writing Tessa really. But I just want to know more. I want to know who this girl was – if she is Violet – and whether she had anything to do with this mystery.'

I reached out and touched the portrait.

'Perhaps there is no mystery at all,' I said, feeling a bit silly. 'But the vicar suggested finding out more might help me with my own story. I told him about my mum dying and he said I should tell Violet's story.'

Ben squeezed my hand. 'It can't hurt,' he said. 'And it could even build some bridges with your dad.'

I grimaced. I didn't want to talk about Dad. 'Priya said she'd help. Well, actually, she begged me to let her help. I'm going to see her at the police station tomorrow.'

Ben grinned. 'Making friends?' he said. 'Solving mysteries? It sounds like you're making yourself right at home in Sussex.'

I gave him a quick hug. 'It's good,' I said. 'It was a good decision.'

I jumped as my phone rang in my pocket. I pulled it out and looked at the screen, then I pushed the button on the top to cancel the call and shoved it back into my jeans.

Ben looked at me. 'Who was that?' he asked.

'Just Dad,' I said. 'He must have sensed you talking about him. It's not the right time to speak to him now.'

'I think you should talk to him,' Ben said.

I made a face. 'Don't want to,' I said, knowing I sounded like Stan.

'He misses you.'

I glared at him. 'Have you spoken to him?'

'No,' Ben said. Then he screwed his nose up. 'Email,' he admitted.

'Ben,' I said, angry at his interference. 'This is my problem to sort out.'

But Ben was defiant. 'You need to speak to him,' he said.

'I will.' Irritably I started gathering together some loose bits of paper on my desk. 'But I'll do it when I want to and not when you tell me to.'

Ben started to speak and I stopped him with a fierce look. 'Okay,' he said. 'I get it.'

He gave me a look that suggested he actually didn't get it, then he kissed me on the temple.

'I'll leave you to your research,' he said, heading for the door. I ignored him. Childish, perhaps, but I was angry that he'd been in touch with Dad.

I took my phone out and looked at the missed call on the screen, then put it away again. Then I changed my mind and took it out again. Just because I wanted to do an images search for the portrait I'd found and see if anything came up. Not in case Dad called again. Nope.

As I took a few photos of the self-portrait, I found my mind drifting to my dad once more. I couldn't blame him for being so overprotective, I admitted. After all, he'd suffered unimaginably when my mum was killed. Her death had changed him almost beyond recognition – not surprisingly.

I couldn't remember Mummy very clearly. I was five when she died, killed in a car accident when she was eight months pregnant with my baby brother. He'd died too, though the doctors had delivered him and tried hard to save him. I'd been at school when the accident happened and I couldn't really remember much about the days that followed.

It was as though I'd gone to sleep one day, happy and safe with a mum who loved me and a baby brother or sister on the way, and woken up in a scary cold place with a bewildered dad, no mum, and no baby.

My first memory of that troubled time was sitting on the stairs, hugging my white kitten. He was called Snowflake and he'd been a present from Mummy and Daddy.

'He belongs to you,' Mummy said. 'He's not to share with the baby – he's just yours.'

But now Mummy was gone, and the baby was gone, and I was alone with Snowflake on the stairs, confused and sad.

There were lots of people in the house. We'd all been to a place to say goodbye to Mummy and the baby, who was called Billy and who was going to heaven too. He and Mummy had been in the same box, called a coffin. I hadn't ever met Billy but I didn't care. I hated Billy for being with Mummy when I wasn't. And I hated Mummy for going without saying goodbye. And I didn't understand why Daddy kept hugging me too tight and for too long.

So now I sat on the stairs with my kitten and hid from all the people in the house who kept kissing me.

'How is Ella doing?' I heard a woman – I thought it was my Auntie Sally – saying.

'Quiet,' Daddy said. I shrank back against the stairs in case he saw me. I didn't like this new Daddy who cried and didn't know how to plait my hair. 'Bewildered. Missing her mum.'

Daddy's voice sounded funny, sort of thick and watery. 'I don't know what to do with her, Sal. I don't know how to look after her. What do I know about little girls?'

'Oh, Jim,' said Auntie Sally. 'You mustn't think that way. You love her. That's enough.'

I peered through the bannisters at Daddy. He looked so sad that I wanted to cuddle him. Instead I pulled Snowflake closer.

'I can't,' Daddy said. 'She needs a mum.' He rubbed his nose. 'Will you take her, Sal? You look after her. Please, Sally, you have to take her.'

'Jim,' Auntie Sally said. 'Think about what you're saying …'

The front door opened and their voices drifted down the path, but I wasn't listening any more anyway. Daddy didn't want me. As it turned out, Sally hadn't wanted me either. At least I'd not gone to live with her as Dad had obviously wanted that day. I'd stayed at home with my sad father, and we'd muddled through together.

But always, hanging over me like a dark cloud, was the memory of him asking his sister – begging his sister – to take me away from him. And the knowledge that she hadn't. What was wrong with me? I wondered. What made me so awful that my own dad didn't want me – and nor did my auntie?

As I grew up I knew I couldn't ever risk doing anything that could make Dad want to get rid of me. So I did everything he asked, from going to bed without arguing to doing my homework. I studied hard. I didn't rebel. I never talked back to him, or acted out. I was a good girl and I wasn't ever going to give him cause to send me away.

Lost in thought, I reached out and absent-mindedly picked up a paintbrush that Oscar had left on my desk – already my special writing space was being taken over by little boys. I squashed the bristles against my cheek, thoughtfully. I couldn't remember much about my mum but I did remember how she wore her hair in a long plait that she pulled over one shoulder. I would cuddle up on her lap and squish the thick end of her hair into my cheek, just like I was doing now with the paintbrush.

In fact, I thought, that was why I'd first written a story. A few months after the accident, my heart still bruised, I had been at school when I'd run my thumb over the bristles on a brush and felt dizzy with painful joy because it reminded me of Mummy.

My teacher, a nice lady called Mrs Williams, had noticed me standing stock-still holding the brush. And she'd gently put some paper in front of me.

'Why don't you paint me a picture?' she'd said. 'Could you draw Daddy for me?'

I had shaken my head. People were too difficult, in real life and on paper.

'Okay then, could you write me a story instead?' Mrs Williams had said. 'What about writing about your kitten?'

So I did. I wrote a story about Snowflake. And then I wrote another one. And another one. I let Snowflake do all the exciting, dangerous, thrilling, cheeky things that I was too scared to do. The things Daddy was too careful to let me do. The things I'd never think of doing in case Daddy got upset and sent me away. And gradually my frozen heart began to thaw.

I thawed a bit more when Dad married Barbara. I was seventeen and about to go to university when they got married so she was never a replacement for Mum. But I wallowed in Barb's warmth and her careful, gentle pushing for me to live my own life. Barb was a solicitor, like Dad, but unlike him she loved art and reading and music. She was the first person who ever read my stories and she encouraged me to write more. Dad only grunted. It was Barb's idea for me to join a creative writing group at university.

'Dad's not interested in creative stuff,' I'd said one weekend when I was home and showing her my latest short story.

Barb had chuckled. 'He reads,' she'd said.

'Military history and the *FT*,' I'd pointed out.

'He'd read something you'd written,' Barb had said. 'He's very proud of you.'

I'd shaken my head. Dad was proud because I was studying law like he'd suggested, I thought. He'd never shown any interest in writing, so I didn't want him to realize it was as important to me as it was. What if he didn't approve?

Barb, though, persisted. She kept telling me to show Dad pieces I'd had published in the university paper, and it was her who'd read my first draft of my first Tessa novel and told Dad all about how amazing it was. She was my cheerleader. I felt like she bridged a gap between Dad and me and I loved her for it. I thought Dad and I were very lucky to have her in our lives and she assured me she felt the same way about us.

Any friction between Dad and me – up until I had my meltdown in the pub – had all been in my head. Though, try as I might, I couldn't ever forget hearing him ask Sally to take me away. I never showed him how I felt. I never, ever let him know my perfect behaviour was hiding my fear that he'd send me away. To Sally, to some unknown relative somewhere, to an awful boarding school like poor Sara Crewe in *A Little Princess*, to I didn't know where. But I knew I couldn't risk it.

I swirled Oscar's paintbrush on my cheek and then ran my thumb over the bristles like I'd done in Mrs Williams's classroom all those years before. Ben was right, I thought. I needed to call Dad. I'd invite him and Barb to stay. He adored the boys and seeing them so happy in their new house would make him realize our move had been the right thing to do. And I'd apologize for all those things I'd said. Maybe I'd even tell him about the mystery. He was logical and methodical and he'd probably be able to help with my research.

I'd call him. But not today. Tomorrow, perhaps. Or the next day. Not today.

Chapter 15

I took a mouthful of tea and made a face.

'Ah yes, forgot to warn you, that the tea here is pretty disgusting,' said Priya, sitting down opposite me in the bleak police canteen in Brighton. She pushed a muffin towards me. 'Have some of this; it hides the taste.'

She smiled at me, her dark eyes searching my face. I thought suspects wouldn't ever be able to pull a fast one with her.

'So has this afternoon been useful?'

I nodded through chocolatey crumbs. 'Very useful,' I said. 'It's good to see how you guys do things down here.'

With Tessa's story in mind, I'd followed Priya round CID, chatting to some of the detectives and taking reams of notes, jotting down every difference I could spot between Sussex and the Met. But while Tessa's investigation was beginning to take shape in my head, it was the Cliff House Mystery, as I was beginning to think of it, that I kept coming back to.

Now I grinned at Priya across the table. 'I've found out some more about our house,' I said.

Priya clapped her hands in glee. 'Tell me everything,' she said.

I took another slurp of horrible tea and outlined what I'd found out about the Hargreaves family – Marcus, Harriet, and Violet. Priya jotted the names down on a piece of paper as I talked.

'And then I found some bits and pieces in an old cupboard,' I said, reaching into my bag and pulling out a folder. 'The dates match up with the Hargreaves bunch. And it's only a hunch but I think they might have something to do with this mystery – otherwise why would the cupboard have been left that way – untouched for more than one hundred and fifty years?'

I pulled the self-portrait out of my folder and opened it up. 'I think this could be a drawing of Violet,' I said.

Priya studied the picture carefully for a minute. Then she put it down and began to leaf through the cuttings with interest. 'God, I can't believe they've lasted this long,' she said. 'Brilliant.'

'It's a really long time ago,' I said, making a face. 'Do your records go back that far?'

Priya nodded. 'Oh we've got them,' she said, clicking the end of her pen, and starting to write in her notebook. 'They're not on the system, though. They're locked away at HQ.'

'Can I get them?'

'If you know what to ask for the archivist will get it for you. You won't be able to sit down for a day and trawl through fifty years of crime reports looking for something that might have happened at your house – they're all stored away carefully. And you can't just run a search like you can on the computer, of course.'

I was disappointed. That was exactly what I'd hoped to do. 'I'll have to try to narrow it down, I suppose,' I said. 'Try to find out if something actually happened. I'm just not sure where to go from here.'

Priya nodded, but she obviously wasn't ready to give up. 'Let me ask around, see if anyone knows anything,' she said. 'There's nothing police officers love more than an unsolved crime, even if it is centuries old. Perhaps someone remembers hearing about it.'

I'd barely made it back to my car, when my phone rang. It was Priya. 'Did I forget something?' I asked.

She laughed. 'I found out about the mystery,' she said.

I was impressed. And slightly dubious. 'No. Way,' I said, doubtfully. 'Spill.'

'Apparently it's legendary,' Priya began. 'But because I've not been here that long, I hadn't heard about it …'

I fished in my bag and pulled out my pad and a pen. I cradled the phone against my ear, and leaning on the steering wheel, I started to write as Priya talked.

'So Marcus Hargreaves built your house,' Priya said. 'He was one of those Victorian philanthropists, you know. He'd made a lot of money somewhere – probably the colonies – and came home to spend it. But he had a conscience.'

I wrote furiously. 'Go on,' I said.

'Well, he lived with his daughter – your Violet I guess. Not sure how old she was when it happened, but she disappeared. Whoosh. Into thin air. Never seen again.'

I stopped writing. 'She ran away,' I said.

'Maybe,' she said. 'But the exact day she vanished, a gruesome crime occurred, right outside her house.'

'You're enjoying this,' I said, chuckling at Priya's undisguised glee. 'What kind of gruesome crime?'

'A murder,' she said in a rubbish Scottish accent. 'And a beating.'

I was already getting out of the car. 'I'm still in the car park,' I said. 'I'm coming back.'

***

'So the neighbours,' I told Ben later, checking my notebook for their names, 'Edwin and Frances Forrest, were attacked that same day.' I was still annoyed with Ben for being in touch with my dad behind my back, and I was even more annoyed that he was right about me getting in touch myself, but I was trying very hard to be a grown-up about it.

'Were they all killed?' Ben leaned over where I was sitting on the sofa and tried to read what I'd written in my notebook. 'Your writing is dreadful.'

I swatted him away. 'Patience,' I said. 'So Mr Hargreaves was away somewhere, and while he was gone something happened. The neighbour, Edwin Forrest, was murdered, and Edwin's wife was so badly beaten that everyone thought she would die.'

'Did she?'

'No, she recovered.'

'And the daughter – your Violet – Mr Hargreaves's daughter. What happened to her?'

'Gone,' I said in a deep voice.

Ben laughed. 'So maybe she was murdered too?' he said.

'Maybe. No one knows.'

'How do we find out?'

'Well,' I said, 'you are lucky to be married to a woman with a brilliant mind for detective work.' I opened my laptop and turned it on.

Ben looked doubtful. 'What are you going to do?'

I gave him a triumphant look. 'I am going to Google Mr Hargreaves,' I said.

'Genius,' Ben said, his voice dripping with sarcasm.

As I typed Marcus Hargreaves into Google, there was a cry from upstairs. Stan. Ben and I faced off for a moment as we waited to see if he'd settle, or which of us would admit weakness first and go to him. I lost, of course. I always did. So I thrust my laptop at Ben and went upstairs.

'See what you can find out,' I said.

By the time I'd tucked Stan back in and waited for his breathing to become regular again, Ben had found Marcus Hargreaves and brought up lots of information about the man who'd built our house. He had his own Wiki entry, he had mentions on several history sites, and he even had a school named after him, down in a dark corner of South-east London. At least he had, until last year when it had become the Excellence Academy. Ben snorted as he read about the name change.

'Read it out,' I demanded as I sat back down next to Ben.

Ben found the Wikipedia page and started to read:

'Marcus Hargreaves (1807–1871) was an industrialist from Sussex,' he began.

'What does it say about his daughter,' I said.

Ben grimaced at me. 'Hold on,' he said and I winced. My impatience always made him want to be infuriatingly slow.

'He was an industrialist who made stacks of cash exporting machinery to the colonies,' Ben scanned the page. 'So no murky slave owning like I assumed when you said he worked in the Caribbean.'

'They wouldn't have named a primary school after him if he was a slave owner,' I pointed out.

'All right, smart arse.' Ben flipped my notebook at me. 'He saw the poverty in the East End, near the docks – crikey he'd be surprised to see the money round there now – and started a school and an orphanage for the children of dock workers.'

I was impressed. 'Does it say anything about his personal life?'

Ben scrolled down. 'Yep. He married Harriet and they had Violet in 1837.'

'What else does it say?' I said. 'Does it say anything about his daughter disappearing?'

'That's it,' Ben said.

'Let me see.' I pulled the laptop towards me and the screen went blank.

'Shit,' I said. 'I need to charge it. The lead's in the car.'

Ben shot me a disappointed look that made me laugh. He swept me into a hug and for a while, Mr Hargreaves was forgotten.

Chapter 16

1855
Violet

It was hot and stuffy in the attic study and I couldn't settle. I sat on the chaise, thinking about Mr Forrest, who I'd not seen for days and days, and of Father, and Mr Wallace, and wondering what would become of my life.

Listlessly I fanned myself with my hat. The day was ending, but it was still warm and the air was close – waiting for a storm to clear the mugginess. I sighed. I felt like I was waiting too, watching and waiting, for my life to begin. I thought, suddenly, of a painting and, with a burst of energy, got to my feet and went to the cupboard in the corner of the room where I kept all my treasured art books, paints, and pictures.

Pinned to the inside of the door was a print of *Mariana*, by my hero John Everett Millais. I'd cut it out of the Royal Academy programme when I'd seen the actual work a few years ago. Father had taken me to the exhibition, not expecting my love of art to be ignited so violently. I allowed myself a small smile at the thought that Father was to blame for my desperation to paint.

Now I gazed at the small picture. It didn't do any justice to the original, which was seared on my memory for ever, but it showed enough. In it, Mariana – from Shakespeare's *Measure for Measure* – was waiting, waiting, waiting for her fiancé, who had rejected her after her dowry was lost. She stood watching, face racked with boredom, at a stained-glass window, but she never saw his ship, because he wasn't coming. She was doomed to wait for ever.

At the Academy, a few lines from Tennyson's poem about poor Mariana had accompanied the painting.

As I had read the poem: 'My life is dreary. He cometh not,' I had been struck by a sense of recognition.

'That's me,' I thought to myself now as I pinned the picture to the corner of my easel. 'But instead of waiting for a fiancé, I'm waiting for life.'

I sketched the outline of Mariana, the window, and the autumn leaves that showed the passage of time. Then I gathered my paints and began to fill in the rich reds, oranges, and blues that Millais had used. But Mariana's face I left blank.

When the light faded in the room, I stopped and went downstairs for dinner. But I spoke little to Father and I went to bed early. Then, the next morning, as dawn broke, I climbed the stairs to the attic again and started work.

Eventually, as afternoon became evening, I stretched and stepped back to look at what I'd done. Narrowing my eyes, I assessed my copy of the painting. It was good; I could see that. But I had to admit the composition and the colours were all Millais's. I'd added my own twist, though. Instead of Mariana's long face and straight, neat hair, I'd painted my own round apple cheeks, dusted with freckles, and unruly red curls. I was Mariana, waiting for something and 'aweary' like the poem said.

It was far and away the best thing I'd ever painted. My King Canute was good, but this was something special, even I could see that. I thought of Mr Forrest again and wondered when he would go to London and see Millais. If I wanted to change my life, I had to take control. I had to get him to take my work to London and this was the painting he should take. This, and maybe some others, but this one certainly. But to get him to take them, I would have to swallow my embarrassment and see him again.

I looked at the painting once more, looking at myself waiting for something that never came, and made a decision. I would wait no longer. I would call on him. That very evening. And I would tell him I had work for him to look at. I shivered at the thought of being so bold.

Later, I put on my hat and gloves, and set off to the cottage next door. The summer air was thick and heavy with storm clouds looming over the sea. I felt light-headed but whether it was because of the atmosphere or nerves about calling on Mr Forrest, I didn't know.

Heart hammering in my chest, I walked up the path and rapped on the door-knocker. It echoed round the house and then all was silent. After a few moments, I heard footsteps and mentally rehearsed what I would say when the housekeeper opened the door. The steps drew nearer and I heard the lock being pulled back.

But it was Frances Forrest who opened the door, her long pale face peering round as though she expected unwelcome guests. A shadow darkened her eyes when she saw me.

'Miss Hargreaves,' she said.

I was so surprised to see her that I forgot all niceties. 'Oh,' I said.

Mrs Forrest smiled slightly. 'You were expecting to see Edwin, I imagine,' she said, opening the door wider and motioning me inside. 'He's not here.'

Finding myself completely out of speech, I said nothing. I had no reasons ready to excuse me from going into the house, so reluctantly I stepped into the cool hallway. Overhead thunder rumbled.

'He's gone to Brighton,' Mrs Forrest continued as she led the way into the drawing room. 'I'm not sure why. Something about work, in all probability. Do sit down.'

I obeyed. I took off my gloves and held them tightly in my hands. My palms were sweating.

'Hasn't it got dark, suddenly,' Mrs Forrest said, sweeping past and turning on one of the oil lamps next to me. 'The storm is on its way. I'm pleased. Some rain will be good for the garden.'

She went to the door and called out. 'Agnes, I have a friend come to call. Could you bring us some tea?'

I heard a muffled shout from the kitchen.

Mrs Forrest sat opposite me and frowned. 'She's terribly ill-mannered,' she confessed. 'But she does make awfully nice cake.'

I was struck by how ridiculous this all was – tea and pleasantries – when really all I wanted to do was give Mr Forrest my painting. I hadn't thought I'd end up having tea with this strange woman with sad eyes.

'I'm so pleased you called,' Mrs Forrest was saying. 'I

97

wanted to get to know you better. I know Edwin is rather taken with you.'

I was taken aback. Had he told his wife about meeting me on the beach?

'And I with him,' I managed to stutter. I paused as Agnes banged a tea tray down on the table between us.

'I'll pour, thank you,' Mrs Forrest said. Agnes stamped out, muttering under her breath. Mrs Forrest smiled again, properly this time. It made her look much younger.

'You look very frightened,' she said. 'Are you feeling well?'

I decided my best chance was to tell the truth. 'I'm disappointed not to find your husband at home,' I began. 'He asked me …' I stopped, then began again. 'I am an artist.' It was the first time I'd ever said the words out loud.

Mrs Forrest handed me a cup of tea but she didn't speak.

I drew breath and started again. 'Mr Forrest expressed an interest in my work and asked if he could take it to London to show his friends,' I said.

Mrs Forrest sat back in her chair. She looked tired. 'Ah,' she said. 'His friends.'

'John Everett Millais,' I said.

'John Everett Millais?' Mrs Forrest repeated.

I was losing patience. Either we were talking at cross-purposes or Mrs Forrest was really rather dim.

I spoke slowly. 'He said he would show my work to John Everett Millais.' I put my cup down without tasting the tea. 'Would you be so kind as to tell him I called? I would be happy to receive him at home.' I didn't mention that Father was hardly ever there.

98

I stood up. 'Thank you for the tea,' I said. 'I will see myself out.'

Back home I went straight to my studio. The sky was dark now and over the sea I could see flashes of lightning. They lit up the wall where I'd pinned my version of *Mariana*. I knew it was good. I knew it. Now I needed some other work – some original work – for Mr Forrest to take.

I curled up on the sofa and imagined myself in a coffee house, talking to Millais and his friends about art. I would bewitch those clever men, dazzle them with my witty talk and exciting ideas. Just because I'd never said anything witty or exciting in my whole life didn't mean I couldn't do it when I needed to.

Father said my favourite artists were dangerous, but I didn't agree. I'd soon have them eating out of my hands, like Daniel in the lions' den. A flash lit up the room again as I reached for my pencil. Daniel. I opened my sketchbook and began to draw.

Chapter 17

1855
Frances

Frances watched her go, the slump of her shoulders the only clue to how disappointed she was not to have seen Edwin.

She wondered if Edwin did know Millais. It was unlikely, though who knew what he got up to in London. She certainly didn't, just like she knew little of what he was doing in Brighton. She suspected he was visiting a prostitute. She didn't mind. If it kept him away from her, so much the better.

She feared for Violet. Edwin was so charming and she could see he was an escape route to a pretty, clever, talented young woman. Violet certainly wasn't the first woman to see Edwin that way, but she didn't know how dangerous he could be.

Frances was torn between her desire to protect her unborn baby by simply staying away from her husband as much as she was able, and her longing to prevent Violent from getting too involved with Edwin. She was helpless.

Chapter 18

1855
Violet

I threw down my paintbrush in exasperation.

'I just think it would look better,' I said.

Philips grimaced. 'I'm sure it would, Miss,' he said. 'But if your father finds out it'll be the end of my job.'

I stared at him in surprise. I was used to Father saying no to me, but this was something new. Philips was normally so biddable. I sighed again. Time for a new tactic.

'Dear Philips,' I said, looking at him through my eyelashes. 'It would mean so much to me.'

He grinned at me, showing dimples in his handsome face, and a broken front tooth. 'Miss,' he said. 'You know I'll help you any way I can. But taking off my shirt is a step too far even for me.'

'Daniel wouldn't have worn a shirt,' I said, irritated once more.

'I dare say he wouldn't,' Philips said.

His calmness annoyed me. I lifted my chin in defiance. 'I order you to take your shirt off.'

Philips stood up and walked towards me. He was closer to me than he'd ever been and he smelled of the garden and sweat. 'I order you to get some manners, little girl,' he said. Then he turned and went, his heavy footsteps echoing through the house as he stomped down the stairs.

I threw myself on the sofa in despair. This was my last chance, I thought. Father had gone to Manchester – he would be away for a good while. And when he got back, he'd made it very clear, he wanted me to meet Mr Wallace. He'd have me married off by Christmas, sooner than I'd ever thought was possible, I was convinced. And then my dreams of a career in art would be over. Unless I could get Mr Forrest to take my paintings to London before then.

I'd wanted to paint Philips as Daniel in the lions' den. Though his lean body was perfect in the pose I'd imagined, I'd always thought Daniel would wear only trousers. But Philips refused to remove his shirt no matter how much I begged. I didn't know what a man's body looked like, not really, because I'd only ever seen them in paintings. How was I supposed to draw something I'd never seen?

But being so rude to Philips hadn't helped me at all. He was my only ally – my only friend, really, sad as that sounded – and I'd be lost without him. I resolved to apologize. I was painfully aware that this longing to be an artist was changing me. I'd never lied as much as I had recently, or been as rude, or as bold. It was like it had taken over my whole life and the sheer frustration of not being able to do what I wanted to do was twisting my whole being. And yet, it seemed worthwhile. It was so important that I couldn't for one moment imagine how my life would be without art in it.

But all that aside, I was left with the problem of Daniel. I stood up and looked at the canvas. It wasn't right, I thought. It wasn't real. I leaned against the windowsill and looked at the painting again. No. Philips simply looked like Philips in the lions' den. I needed Daniel. I needed another model.

Leaning my forehead against the cool glass, I gazed out at the sea. There was another storm coming. Fat drops of rain splashed against the window. Down on the beach, a figure caught my eye.

Mr Forrest, I thought. Without hesitation, or any thought of the awkwardness I had felt the last time I had seen him, I picked up my shawl from the sofa, skipped down the stairs and out on to the lane. The rain splattered on to the scorched earth, splashing on to my feet, but I walked quickly, undeterred, scrambling down the steep path faster than ever before. The beach, though, was deserted. Disappointed, I stood for a moment, watching the grey waves pounding the sand, damp and shivering in my thin shawl.

'Violet?'

I looked round. Mr Forrest was standing beneath an overhanging rock behind me, tucked into a shallow cave and sheltering from the rain. He gestured with his head that I should join him and gratefully I ducked beneath the rocky shelf, glad to be out of the rain.

'It's getting worse.' Mr Forrest didn't look at me; instead he stared out at the clouds looming purple over the waves.

A rumble of thunder sounded and the rain increased. I shivered and Mr Forrest looked at me, concern etched on his face.

'Dearest Violet, you're freezing,' he said, slipping off his jacket. He took off my shawl and draped his warm coat over my shoulders, then he hung the shawl from the rock.

'It should dry soon,' he said.

I smiled, shivering at the memory of his touch on my skin now, instead of from the cold. 'Thank you, Mr Forrest,' I said.

He waved his hand. 'Call me Edwin,' he said. 'I think we're friends, don't you?'

I nodded and Edwin looked pleased.

'Let's sit a while and wait for the storm to pass.'

He sank down on to the sandy floor of the cave, his back against the stony wall. After a second, I joined him, spreading out my wet skirt so it would have more chance to dry. It felt as though we were in our own little world, away from the ordinary rules of society where Edwin wouldn't even have called me Violet, let alone asked me to sit with him, away from the comforting watch of a chaperone. I felt heady with anticipation. Anything could happen here. Anything at all.

'So tell me,' Edwin began. 'What brings you out in a rainstorm?'

'Frustration,' I said. 'I'm beginning a new painting and it's not going well.'

Edwin frowned. 'Tell me,' he said.

I flushed, thinking of how rudely I'd spoken to Philips. 'I have a problem with the model,' I admitted. Cautiously, I explained what I'd wanted Philips to do, and Edwin laughed.

'It was not funny,' I said, hurt. Then I realized actually it was and laughed too.

We sat in easy companionship, while the storm lashed the beach, and chatted about my painting. Edwin offered ideas about how I could compose my work and I tried hard to remember his suggestions.

After a while I realized his arm was lying loosely about my

shoulders. I knew I should move away but it felt so natural I couldn't bring myself to shift across the sand.

'So your model,' Edwin was saying. 'There is no persuading him to do as you wish?'

I shook my head. 'None at all. He is too afraid of my father. And I can't say I blame him.'

Edwin turned his head to look at me. His face was very close to mine. Again I thought I should move and again I stayed exactly where I was.

'I,' Edwin said. 'I am not afraid of anything. Not the thunder.' His face moved closer. 'Not lightning.' He moved closer still. 'And certainly not your father.' So gently I barely noticed him do it, he pressed his lips to mine. 'I will model for you, sweet Violet.'

I was dizzy. Whether it was the kiss, the joy of finding a new model, or simply the closeness of the air in the cave, I didn't know.

I have been good for many years, I thought as I sank into Edwin's embrace. I have done everyone's bidding but my own. Not any more.

Chapter 19

Present day
Ella

The next day was gloriously warm. We'd definitely moved to Sussex at the right time of year. We were into August now and I was starting to think about school uniforms for Oscar and getting Stan ready for nursery. I thought the tiny village school was going to be a big change from their large London primary, but I hoped they'd settle down quickly. Meeting Priya had definitely helped, because Oscar had already met Amber and Priya had promised to arrange a few play dates with some other children from their class before term started.

Ben went off for the final training session before the football season started – he was nervous and antsy and I was glad to see the back of him for a few hours. And I decided to make a few more notes for my plot, then go for a walk along the cliff top and scout for a location for the supposed murder in my novel. I went upstairs and threw open the windows of the study, smiling as I heard the sound of the children playing in the garden with Margaret and Dumbledore the puppy, and got to work.

After an hour or so, I wiped the sweat from my brow, and read through my notes. I'd plotted out the whole novel and I was quite pleased with it. Ish. I was so determined to make things work now we'd moved that I could see the positives in writing anything at all, but I still wasn't sure I was feeling this new story.

I thought I'd email it to my agent and see what she thought, before I wrote any more. I'd found myself glancing over at the self-portrait, which I'd put back in the middle of my whiteboard, while I was writing and wondering if she was the missing Violet. I'd even mixed up names a few times and written Hargreaves when I should have written something else. Maybe that was the story I should be writing, I thought. It was just a shame I didn't know what the story was.

I stood up and stretched, then walking to the window I breathed in the late summer air and smiled to myself. I saw the children bundling inside – for a drink, I assumed – and decided to go and join them for ten minutes before I headed off for my walk. But as I turned from the window, the cupboard in the corner of the room caught my attention again. The door edged open, gently, as though inviting me to look inside. There was much more to investigate in there, I knew. I'd only just scratched the surface of everything that had been shut up inside. And obviously I couldn't resist.

It was a big cupboard, with a sloping ceiling down to the floor. The space inside smelled old and fusty, its floor lined in old, long-since-changed carpet. I discovered I could step inside, if I ducked my head; so I did, holding the door open in case it swung shut and trapped me. There were books on the shelves and, propped in the corner, a roll of papers tied with string. I picked it up, backed out of the cupboard and shut the door again. My heart was beating fast.

I sat on the floor and pulled the string down to the bottom

of the roll. The papers sprang open. I took them apart and spread them out on the floor.

There was a large painting, then several smaller pencil drawings. I smoothed them out but they rolled up again persistently, so I went to my own shelves and pulled out some heavy books to weigh them down.

The sketches were all of a man, maybe in his early forties. In one he was wearing a suit and shirt with a high collar and in the rest he was stripped to the waist, seated on the ground, with indistinct shapes of animals – they looked a bit like big cats, lions perhaps – sketched around him. He was handsome with broad shoulders and thick hair and looked serene and calm in most of the pictures, more bold and slightly defiant in the one where he was wearing the suit. I wondered if the suited drawing was the one that showed him as he really was – in his comfort zone, as it were.

The drawings were very good. They seemed to be preparatory sketches, the beginning of another work, and they had a storytelling feel to them – though they were telling a story that I felt I almost knew, but couldn't quite remember.

I turned my attention to the painting. It was larger than the drawings and full of muted oranges and reds. It glowed in the sunlight in the attic room.

It showed a woman in a blue dress standing in front of a stained-glass window. She was leaning back, massaging the small of her back, a look of boredom on her face.

I looked closer. The painting was familiar. I'd seen it somewhere recently...

With sudden inspiration, I got up and went to my desk where I'd left the copy of *Illustrated London News* I'd taken from the cupboard. Carefully turning the soft, aged pages, I scanned for the picture and found it. This was where I'd seen it before.

Mariana *by John Everett Millais*, I read. *Today we have an engraving of a new painting by Millais, currently being exhibited at the Royal Academy …*

So what was this? The original? Surely not? Though I didn't know much, I'd heard of Millais and I knew he was a well-known British artist. Had I stumbled upon some hidden masterpiece? Could I be one of those people on *Antiques Roadshow*, gasping as they told me how much this treasure was worth (I conveniently ignored the fact that we didn't own this house and any riches would go straight to our landlord).

I squinted at the picture again, as I looked for a signature, and breathed out as I read Violet Hargreaves in the corner.

'Violet Hargreaves,' I said out loud. So Violet really was the artist, then. Marcus Hargreaves's missing daughter had been a painter. No riches for me, then, for finding a missing Millais, but even better – another clue in the Hargreaves mystery.

I scrambled to my feet and took down the self-portrait. Even to my untrained eye, it was obviously drawn by the same artist. So the girl in the picture with the flowery dress and the sweet smile definitely was Violet.

'Hello, Vi,' I said. The girl in the picture stared back at me.

Intrigued now, I sat at my desk and typed '*Mariana* by John Everett Millais' into the search page. Up came a page about the Pre-Raphaelite Brotherhood with the illustration, the same bored woman in the blue dress.

I pulled the screen closer and gazed at the picture. This one was signed John Everett Millais with the initials PRB beneath the name. Violet Hargreaves had painted a rather good copy.

Downstairs, the front door slammed and I heard the puppy barking as Stan shouted, 'Daddy!'

Ben will be interested in this, I thought. Carefully, I rolled up the pictures again, took the self-portrait from my whiteboard, and picked up my laptop, then I went downstairs to show him.

Chapter 20

Ben was wearing a club T-shirt and shorts, leaning against the kitchen sink, and drinking a glass of water. Stan and Oscar were still in the garden, shouting to each other, and Margaret was sitting on the patio, watching them. She waved to me as I came into the kitchen and I waved back.

Ben raised an eyebrow at me. 'What have you got there?' he said.

'How was training?' I asked, ignoring his question and starting to unroll the pictures on the table.

'Good,' he said. 'Everyone's fit. Ready for the new season.'

'Nervous?' I said.

He waved his hand. 'Nah.'

I grinned at him. 'Truth?'

'Absolutely bloody terrified.'

I gave him a kiss.

'It'll be fine,' I said. 'You're a brilliant physio and they're lucky to have you.'

Ben gave me a weak smile. 'What's all this then?' he said. 'Trying to distract me with old bits of dirty paper?'

I made a mock-outraged face. 'These are not just any old bits of dirty paper,' I said. 'I've found some more pictures.

Violet was definitely an artist and it's definitely her in the self-portrait.'

I carried on unrolling the pictures, weighing them down with the salt and pepper cruets and Stan's plastic beaker. Seeing something interesting happening inside, Oscar and Stan both came into the kitchen and crowded round to see. Margaret lifted Stan up so he could see.

'These are Violet's sketches – see she's signed them,' I explained. 'And this is a painting she did. It's a copy of a work by John Everett Millais. The original is here …'

I opened my laptop and turned it round so everyone could see the picture while Ben peered at the paintings.

'I'm no expert,' he said. 'But these are very good, aren't they?'

I nodded. I smoothed out Violet's version of the picture and realized something. 'Oh look,' I said, pointing at the face of the woman in the original painting on the screen, and then the one in Violet's painting. 'I didn't notice when I was looking at it upstairs, but she's different.'

Ben wrapped his arms around me from behind and looked over my shoulder. 'You're right,' he said.

The woman in the original painting had a long, pale face and neatly tied hair. In Violet's copy the woman's face was rounder with apple-like cheeks and untamed curls.

Oscar hung off Ben's arm.

'That's the lady,' he said, pointing to Violet's self-portrait. 'The same lady.'

'Oh he's right,' I said, looking from Violet's portrait to her copy of *Mariana*. 'She's painted her own face into the picture. Why would she do that?'

'I guess we'll never know for sure.'

I gave Ben the look I always gave him when I was disappointed in him. 'I'm sure there are ways to find out,' I said, a bit more sharply than I'd intended.

I read the blurb on the website.

Mariana *is an 1851 oil-on-wood painting by John Everett Millais. The painting is based on the lonely Mariana from William Shakespeare's* Measure for Measure, *and the poem by Alfred, Lord Tennyson. In the story, Mariana was to marry, but her dowry was lost in a shipwreck and she was spurned. She waited in vain for her lover to come.*

'Perhaps she identified with this Mariana,' Ben said, obviously keen to make amends. 'Maybe she was waiting for someone.'

'Or something,' I said. I touched the woman's face in the picture. 'Poor Violet.'

'What about the other drawings?' Ben said.

Oscar had climbed on to a chair and leaned over the sketch of a man sitting on a stool, surrounded by what looked liked big cats. 'It's Daniel,' he said.

'Who's Daniel?' Ben asked.

'Daniel in the lions' den,' Oscar said. 'Look, he should be scared because of all the lions, but they've all sat down. They're not going to eat him, because of God.'

Ben and I, who only went to church for weddings, exchanged a look over his head. Oscar sighed, obviously exasperated at how slow his dense parents were being.

'This is Daniel,' he said with exaggerated patience, pointing at the man. 'And these are the lions.'

Ben looked closer. 'I think he's right,' he said. 'It's a Bible story but it looks very real.'

I nodded, understanding. 'I read about the Pre-Raphaelites in one of the newspapers I found,' I said. 'They often painted biblical subjects but from real models. Caused quite a stir at the time, apparently.'

Oscar had lost interest. 'It would be better if the lions ate Daniel,' he said. 'Raaaarrr.' He pretended to eat Stan's feet and Stan squealed in delight. Margaret herded the children out of the back door, laughing along with them.

Ben looked at the pictures again. 'So does this mean Violet was a Pre-Raphaelite?' he asked. 'Do you know anything about them?'

I wrinkled my nose up. 'Only what I remember from A Level, and from George telling me bits and pieces at uni,' I said. 'Which is enough to know they're not my cup of tea. But I can't imagine that Violet was part of that gang – a middle-class woman would never have been able to pursue a career in art in those days. I think they were a bunch of young men, drinking and having their pick of gorgeous models.'

'Sounds like a good life,' Ben said. I gave him a disapproving look and he grinned at me.

'Maybe Violet wanted to be an artist,' he pointed out. 'She seems to have been good enough.'

'It's sad, isn't it,' I said. 'She had the talent, but she couldn't do it because she was a woman. So unfair.'

I picked up the drawing of the man wearing a shirt and trousers. 'I wonder who her model was. She must have known him well to paint him without clothes. But it can't be her husband, because she was still called Hargreaves. And she would only have been about eighteen in that self-portrait.'

'Perhaps there was a scandal,' said Ben with glee. 'Perhaps she was cast out of the community and that's why she went missing.'

'I'm going to find out,' I said, making my mind up. 'I'm going to find out what happened to Violet.'

'Well, surely it can't be that hard to discover more about her,' Ben said. 'Maybe even track down a photograph?'

I shook my head. 'Too early for photos, I think,' I said, thinking of the newspapers, which were all illustrated with sketches. 'But I bet there's a portrait of her somewhere.'

I stood on my tiptoes to kiss him.

'I'm going to find her,' I said again.

Chapter 21

In these days of Google and information at your fingertips, I'd sort of forgotten how labour-intensive research could be. And after more than an hour in the central library in Brighton a few days later, I was beginning to regret my decision to track down Violet Hargreaves.

My mistake – I thought, as I sat on the library carpet, surrounded by books – was trying to combine school-uniform shopping and research. The boys and I were all hot, tired, and bored. I'd thought spending time in the air-conditioned library would be a nice break from the crowded shops, but it had turned out to be a bit of a thankless task.

I'd found a pile of local history textbooks and I was busy leafing through, looking for any reference to Marcus Hargreaves or Violet. So far, I'd found nothing relevant though I'd read quite a lot about Victorian Sussex and way too much about how they brought the railways to Brighton. I was, if I was completely honest, bored out of my mind. The kids were listless and Stan's eyes were drooping and I knew if I didn't want a nightmare at bedtime I had to make sure he didn't go to sleep.

'Five more minutes, kids,' I said. 'Then we can go for ice cream.'

Oscar didn't look up from his book about dinosaurs. 'Chocolate?' he said.

'And strawberry?' asked Stan, who was lying on a beanbag, flicking the pages of a copy of *The Gruffalo*.

'Yep,' I said. I picked up another book and flipped to the index, scanning for the name Hargreaves. This time I struck gold. In yet another section on the expansion of the railways, was a mention of Marcus Hargreaves. Sitting up a bit straighter, I read about Marcus's philanthropic nature and how the spread of the railways allowed him to travel round the country to his various businesses. Yawn. Then further down the page, something caught my eye.

Friends of Marcus Hargreaves at the time believed his devotion to doing good work stemmed from tragedy in his personal life. He lost his wife, Harriet, and his young daughter was brought up for a short while by relatives. Later, the same daughter was a victim of a violent crime and disappeared. She was never found.

I stared at the page in astonishment. Violet was sent away, I thought. Her father sent her away, just as mine had wanted to do with me. Poor, poor girl. Again I felt the pull towards this long-dead teenager because of the similarities between us. I had to find out what happened to her.

I wondered what Violet had been like and whether her father had been supportive of her art. Somehow I doubted it – I thought middle-class daughters of Victorian philanthropic industrialists would not have been expected to have a career as an artist. Maybe her dad was against her painting and she did it anyway. Perhaps she didn't worry about him sending her away because he'd already done it. Or maybe she just didn't care. I felt a flush of pride for Violet.

'Well done, girl,' I whispered under my breath. 'Well done for doing it anyway.'

Oscar looked up and gave me a withering look.

'One more book,' I said. 'Then we'll go, I promise.'

I put the book with the mention of Marcus to one side to borrow, and picked up the final text I'd found. Again I turned to the index and looked for mentions of Hargreaves and again there was nothing. Ah well, it was time to give up anyway. I flicked through the pages of pictures in the centre of the book at random, looking for what I didn't know, and stopped in astonishment as I came across Violet's sketch of the handsome man. It was a slightly different pose, but he was wearing the same clothes and it had obviously been drawn at the same time.

'Look, Oscar,' I said, turning the page round so he could see.

With some effort he raised his eyes from a picture of a T-Rex and glanced at the book. 'It's the man from the picture of Daniel,' he said, without interest.

I ruffled his hair and turned my attention back to the page, scanning the text until I found the section about the man, and began to read.

Sussex solicitor Edwin Forrest (pictured, artist unknown) was murdered in 1855. His pregnant wife, Frances, was also attacked and badly injured. A neighbour of the couple, Violet Hargreaves, who disappeared at the same time, is thought to have drowned, although no body was ever found and some people at the time believed she had also been murdered by the same attacker who was never caught.

So more pieces of the jigsaw fell into place. The mystery model's name was Edwin Forrest. And he was the murdered neighbour. I felt a wave of sadness for poor Violet, consigned to history as an unknown artist. I was even more determined to find out what had happened to her. She was so young in 1855 – just a teenager. Had she drowned? The sea near our house was unpredictable and rough as it crashed on to the rocks. I was sure there had been accidents there in the past. Or maybe she really had been murdered by the same attacker who killed this neighbour and his wife? I looked at the page again. No, his wife hadn't died. She'd just been injured. How awful to be attacked when she was pregnant. Had she lost the baby? Probably, I thought with a shudder.

This was all fascinating and I was itching to write it all down. For the first time, I admitted to myself that Tessa's next case might have to wait a while because Violet's story had intrigued me so much I could no longer ignore it. I felt a strong connection to the girl who'd lived and died so long ago, and I knew it was because I thought we were similar – both having lost our mothers and grown up with our fathers, and now I knew she'd been sent away too I was even more drawn to her tale.

I looked at the picture in the book again, sure that finding out more about Edwin Forrest would be my next step. Then I tucked that book and the other one under my arm and scooped up my bag.

'Right, boys,' I said. 'Who's for ice cream?'

When we got home from the library, I phoned Priya, who was at the police station.

'So now we've got a date to go with the names of the victims,' I told her.

At the other end of the phone, Priya laughed. 'You're better at detective work than we are,' she said. 'I have found out, though, that it all happened too long ago to be in the archives at HQ – there's a records archive in Lewes where everything is kept. If you like, I'll email them and let them know you're coming and what you want to see. I'll give you a call when it's sorted.'

'That would be great,' I said, gratefully.

Ben had taken the boys out to the shop to buy some milk – and stop Stan sleeping, poor boy – so the house was quiet and I felt restless. I knew I should be writing but I couldn't settle to Tessa's story when Violet was who I was really interested in. Instead I made myself a – black – coffee then wandered aimlessly into the garden.

I walked to the end of the lawn, then turned and looked back at the house. The small window in the attic looked at me blankly. It was above the boys' bedroom as far as I could tell. The window was tiny, no more than one or two bricks wide, and lower down than the rest of the windows in the room. I went round the side of the house and looked up. There was nothing on that side. No clues about what the window was. It must just be for ventilation at the top of the house, like Ben said. It did get very hot up there, when the sun was shining.

I wandered back upstairs to the attic, feeling a bit guilty for wishing that the weather would cool off a fraction, and stared out of the windows at the garden, where I'd just been standing.

Opening the large window, I leaned out as far as I dared

and twisted to look at the window that belonged to no room. It offered me no clues. It was really frustrating.

'Ella.' Ben – who I'd not heard come home, though now I could hear the boys shouting downstairs – had come up beside me unnoticed. 'The boys said you went to the library? Did you find anything?'

'I did,' I said, triumphant in my discovery. I had put the sketches up on the whiteboard, alongside Violet's self-portrait and the beautiful copy of *Mariana*. Now I pointed at one of the Daniel sketches.

'This is Edwin Forrest,' I said. 'He's the man who was murdered when Violet disappeared.

Ben looked impressed. 'Blimey,' he said. 'This is a proper mystery, isn't it?'

I grinned. 'Bloody well is. I want to find out what happened to Violet. So I need to find out more about this Edwin and his murder, I think. I'm going to go to the police archive and root around in the old records. Priya said she could set it up for me.'

Ben looked a bit shell-shocked. 'Good,' he said. 'I think.'

'And I'm going to email George,' I told him. George was my art historian friend. 'Use his expertise. He owes me anyway, after I sorted out the mess he'd made of his taxes.'

Ben smiled at me. 'And Tessa?'

I shrugged. 'She'll still be there when I've found out more about Violet.'

'Then do it,' Ben said. 'Because, I think you've found your next book.'

Chapter 22

1855
Violet

Edwin didn't touch me for days and days after he'd kissed me on the beach during the storm. It was like the most delicious torture I had ever experienced because I saw him almost every day. I always began a painting with preparatory sketches and Edwin had volunteered to pose for those, too. I wanted to get to know him, to understand every part of his body – the golden downy hairs on his thick forearms, the thick wavy hair on his head that made him seem leonine and a perfect fit for Daniel, his broad shoulders, and narrow waist.

At first, we went back to the beach. With autumn around the corner, it was normally deserted and the few people who did saunter by kept to the firmer sand close to the waves, where it was easier to walk.

I set up my easel in the shade of an overhanging rock on the first day and sketched the scenery while I waited for Edwin to arrive. My stomach was knotted but whether it was anxiety or excitement or a mixture of both, I couldn't tell. I tried to concentrate on my sketching, watching how the waves broke on the rocks at one end of the beach and trying to capture the movement with my pencil strokes. A stone skittering down the cliff path made me jump and I looked up to see Edwin coming towards me. He nodded at me and lifted his hat.

'Miss Hargreaves,' he said, formally, as though yesterday he had not pressed his lips to mine just yards from where we now stood.

'Violet,' I said. 'Call me Violet.'

He smiled at me then, a smile that made my heart lift and my legs tingle. Was this love? I had no clue.

'Shall we get on?' Edwin said briskly. 'I do have some work to do later.'

I realized I was staring at him. Flushing, I picked up my pencil. 'Certainly,' I said. 'Could you sit on that rock?' I gestured and Edwin sat down, looking out of place on the beach in his smart, dark suit.

'If you could stay in that position for now,' I said, beginning to move my pencil over the paper. 'Try to relax.'

I worked quickly; I always did, but I'd never been so aware of my subject before. I exhaled every breath along with Edwin, and felt the weight of his gaze.

Eventually after an hour or so, Edwin stood up. 'I must go,' he said, brushing sand from his trousers. 'Frances will be wondering where I've got to.'

I understood the unspoken assertion that Edwin didn't want his wife to know where he'd been, something that thrilled and scared me equally.

I looked at Edwin over the top of my easel. 'Can you come again tomorrow?' I asked, astonished at my own bravery. 'I'd like to sketch you some more.'

Edwin picked his hat up. 'I shall try,' he said. 'Good day.'

I watched him go, wondering how I would get through the hours until I saw him again.

After that my days fell into a rhythm of sorts. Each day, after breakfast, I would struggle down to the beach and set up my equipment. I had hit a stumbling block with my sketches – so eager had I been to find a model for Daniel that I'd not considered the difficulty of painting a lion. So I watched the dogs that ran on the beach each day, chasing each other and barking at the surf.

Edwin had work, of course, so I knew I wouldn't see him in the morning. But as the shadows lengthened and the sun began to sink behind the horizon, I looked hopefully at the path. When I saw him striding down towards me, my heart would thump.

The second day passed without him touching me, again. When he bade me goodbye that evening I was listless and confused. Had I dreamt our time in the cave? Had I imagined the feeling of his lips on mine?

The third day he didn't come at all, and I thought I might stop breathing, so disappointed was I. Where was he? My whole body ached with longing. My skin was raw, my nerves tingling. All I thought about was Edwin. All I cared about was Edwin. He had overwhelmed me.

The next day Edwin appeared on the beach, just as I was beginning to think I'd never see him again. It was all I could do to stop myself dancing a little jig as I watched him carefully climb down the steep path.

'Violet,' he said. He took my hand and raised it to his lips, brushing my skin with the bristles on his face. I drew my breath in sharply. I was so aware of him – of his presence, his maleness – that I thought I might faint. Edwin was dressed more casually today, in a loose shirt. He looked relaxed and handsome. My pencil flew across the page, capturing him as he sat on the rock, gazing up at me with a slight smile on his pink lips.

Later, as I packed up my things, Edwin came to where I stood.

'Can I see?' he said, looking at the sketch clipped to my easel.

My hair blew in the sea breeze and whipped across my face. Edwin reached out and gently pushed the strand behind my ear. I froze, my whole body tingling in anticipation of his kiss. Edwin stroked my cheek, I tilted my face towards his … and then he smiled.

'Goodbye, Violet,' he said.

Chapter 23

I thought I was in love. It was the only explanation for the way I was feeling. I thought about Edwin all the time. I spent hours just lying on my bed, thinking about our life together. I wondered what illness Frances had and imagined it could kill her. Dreadful as it sounded, I hoped it would kill her. I felt a brief – very brief – flash of guilt as I imagined the funeral at the village church. It would be raining, I thought. A handful of mourners – not many. I didn't think Frances had friends. Edwin, thin-lipped with sadness but stoic and brave.

I planned how I would comfort Edwin, the grieving widower, and then – after a respectable amount of time – we would go to Father together and tell him we'd developed feelings for one another and we could marry. I even imagined our children. Two boys, just like Edwin, and a little girl.

I didn't really know much about what went on with men and women – though I wasn't completely in the dark; I had grown up in the country, after all. I'd seen animals together, but somehow I couldn't make that work with men and women in my head. I considered asking Mabel but the shame of that conversation, even in my imagination, made me shudder.

Instead I trusted that Edwin would lead the way. He was married, after all. He would know what to do.

At night, when my room was dark, I allowed myself to think about our kiss. The feel of his lips on mine. His breath on my face. And the way my whole body reacted. I'd felt a tugging in my stomach, and a pulse beating between my legs, and a tingling in my chest. I found I could re-create that feeling, just by thinking about that moment, but that wasn't enough. I wanted it again. I wanted more, even though I knew it was wrong.

In my more sensible moments, I respected Edwin's distance from me. I understood he must have decided to obey his marriage vows until the time we could be together. But that didn't make it easy – especially when we were spending so much time with each other and I was studying his body so closely.

One day, I walked into the village, just for something to do. I was walking past the greengrocer's shop when I saw Edwin coming towards me. He was with Frances, much to my dismay, but as I watched them, Frances went into the butcher's, and Edwin waited outside. And then he saw me. As our eyes met, I smiled widely – I couldn't help it and Edwin smiled back.

It was fairly busy in the village with people strolling by, going into the shops, or chatting, so it wasn't the same as when it was just him and me together on the beach. But I was so pleased to see him I didn't mind too much.

As I approached him, he lifted his hat.

'Miss Hargreaves,' he said.

'Good morning, Mr Forrest,' I said. I was impressed by how normal my voice sounded, when my heart was pounding.

'Running some errands?' he asked.

'Killing time,' I admitted. 'Father is away again and I am bored to death.'

Edwin looked sympathetic. 'It's hard for me to get away,' he said in a low voice. 'Frances is very demanding and insists on me being with her at all times.'

I glanced into the shop, where Frances was chatting with the butcher and laughing. She looked quite happy and relaxed to me, but Edwin wouldn't lie. As I watched, Frances handed over some money and the butcher gave her a wrapped parcel. Realizing she'd soon be coming out on to the street, I gave Edwin a brief smile.

'I must go,' I said, fixing Edwin with a meaningful stare. 'Back to my empty house.'

Edwin raised his hat once more. 'It was nice to see you,' he said. 'I hope we shall see each other soon.'

I turned and walked slowly back towards the house, wanting to scream with the frustration of it all. It was like talking in code. Still, Edwin knew Father was away again and I hoped he would call round. I wanted so desperately to be alone with him, in private.

Chapter 24

1855
Edwin

Edwin watched Violet go, a smile playing on his lips. He was reeling her in, he thought. It wouldn't be long before she gave herself to him entirely.

His eyes followed her as she walked away from him, admiring her narrow waist and the curve of her breasts. She was like fresh snow, untouched by human hands. Until now. The thrill of being her first would be worth this elaborate chase. This hunt.

He would handle it better this time, he thought, remembering Beatrice. That had all gone horribly wrong though she was responsible for her own fate, ultimately. Edwin's conscience was clear on that front.

As Frances came out of the butcher's shop and they walked on, Edwin remembered the first time he'd seen Beatrice. She was a daughter of a valued client, Mr Sanderson. One of two daughters actually. He'd met them on several occasions, two girls with dark hair and flashing brown eyes. They were always together, whispering into each other's ears and laughing.

He'd thought they were twins, at first. That thought had sustained his night-time fantasies for a while, imagining bedding them both at the same time, and then taking healthy amounts of money from their oblivious father at work the next day.

But then Beatrice came to the office on her own with her father and he discovered her sister – who it turned out was three years older – had married and moved to Norfolk. While Mr Sanderson went through some papers with a colleague, Edwin chatted with Beatrice, who was fed up and missing her sister, Louisa. She was younger than he'd thought – just seventeen years old – but very pretty and gratifyingly thankful for his attention.

She loved music and dancing, she told him. She loved concerts and she longed to go to the Canterbury, the new music hall everyone was talking of, and watch the performances but her father wouldn't allow it. As she talked, Edwin watched the swell of her chest and the fullness of her lips and wished he could unlace her corset right there and then. He'd push her back on to his desk and ...

'Mr Forrest, are you well?' Beatrice said. She'd stopped talking and was gazing at him, wide-eyed with worry.

Edwin smiled. 'I'm so sorry,' he said, recovering his thoughts. 'I was thinking about a friend of mine who owns a music hall. It's called the Berwick Rooms. It's not as splendid as the Canterbury, but if you could get away, I would gladly accompany you one evening.'

Beatrice glanced at the closed door between her and her father. 'I don't think so,' she said.

'No, no, you're probably right,' Edwin said, thinking of a poster he'd seen on the way to work that morning. 'Such a shame, as I know the singer Rose Roberts is performing and I hear she is popular. My friend is keen to introduce me ...'

'Rose Roberts?' said Beatrice. 'I could meet Rose Roberts?'

'I'm sure I can arrange it,' Edwin said with a smile. 'I could ask your father.'

'No,' Beatrice said in a rush. 'Don't ask him. I will arrange it.'

After that it was easy. Edwin spent a few evenings at music halls with enraptured Beatrice and told her that his (completely fictional, of course) friend was away but would be back soon to make the introductions. One day, after a performance that Beatrice adored and Edwin found embarrassing, he kissed her and mentally applauded himself as she relaxed in his arms.

After that it was simply a matter of time before their frantic kisses in shady corners grew more urgent. At home, Frances was turning away from him because she'd lost a baby and she was still feeling fragile, much to his annoyance. So instead, he took a room in a boarding house and one evening, he led Beatrice there instead. She resisted at first, of course, as he unlaced her corset as he'd imagined. But not for long.

'I love you, I love you, I love you,' she whispered the whole time he was on top of her. Edwin didn't reply.

After a few months, however, things started to go wrong. Edwin was bored of Beatrice by then, making excuses and pretending Frances was ill and he couldn't leave her. Beatrice grew sullen and thin. When she came to the office with her father one day, Edwin noted, with some dismay, that her curves had all but disappeared. Still, it meant he'd made the right decision when he'd stopped wooing her. She held no charms for him now. He avoided her gaze when she tried to catch his eye and offered to take her father through the papers so he wouldn't be forced to be alone with her.

Beatrice was getting married, her father told him as he signed his documents in Edwin's office. A man called Walter James. Edwin smiled to himself, knowing Beatrice was no longer a worry for him.

And then Walter James himself turned up at the office. He strode in, demanding to see Edwin – and on a day when Edwin's father-in-law was working too.

'My fiancée Beatrice Sanderson says she is in love with you, Forrest,' Walter James said. 'She has told me she cannot marry me, because you are the only man she wants.'

Luckily, Edwin's father-in-law watching the whole sorry drama, took his horrified face for incomprehension and believed Edwin when he said he'd only ever met Beatrice a handful of times.

Walter crumpled in the face of Edwin's charm.

'I have, I admit, spoken to her at length about her love of music,' Edwin confided. 'Simply to distract her while her father was in a meeting. Perhaps she misinterpreted my interest in her hobby for interest in herself?'

Walter, who was easily convinced of the weakness of the female mind, agreed. A few weeks later he and Beatrice were married. And that was that, thought Edwin.

But Beatrice did not agree.

She took to turning up at the office when she knew he'd be leaving for home. Running along the street next to him, begging Edwin to free her from her marriage. She told him she loved him. She even arrived at their house one day, threatening to tell Frances what they'd done on those nights in the boarding house.

Edwin saw her round Brighton. She was like Banquo's ghost – lurking round corners wherever he went. She sat on the wall outside his office, staring up at his window for hours at a time. She followed Frances when she went out to meet a friend. It was – to say the very least – not ideal.

Finally, one day, Edwin was forced to act. Beatrice was waiting for him outside the office one morning.

'Edwin,' she said desperately as he walked by. 'Edwin, darling, please …'

Edwin felt icy rage.

He turned to Beatrice, taking in how thin she was, how her cheeks were hollow, and her olive skin had turned sallow.

'Beatrice,' he said. 'My darling. My one true love.'

Beatrice started to cry. 'Oh, Edwin,' she said. 'I knew you felt the same. I knew it.'

Edwin offered her his arm. 'Let's go to see your husband,' he said. 'We can explain.'

But when they reached Walter James's warehouse, Edwin allowed his cold fury to show.

'Your wife,' he hissed at James, who recoiled in the face of such anger, 'is ruining my life. She is mad. Quite, quite mad. She is tormenting me, and my own darling wife – who has been made ill with the worry of it all. She needs to be locked up for her own protection.'

James jabbered apologies while Beatrice sat on the floor of the warehouse, surrounded by sawdust and watched by bewildered craftsmen, and wept.

The next day she threw herself off the West Pier and drowned.

Frances took it quite well, considering, he thought now as they walked towards home. She fixed him with a resigned stare, then shrugged as her father explained it was not Edwin's fault. None of it. Beatrice had been weak-minded and fixated on him without her feelings being reciprocated. Then she'd merely told him that she could no longer live in their house – with its stunning views of the West Pier. She wanted to go somewhere quieter, away from people and gossip and chatter.

Shortly after that her father died, leaving his firm in Edwin's capable hands, and making it easier to leave Brighton. And so they came here, to Heron Green, where it was quiet and peaceful. Frances seemed, if not happier then at least more settled and 'I,' Edwin thought as he glanced down the lane at Violet's house, 'have found a new hobby to occupy myself.'

Chapter 25

1855
Violet

I thought I'd never been so happy or so frustrated. I lay on my bed, replaying every word I'd said to Edwin, examining every nuance in how he had stood, or walked, or how he had cupped my face in his hand. Why, why, why hadn't he kissed me again? I thought I would burst with confusion.

Edwin was married; that was the awful, unchangeable truth. Perhaps that was why he hadn't touched me. I felt very sorry for him, trapped in a loveless marriage, forced to live out his days in the company of his dull wife. He was so honourable, I thought. What a loyal man he must be to ignore this connection we had. Fighting it. All for the sake of a marriage that gave him no joy.

I was in love with Edwin; I had no doubt about that. Admittedly, my knowledge of love was shaky. I had no girlfriends with whom I could discuss such things. I would never speak to Mabel about it – though I knew Mabel was sweet on a lad from the village and would probably give me the advice I felt I needed, the shame of asking put me off.

I wondered if Father and Mama had felt this way about

each other. If Father's kisses had made Mama feel the way Edwin made me feel. Like I was about to burst into flames, and yet so icy cold I was shivery. It seemed unlikely. Father never touched me – he had never cuddled me or kissed me even when I was small – so I couldn't imagine him being affectionate with my mother. I had no memory of ever seeing them together in fact. I had few memories of Mama – they were more feelings than solid remembrances.

I remembered the way she smelled and the softness of her cheek against mine. Unlike Father, Mama had been affectionate. She had been shy, I thought, and that was why she chose to live in Sussex though Father's work took him all over England. I didn't remember Mama going to dances or accompanying Father when he travelled. Instead she stayed with me and took me walking on the beach, or encouraged me when I drew pictures on the slate I used to learn my letters in the nursery.

I had been five when Mama died, though she had been poorly for a while before she finally passed away, with a fever caused – so Betsy, our housekeeper at the time, had said – by the baby inside her. I hated the baby.

One night I'd been woken by my mother's cries, and footsteps running up the stairs. Scared, I had knelt by the window and looked out into the night to see a man riding up on a horse and coming into the house. He was the doctor, I'd learned later. But whoever he was, I somehow knew that a late-night visitor wasn't good news.

In the morning, there was silence. I'd gone downstairs, barefoot and still in my nightgown, and found Betsy, the housekeeper, hanging heavy drapes at the window and crying. When she saw me, she gathered me into an embrace and I felt her tears dripping on to my sleep-tousled curls.

'Your mama is gone,' Betsy said, sniffing. 'Your mama and her baby boy.'

I had blinked at her, not fully understanding at first. Later, I'd gone to see Daddy, who was sitting in his leather chair by the window of his study, looking out over the sea.

Feeling sad and confused and so alone, I had wanted to climb on to his lap and snuggle into his chest and have him tell me everything was going to be fine. I wanted him to say that I was safe and he wasn't going to leave me the way my mother had. But he didn't look at me. Instead he spoke in a gruff tone.

'You are to go and stay with your Uncle Alistair and Aunt Gert.'

I wanted to protest. I loved my Aunt Gert, who was Mama's sister, but I was scared of Uncle Alistair who had a tickly moustache and an unfamiliar Scottish accent, and I really disliked my cousin, Peter, who pinched me and teased me. But the set of Daddy's jaw made me think again. It was clear I was going whether I wanted to or not.

As it happened, I only stayed a few months with Alistair and Gert in their draughty Tunbridge Wells home, because Uncle Alistair was sent to India and Daddy didn't want me to go, though I nearly did at first. My ticket was bought and my place on the ship confirmed before Daddy decided I should stay – and instead I came home where I was cared for by Betsy and educated haphazardly by a series of miserable governesses.

I longed to go to school, but Father wanted me at home where I had no friends, no mother, no father to speak of, since he travelled such a lot. I had been starved of affection and attention. And now Edwin was giving me both. I craved his love like the desert craved rain, I thought. And I knew – I knew – that he returned my feelings, wife or no.

I thought of him now. The way the breeze lifted his reddish-gold hair, how his strong arms were dusted with freckles, the way – when he gazed at me – his blue eyes darkened.

Lying on my childhood bed, I ran my hands over my body and wondered how it would feel to have Edwin do the same. I thought about the novels that Mabel read and that I'd sneaked a look at, and pictured myself in the place of the heroines, but that wasn't nearly detailed enough. All I knew was that until Edwin kissed me again, I wouldn't rest.

The next day, after I'd finished yet another sketch on the beach, I stepped back from my easel and took a breath. 'Would you like to see it,' I asked Edwin.

He smiled at me and crunched across the shingle to look. 'Excellent,' he said, standing close to me. 'You are indeed very talented.' I breathed in the smell of his cologne. I couldn't speak. Edwin took my hand and for a moment I thought I would pass out.

'Violet,' he said. 'You are so special to me.'

Then he bent his head down and kissed me. My knees buckled and I felt that pulse pound between my legs – how could that be?

Then Edwin released me.

'I have to go,' he said. 'Frances is expecting me for dinner.'

I sank on to a rock, weak with desire, and watched him climb the path to the village without looking back at me.

I loved him completely; I knew that now. I was his.

Chapter 26

Present day
Ella

From: elladaniels@writemail.com
To: ggriffiths@unimail.com
Subject: Research!

Gorgeous George,

How is the academic life treating you? Do all the students seem terribly young? Do you remember how grown up we thought we were back then?

So, here we are in Sussex and I'm supposed to be writing my latest novel. But instead I'm digging into a mystery! I've found out that an artist lived in our house. She disappeared without a trace in 1855, and though at the time people thought she'd simply run away, I think something might have happened to her.

Her name was Violet Hargreaves and she was a contemporary of your buddies the Pre-Raphaelites (by the way, I've been reading a lot about them too and beginning to appreciate them, you'll be pleased to hear). She seemed to paint a chap called Edwin Forrest rather a lot.

I've been trying to find out more about her, but there

are so many books about the Pre-Raphaelites I'm at a loss as to where to start – and let's be honest, there's very little written about female artists anyway. So could you possibly, pretty please, see what you can dig up about my Violet? I'll be so grateful.

And if you ever want a weekend by the sea (the English Channel I mean, rather than the bracing North Sea) then you know you are always welcome. I attach some pics of the new house and the kids.

Much love
E
Xxx

Chapter 27

1855
Violet

'Are you certain you don't mind?' I looked at Edwin over the top of my easel.

He gave me the half-smile I was growing to love, and shook his head. 'Such sacrifices I must make in the pursuit of art,' he said. He laughed at my worried face and came to kiss me, sending shivers through my body.

'Darling V,' he said. 'Of course I don't mind.'

Father was still in Manchester and I was making the most of my time alone. Now I was accustomed to sketching Edwin and felt I had got used to his stance. He was a natural model, aware that he was a handsome man, and I sensed he knew I thought so too. I had so far simply sketched him in poses I thought of as 'Edwin poses', perched on his rock or standing, hands clasped behind his back, staring ahead, as he had been the first time I saw him.

But now I had decided the time was right to begin my sketches for the final work – I needed to sketch Edwin in my studio and I needed him to take his shirt off.

I had met him as usual on the beach that afternoon, but had asked him to come to the house with me. He had agreed, but followed me five minutes later to make sure no one saw us together.

'The villagers have an ear for idle chatter,' he said. I wondered if it was Frances's eyes he wanted to avoid but I didn't ask.

I had waited just inside the front door, then let him in when he arrived, bustling him upstairs before Mabel saw. But then I'd had to ask Philips to bring up a stool. He had done so in silence, glancing at Edwin as he passed.

'Is everything all right, Miss?' he said.

'Quite all right, thank you, Philips,' I said, feeling awkward. I knew it was silly but I was still stinging from the way he'd rebuked me when I'd asked him to pose for me.

When Philips went down the stairs, I positioned Edwin on the stool.

'Imagine you've been in the lions' den all night,' I said. 'But they've not harmed a hair on your head.' I pulled him forward so he was leaning with his arms on his knees. His hand skimmed the back of my skirt and I flushed.

'Now look up at me,' I said. Edwin looked at me through his long eyelashes and I bit my lip. He was a fine man. That was when I asked him to remove his shirt and he came to kiss me.

He stood close by as he took off first his shoes and socks, then loosened his tie and unbuttoned his shirt. I breathed in the smell of his sweat as he slipped his shirt off his broad shoulders.

He was lean, with well-defined muscles on his stomach and a sprinkling of golden hair across his chest. It took every bit of self-control I possessed not to reach out and touch him. He saw me looking and smiled again.

'Sit back on the stool,' I said, my voice shaky, my head reeling at seeing a man's body for the first time. I retreated to the safety of my easel, using it as a shield.

Edwin sat down, still holding my gaze. He almost assumed the same pose as before, but his arms were different.

'Just slightly forward,' I said.

'Show me.'

I moved towards him and took his upper arms in my hands. My fingers looked tiny compared with the width of his muscled arms. Gently, I pulled him forward, then – as though my hands had a mind of their own – I traced a soft caress up to his shoulders.

'Violet,' Edwin said. He leaned forward and rested his head on my breast, his arms round my waist. I stroked his back.

We stayed for a while, locked together, then Edwin stood up, his arms still around my waist, tipped his head and kissed me.

Until now our kisses had been dry and chaste, but this time everything was different. Edwin's lips pushed against mine until I opened my mouth.

'Edwin,' I gasped. 'I ...'

'Hush, my darling,' Edwin said. 'No one need know.'

In shock I realized Edwin's strong fingers were busy unbuttoning my dress from the back. He kissed my neck and walked me backwards to the chaise longue where his shirt lay.

With a practised move, he pulled my gown from my arms and pushed me on to the sofa.

'Edwin,' I said again. I wanted him to stop, but I didn't know how. I had started this and now I felt powerless to stop it. A breeze blew across my bare arms and I shivered, feeling horribly exposed.

With swift hands, Edwin removed my underclothes and stepped out of his own trousers.

'Beautiful girl,' he said, running his hand down my body. It was just as I'd imagined those nights in my room on my own, only this didn't seem romantic or loving. It was just frightening. I shut my eyes. I didn't want to see him seeing me.

Then suddenly he was on top of me. I could hardly breathe. There was a sharp pain and Edwin groaned as he started to move. I stayed still, paralysed with fear as Edwin pushed into me once more, hard, and then collapsed on top.

I started to cry, hot tears running into my hair as I lay on the chaise.

Edwin sat up. 'Darling V,' he said. 'Whatever is wrong?'

Trying to act like the grown woman I thought I now was, I forced a smile. 'Nothing is wrong,' I said.

I wiped my tears and pulled on my underclothes, stifling a gasp as I saw blood on the upholstery of the chaise. Edwin wiped it with his handkerchief.

'It won't hurt so much next time,' he said, putting on his own clothes.

I had no words. I sat, silent, staring ahead. Another tear rolled down my cheek.

'Dearest,' he said. 'I'm sorry it was so quick. Your beauty quite overwhelmed me.'

He pulled me into him and, bewildered about what had happened, I clung to him. He kissed away my tears, stroked my hair, and murmured calm words of endearment until I stopped crying. Then, carefully, he helped me into my dress, as though I were a child, and kissed me gently once more.

'I must go,' he said. 'But I shall return tomorrow – if you still want me?'

I nodded. My mind was a tangle of love and pain, but I knew I wanted to paint him, still.

'Goodbye, sweet Violet,' he said, picking up his coat from the chaise. 'Until tomorrow.'

Chapter 28

1855
Frances

Frances was reading when Edwin came home. He poked his head round the door to the drawing room and gave her a broad smile.

'Hello, darling,' he said. 'I have a mind to take a bath. Could you ask Agnes to draw one for me?'

Frances nodded and put her book to one side. 'I'll send her up,' she said, knowing Agnes would grouse and grump about being asked.

She heard Edwin singing as he went up the stairs and knew his seduction of young Violet had been successful. He was nothing if not predictable, she thought as she went to find Agnes. His adultery always followed the same pattern. Time was she would have been crushed by his finding someone else he believed worthy of his affection, but it had happened so often during their marriage that she no longer cared.

This time, indeed, she was almost pleased. While he was wooing Violet he was paying her no attention. She could continue to hide her money and plot her escape. Though, after everything that happened in Brighton, she did have concern for Violet herself. She was very young and, if she had lived her whole life in this quiet village, then Frances feared she would be very unworldly. She may not be able to cope with Edwin, who was ruthless in his assumption that he could simply have anything he wanted.

Once more she felt an almost maternal protectiveness towards the ungainly girl who lived next door and tried to quash it. She had to think about herself now, herself and her baby, not the teenager seduced by her husband.

She waited until she heard Agnes stamp down the stairs, and Edwin retreat to his dressing room where his bath was. Then she went into her own room, shut the door, pulled a small table in front of it, and loosened the floorboard. Inside she had a bag of money – a good amount now – a diary and a book.

The book was about Scotland, which was where she had definitely decided to go. She liked the sound of a small town called North Berwick, close to Edinburgh, but she knew it would take time to get there. She planned to go first to Manchester, then Glasgow, and then make her way east. She'd befriended the stationmaster at Brighton station and, professing an interest in the ever-expanding railways, had asked him the best route.

In her diary she had been practising her new name. She'd decided to call herself Florence after a great-aunt she'd had a fondness for. And for a surname she'd chosen Bennett. She felt both names were just unremarkable enough. She picked up her pen and signed her new name with a flourish. She'd also written a life story for herself. She was a widow from Manchester. Her fictional husband – Alfred – had been killed in a factory accident and she'd decided to start a new life with her baby away from the memories of him and closer to her imaginary family who lived somewhere near the border.

She shifted on her chair and loosened the waistband on her skirt. She was definitely thickening round the middle. Soon she planned to leave off one petticoat, then another, as her baby grew inside. She felt sure that would buy her enough time to make her escape plan perfect.

'Frances?' Edwin called from the other room, jolting her from her daydreams. She put her diary, papers, money, and the book under the floor once more, replaced the floorboard, and put the small table on top. Then she smoothed down her hair and went to see her husband.

Chapter 29

1855
Violet

After the first, terrible time, Edwin came to visit me every day. I was in turmoil. I loved painting him; 'Daniel in the Lions' Den' was coming along very nicely and the sheer joy of drawing every single day made me want to sing with happiness.

About Edwin himself, I was conflicted. He made me feel so precious, calling me darling and dearest, complimenting my painting, my character, and my beauty. But after the drawing, came his heavy kisses, his breath hot on my face, and then inevitably, he would push me back on to the chaise.

After the first time, I screwed my courage up and tried to talk to him.

As I washed out my brushes, he came behind me and wrapped his arms around me.

'My darling,' he said, kissing my neck.

I froze. I didn't want this. Not again. 'Dearest Edwin,' I said, my voice small and shaky. 'While I have an enormous fondness for you, I fear we must not forget that you have a wife …'

'Frances is ill,' said Edwin, tugging at my petticoat. 'Her nerves are bad. She cannot give me what I need. No one could judge me for wanting you.'

I tried to move away, but I was trapped between the table where I kept my brushes, and the wall. I felt a chill of fear. 'But, Edwin,' I said.

'Hush.' Edwin squashed his lips on mine so hard I felt sure he would leave a bruise. Beginning to panic, I put my hands on his upper arms.

'Edwin,' I said. 'No.'

I pushed firmly against him but he pushed back so I was against the wall. It felt cold against my back. Edwin towered over me and I was struck once more by how small I was compared to him and felt, again, a flash of utter fright.

'Darling Violet,' he said and crushed his lips on mine again.

I thought about the pain of yesterday and how it had felt when he was on top of me. I didn't want that again, no matter how I felt about Edwin. Summoning every bit of my strength, I braced my arms on his and shoved him hard. He stumbled back and fire flashed in his eyes.

Seeing a way out, I ducked under his arm. I was close to tears. 'I am so sorry,' I said. 'I just, I can't …'

Edwin's fist flew towards me. Pain flared in my jaw and, confused, I found myself sprawled on the floor. It was a moment before I realized what had happened and I stayed slumped on the white floorboards as I tried to make sense of it. Surely it had been a mistake? Edwin couldn't have meant to hurt me.

I looked up at him where he stood, and his face softened. He bent down to me, and wrapped his arms around me. Just like last time, I hung on to him, like a drowning woman, sobbing as he stroked my back and spoke soothing nothings into my hair.

'Sweetheart,' he cooed. 'Violet, my angel. I'm sorry, darling. I'm sorry.'

It was the heat, he explained. And worries at work. And he'd so been looking forward to spending time with me, and to be disappointed, well …

When my sobs eased, he gently picked me up and led me to the chaise. He sat me down and carefully unbuttoned my dress, still talking.

'Darling girl,' he said, dropping a kiss on my exposed collarbone. 'You're so beautiful.'

I was trembling. My face ached and my side was raw from where I'd fallen on to the floor. With shaking hands I touched my jaw and winced as I felt tender swelling. And still Edwin was busy, pulling up my petticoats and pushing me back on to the couch. I began to sob once more as he clambered on top of me, turning my face away so Edwin wouldn't see. After everything that had happened, I still didn't want to upset him.

Afterwards, Edwin kissed my tears as they fell and told me again how much I meant to him. He didn't help me dress this time, though. Instead, he left me dishevelled and bruised, on the sofa, watching in silence as he pulled on his trousers and straightened his hair.

'I have a mind to go to London at the end of the week,' he said, as he picked up his jacket.

I tried to smile, but my swollen cheek prevented me. 'Will you be seeing Mr Millais?' I asked, my voice shrill as I fought more tears. Would this all be worthwhile in the end?

'I will certainly try,' Edwin said. 'Will you be ready?'

At that moment, I thought I might never paint again, but I nodded.

'Good,' said Edwin. 'Until tomorrow, sweet Violet.'

I heard him whistling as he went down the stairs. Still I sat, half-dressed, wondering what was happening. Was this love? Was it being an adult? And was it the price I would have to pay to be an artist?

As the sun set over the sea and the room darkened, I finally pulled myself to my feet and buttoned my blouse. I was sore. My face was swollen and my hip stiff. Slowly, I walked downstairs to the kitchen to find Mabel.

She gasped when she saw my face and fussed around me.

'Oh, Miss Violet,' she said, bustling me on to a stool and pushing me down. 'What happened?'

My eyes burned at her kindness. 'I slipped,' I lied. 'Upstairs.'

Mabel looked at me closely, but she didn't question me further. 'You need something cool on that,' she said. She fetched a rag and soaked it in cold water. Then she folded it up and held it against my painful face.

The icy water ran down my neck and I rested my head against Mabel's chest, feeling safe for the first time since it had happened.

Mabel stroked my hair, mothering me though we were almost the same age.

'There, there,' she said. 'It'll be better in a few days.'

'How did you slip?' I hadn't noticed Philips in the corner of the kitchen, mending a cupboard door.

'I'm not sure,' I stammered.

Philips stood in front of me and for a frightening moment I was reminded of how Edwin had loomed over me. I felt myself cower backwards and wished I hadn't.

'Show me,' he said.

Mabel lifted the cloth away from my cheek and Philips winced.

'Painful,' he said. 'Reminds me of when that lad from down the way had too much ale and started on me.'

'I slipped,' I said again. I took the cloth from Mabel and put it on my cheek myself.

Philips gently pushed back the stray lock of hair that had fallen over my face as usual and studied my face for a moment.

'You be careful, Miss Violet,' he said. 'You just be careful.'

And after that, I didn't fight Edwin any more. Each day he would come and I would paint him. And then, when he grew tired of standing or sitting, he would get up and walk to the window, shaking out his limbs, and I knew what was coming.

I would put down my pencil, or my brush, and go to the sofa. Then I would unhook my dress, and slip off my petticoat. I'd taken to wearing fewer layers, just so it would be over more quickly and I found I could shut my mind away from what was happening. I would close my eyes and imagine myself looking at my own painting hanging in the Royal Academy. And I found I could ignore Edwin's breath, hot against my cheek, his heavy limbs, and the pain as he thrust inside me.

Afterwards Edwin would go down the stairs, whistling to himself, and I would watch out of the landing window until I saw him disappear through his front gate. Then I would go down to the privy with a basin of water and clean myself up. I took a sort of grim comfort in this restorative routine; bringing myself back after Edwin had taken me away.

I felt completely alone. Father was still away, and Philips, who had long been my confidant, kept his distance. I couldn't have confided in him anyway. This was too base, too raw, to be talked of. A thousand miles from chatting about my artistic ambitions, or the plans Philips had for his own market garden and shop.

For a few days after Edwin hit me, I stayed indoors. The village was small and the locals too enthusiastic in their gossip for me to feel comfortable outside. But eventually, after a week had passed, I stood in front of the mirror and examined my injuries.

Edwin had caught me across the jaw and a smear of yellowing bruise showed down the bone and up towards my cheek. But the worst had passed and I felt sure no one would notice. In any case, if any villagers were too interested I would simply say I had slipped and change the subject.

Since the rainstorm the day I'd met Edwin on the beach – oh how long ago that seemed now, back when I was still a child – summer had all but given up and was slinking into autumn without much of a fight. I pinned on my hat and wrapped a shawl across my shoulders to guard against the chill, put my chin in the air, and left the house.

It was good to be out after so much time stuck inside. I strolled into the village and looked in the windows of the shops. I stopped and chatted with a friend of my father's, and I felt more like myself than I'd felt for a week.

I had promised Mabel I would collect the clean linen – not much of a bundle now I was alone in the house – and so I went to the laundry. As I went into the shop, Frances Forrest was coming out.

Feeling my heart pound against my breastbone, I held the

door open and dropped my eyes, fearing Frances could tell what I had been doing with her husband.

'Good day, Miss Hargreaves,' Frances said.

I nodded, worried any response at all would give me away.

But it seemed even that simple nod had been my undoing because when I came out again, Frances was waiting. I felt sick. Was Frances waiting to question me about where Edwin had been every day?

I put my head down and went to scurry by, but Frances fell into step next to me.

'Miss Hargreaves,' she said. 'Violet.'

I walked on. I was consumed with guilt and I didn't know how to react, what to feel, or what to say.

'Stop.' Frances pulled my arm and I stopped walking.

Cautiously, I raised my eyes to Frances's and was astonished to see only concern – not the hatred or confrontation I was expecting.

Gently Frances reached out and cupped her hand around my jaw, where Edwin's fist had left the bruise.

'Oh, my dear girl,' she said. 'My dear girl.'

I winced away from her fingers. The bruise no longer hurt too badly, but the worry in Frances's sweet face was too much. For days I'd forced myself to shut my feelings away, but suddenly I was flooded with emotions. At once I felt horribly guilty, but also I had a strange longing to throw myself into Frances's arms, to let her look after me with the gentle concern she'd shown as she touched my aching face.

'I'm so sorry,' I said.

Frances shook her head. 'No matter,' she said. 'It is nearly over for me. But you must look after yourself.'

I was confused and nervous about what she knew. Did she realize what Edwin had been doing when he wasn't with her? And I was scared. So scared that she knew everything and would confront Edwin. Would he be angry? Would he never speak to me again? At a loss as to what to say, I decided to play ignorant.

'Are you well, Mrs Forrest?' I said. She didn't seem ill, but she never had in the time I'd known her, and Edwin had spoken often of her illness.

'I am indeed,' Frances said. 'It is your health I am concerned for. Violet, you must …'

I fought the desire to run away. An image of Edwin, trousers off, panting and red-faced on top of me, crossed my mind and I felt I would die with shame. Why, why, was Edwin's wife being so nice?

'I do feel weak,' I said, interrupting Frances's talk. 'I must go.'

I hoisted the laundry bundle into my arms, turned on my heel, and fled.

Chapter 30

1855
Frances

Frances felt completely helpless. She knew Edwin's marks when she saw them; she'd been on the receiving end of that fist too many times. But it had happened so soon for young Violet. Normally he wooed them for months before showing his true colours.

Frances walked slowly in Violet's footsteps back towards the house, wondering if the younger woman had resisted Edwin's advances. Perhaps that's why he had struck her. That was good, she thought. The girl's spirit could keep her safe. If only Frances had had an ounce of her wilfulness, perhaps she'd never have fallen so hard for Edwin's charms.

And yet, Frances had a shadow of doubt. She wasn't sure Violet had completely understood what Frances was trying to tell her. It was a difficult situation. Should she come straight out and say: 'I know you are having relations with my husband. He is dangerous. Leave him'?

If by any small chance she was wrong about Violet and Edwin, she would have smeared the young woman's character terribly.

But if she was right – and she was almost sure she was – then Violet may not believe her. Edwin's charm was considerable.

For a young woman in the grip of first love, it would be hard to imagine another woman didn't want her man. Violet may assume she – Frances – was simply a bitter, spurned wife. And what if Violet told Edwin what she had said? He would be furious.

Frances was worried about Violet, there was no doubt, but her biggest concern was for her own child. Now she had her baby to think about, she couldn't do anything to risk his or her safety. If she said anything to Violet all her plans to leave could be at risk – her one chance for a future away from Edwin.

So it seemed she had to continue with the softly-softly approach. At least for now. She stared up ahead where Violet was whirling down her garden path, skirts and hair trailing behind her. She just hoped Violet would understand.

Chapter 31

Present day
Ella

From: ggriffiths@unimail.com
To: elladaniels@writemail.com
Subject: Success!

Darling Ella

What a house! Lovely stuff. So pleased things are looking up for you and that handsome husband of yours. I have been watching the progress of his football team with a new-found eagerness. Who knew football could be such fun? ;-)

I have good news and bad regarding your mystery artist. Of Violet Hargreaves I found nothing. Not a trace. If she was painting back then, she obviously just did it for her own pleasure and not for commercial gain. Sorry.

Regarding Edwin Forrest I had a bit more luck. I have found two works by him – not of him, as you asked. I attach them as jpegs. They are very good. One is King Canute turning back the tide (it is on display in one of those rather exclusive private members' clubs in London called

the Jermyn Club) and the other of Daniel in the lions'
den (part of the collection at Manchester University).

Apparently his career was short-lived because he was
brutally murdered not long after he began – I'm guessing
that's related to this mystery of yours? Tell me more – I'm
desperate to hear all about it.

Hope that helps. If you need anything else, give me
a shout. I would love to come and check out your new
pad and see those lovely boys of yours. I'll give you a call
in a few days.

Look after yourself.
George x

I opened the two attachments George had sent with the email
and looked at the pictures in surprise.

Ben was in our bedroom, putting together a new chest of
drawers. I went out of the study and leaned over the bannister.

'Ben,' I called. 'Ben, come and look at this.'

He came out of the bedroom and looked up at me. 'I am
very busy,' he said, waving the screwdriver at me. 'It's like
DIY SOS down here.'

I laughed. 'Well I hate to interrupt, but could you come
and see what George has sent?'

Ben took the stairs two at a time, so eager was he to aban-
don his flat-packed furniture.

He perched on the desk where I'd been drawing arrows
between names on a piece of paper, trying to force myself to
concentrate on Tessa's story instead of Violet's.

'Plot?' he said.

'Plot schmot,' I said, shoving the papers to one side. I showed him the pictures George had sent.

'He says they're by Edwin Forrest,' I explained. 'But they're Violet's. At least one of them is, so I think the other one must be, too.'

'Are you sure?' Ben said.

'It's Daniel in the lions' den,' I said. 'It's the finished painting from the sketches we've got. And she signed those sketches.'

'Ooh the crafty bugger,' Ben said. 'Do you think he passed off Vi's work as his own?'

'Looks like it,' I said, chewing my lip. 'I suppose she could have known about it, though. It could have all been her idea; from what I've read, female artists weren't well received back then.'

'Could they all be Edwin's?' Ben asked. 'The sketches too?'

I shook my head. 'I don't think so. It's fairly obvious that these are drawn by the same artist as the sketches, and like I say, those are signed by Violet. And of course people paint self-portraits, but I think it would be strange for an artist to paint himself into a story – like Daniel. I've been reading lots about these Pre-Raphaelites and I've not come across anything like that.'

'Violet painted herself into *Mariana*,' Ben pointed out.

'S'pose,' I said. 'Though not if Edwin was the artist.'

I narrowed my eyes as I thought back to what I'd read about the artists of the time. 'I really think Violet did that painting, though. From what I've read, Millais painted *Mariana* as a kind of comment on women's place in society at the time. Violet would have known that; it was quite controversial

162

then – there's a big write-up about it in that paper I found. Maybe she painted herself into *Mariana* because that's how she was feeling. Remember, it's all about a woman waiting for a man, and not being able to act by herself.'

I turned the laptop back to myself and scrolled through the two paintings on screen, zooming in on the signature. It said Edwin Forrest in a confident, blue scrawl.

I shook my head. 'I just don't believe Edwin was an artist,' I said. 'Violet's the artist. Surely …'

A thought struck me.

'Maybe she was angry that Edwin got the credit for her work,' I said. 'Maybe she was the murderer?'

'How much credit?' Ben asked. 'Was he successful?'

'Ah,' I said, thinking of George's email. 'No, not really. That ruins my theory. He seems to have sold two paintings in all.'

'Because he was killed,' Ben said. 'His death stopped his art career.'

'Or rather it stopped Violet's career,' I said. 'So why would she kill him if he was her route to success?'

'Maybe that's why she ran away, to follow her dreams of becoming an artist,' Ben said.

'Perhaps,' I said doubtfully. 'I'd love to think she ran off and saw out her days painting, but …'

'But?'

'George didn't find anything by Violet Hargreaves, for a start,' I said.

'She could have changed her name.'

'I don't think this story has a happy ending, you know …'

'I can hope,' Ben said.

'Softie,' I said, with affection. I pulled my notebook and pen towards me, then I wrote Violet and Edwin on my paper and joined them with an arrow.

'If I was writing this story,' I said, 'they'd be having an affair.'

'That makes sense,' Ben agreed. 'It would explain how she came to draw him and why his name ended up on her paintings.'

'So maybe it was Edwin's wife who killed him in a jealous rage,' I said. I wrote Frances down, frowning as I did so. 'It's a bit obvious, though.'

'Maybe it was just a love triangle,' Ben said.

I sighed, feeling inexplicably disappointed. 'A love triangle,' I said.

'Maybe Violet was having an affair with Edwin,' Ben said. 'Frances found out and killed them both – Edwin and Vi.'

'No.' I shook my head because something about what he was saying didn't add up with what I thought I knew. I leafed through my notebook until found the page I was looking for. 'Priya said Edwin was killed and Violet disappeared, but Frances was also badly injured. Beaten so violently she almost died herself. She couldn't do that to herself.'

Ben smiled at my enthusiasm. 'Are you writing this story in your head?'

'I am, a bit,' I admitted. 'I can't settle to Tessa when this is more interesting.'

'So what's next?' Ben asked.

'We need to find out exactly what happened,' I said. 'Priya said she could get me into the police archives in Lewes. I'm going to ring her now and see if she's got me an appointment.'

I looked down at George's email.

'And I might see if George fancies a trip to London,' I said, half to myself. 'I'd like to go and see Violet's painting for myself.'

Chapter 32

'Has your dad seen the house?' Priya asked a few days later. It was another hot day and we were in our garden watching my boys and her girls play in the paddling pool.

I shifted on my deckchair uncomfortably. 'Not yet,' I said. 'It's a bit complicated.'

Priya looked at me, but she didn't say anything.

'We had a bit of an argument,' I admitted. 'And I said some horrible things. He's been calling me but I've not answered.'

'Oh, Ella,' Priya said. 'If being in my line of work has taught me anything, it's that life is short. Don't wait too long to speak to him.'

I sighed. 'I know. You're right. I need to call him.'

Priya picked up my phone and held it out to me. 'No time like the present,' she said. 'I'll watch the boys.'

I didn't take it. 'I don't want to,' I said.

Priya raised an eyebrow.

'The signal's patchy in the garden.'

'Go inside.'

'He might be busy.'

'So leave a message.'

Reluctantly, I took the phone from her outstretched hand and scrolled through to find Dad's number.

He didn't answer but he never did – his phone was probably in the bottom of his bag, or on a shelf somewhere. Or he might be at work – he still did the odd bit of work for his old firm, even though he was in his sixties now. I took a breath as the ring switched to voicemail.

'Dad?' I said in a small voice. 'It's me. I was just phoning to …'

I paused and Priya gave me a little nod of encouragement.

'Just to see if you and Barb want to come down next weekend. It would be really lovely to see you and the boys have missed you.'

I paused again.

'I miss you too,' I said in a hurry.

I ended the call and looked at Priya.

'Feel better?' she said.

I did, actually. It was a start, at least.

'Things are tricky between me and Dad,' I said. 'Though I'm not sure he'd see it that way.'

Priya raised her eyebrows.

'I kept a lot of stuff bottled up and when he questioned us moving here, it all just exploded,' I said.

'Ouch.'

'Ben's been emailing him.'

'Double ouch.'

I shrugged. 'I was annoyed when I found out, but he was right to,' I admitted. 'In the end, family's the most important thing.'

Priya made a face. 'I've seen some pretty awful families

167

over the years,' she said. 'And I wouldn't say it's always blood relatives who are the ones to stand by you. My family weren't great when I married Nik. They didn't like the thought that he'd been married before. But Nik's parents are wonderful and they've been a big support with the girls.'

I thought of Barb and how she had fitted right into our lives, and nodded.

'But when family is good, it's great,' Priya went on. 'And you shouldn't throw it away because of a silly row.'

'You're right,' I said. 'Ben's right. I just hope Dad calls back.'

'He will,' Priya said. 'What did you row about anyway?'

'Oh moving here,' I said. 'Giving up work. All sorts.'

I looked over to where Oscar and Amber were lying on their tummies in the water and laughing uproariously.

'He thought we were taking a big risk and we were. But look – the boys have settled in and they're making friends – and so am I.' I smiled at Priya and she smiled back. 'Ben loves his job … it's all good.'

'What about the writing,' Priya said, picking up her glass of water from the garden table and resting it on her bump. 'God it's hot.'

I stood up and adjusted the parasol so she was in the shade. 'Don't overheat,' I said.

'Don't change the subject.'

I sat down again. 'It's going very badly,' I groaned. 'I've written a plot for Tessa, but I just can't get started. I'm not interested in her mystery – I'm interested in my own.'

'So write that one instead,' said Priya.

'Well, I've got nothing to write yet,' I pointed out. 'I don't know what happened to Violet.'

'I'm still waiting for the archivist to get back to me,' Priya said. 'But there must be something else we can do.'

'What do you do, when you're investigating a crime?' I asked.

'What do I do?' Priya said. 'You know all this, surely?'

I nodded. 'I know the procedure, but if you talk it might give me an idea.'

'Well it's all to do with the scene, of course,' Priya said. 'If someone's dead, then we go to where it happened.'

Her phone rang and she looked at the screen, then answered. 'Oh lovely,' she said. 'We're at Ella's. It's the Cliff House, you know? We're in the garden so come round the side.'

I looked at her, wondering who she'd invited round.

'Jasmine,' she said. 'She's home from uni this weekend and she was in the village and wondering where we were. She's going to pop in.'

Amber hurtled past us, to the side gate. 'Jassssssssssss,' she bellowed.

I looked round as Jasmine came in to the garden. She was only wearing denim shorts and a plain black vest top with flip-flops on her feet but she was film-star gorgeous.

Amber pulled her towards us. 'This is my sister,' she said proudly. 'My biggest sister.'

We all said our hellos, Jas engulfing Priya in a huge hug as much as she could with the bump in the way. I watched them, thinking about what Priya had said about family as I poured Jasmine a glass of water too. As Amber dragged her off towards the paddling pool, Priya stopped her.

'Jas, can you watch the kids for a minute? Ella and I just have to pop next door.'

'Next door?' I said in surprise, as Jas nodded and headed to the water with the children. 'Why?'

'Crime scene,' said Priya, heaving herself out of the chair. 'Might give you inspiration.'

'Nice thinking,' I said, following Priya as she waddled round the side of the house and out on to the lane.

'So according to the people at the station, the attack happened outside the house,' Priya said, squinting in the sunshine at the house next door. 'But by the look of it, the house has been completely rebuilt – that's not a Victorian house, is it?'

I looked at the house, which was double-glazed and red-roofed, with a huge extension on the side and a large conservatory to the back.

'Guess not,' I said, disappointed. 'Mind you, if someone had been murdered in my house, I'd probably want to knock it down and start again.'

Priya nodded, a grim expression on her face. 'Got that right,' she said.

'But whatever the house looks like now, this is where Edwin Forrest lived,' I said. 'With his wife, who was pregnant …'

'Poor cow,' Priya muttered.

I chuckled. 'And where he died,' I added, seriously.

We looked up and down the lane as if trying to picture what had happened.

'My friend George is an art historian and he found some

paintings,' I said. 'I asked him to find stuff painted by Violet, but what he found was two paintings by Edwin Forrest.'

'So he was an artist too?'

I shrugged. 'I think he's signed Violet's paintings,' I said. 'Because I think the work George found is drawn by the same artist who drew the self-portrait, and that's Violet, obviously.'

Priya looked thoughtful. 'Is there any way to find out for sure?'

'Don't know,' I said. 'But George is coming down in a few days and I'm going up to London to meet him. We're going to see one of the paintings in real life.'

'Oh brilliant,' Priya said. 'Because if he nicked her work, that gives her a motive for murder.'

'Oh,' I said.

'Maybe Violet killed Edwin and then went on the run,' Priya said. 'Changed her name and fled the country. Maybe she's sunning herself down in Spain as we speak.'

'Priya,' I said, giggling. 'Be serious.'

She stuck her tongue out at me. 'She would be a suspect, though,' she said.

I made a face. 'So what would you do next?'

Priya leaned against a tree and fanned herself as she gazed at the house next door. 'I would follow the artwork,' she said. 'I'm assuming there would have been money in it. It always comes down to money in the end. That or sex.'

'Or both,' I said, wondering again if Edwin and Violet had been having an affair.

'Go to London and see what you can find out about the paintings,' Priya said. 'I'd come with you but I can't face the train in this heat.'

I gave her a sympathetic smile. 'Don't worry, George knows what he's doing,' I said. 'I just need you to get me into the archives.'

'I'll email them now and chivvy them along,' Priya said.

A shout and loud laughter drifted along the lane from our back garden and we looked at each other.

'Let's go and rescue poor Jasmine,' I said.

'Or,' said Priya, 'we could go to the pub, sit in the garden, and share a jug of Pimm's.'

With a rueful look along the lane towards the pub, we both turned and walked back to the house.

Chapter 33

1855
Edwin

Edwin stared at Violet and she stared back, chin lifted and eyes gleaming.

'I want to come with you,' she said. Her travelling cloak was wrapped around her shoulders and a small bag lay at her feet. In her arms, like a baby, was a rectangular parcel, wrapped neatly in brown paper and tied with string.

'I want to come to London,' she said.

Edwin chuckled. 'Darling V,' he said. 'London is no place for a girl like you.'

Violet's eyes sparked with defiance. 'I am not like other girls,' she said. 'I have my paintings ready to show Mr Millais.'

Edwin looked round. They were standing by Violet's front gate where any passer-by could see them together.

'I will gladly take your paintings,' he said. 'But I cannot take you. I will be working.'

Violet snorted. An unbecoming sound for a girl so beautiful. 'Are you afraid I will tarnish your reputation?'

Edwin picked up her bag and took her wrist, holding it hard. 'Come,' he hissed at her. He pulled her, quite roughly he had to admit, round the side of her house and into the garden where he pushed her down on to a bench.

'Violet,' he said, standing over her. 'I will not take you to London. I am married. What would your father say? I cannot encourage you to socialize in the taverns of the city.'

Violet gripped her parcel tighter. 'I can't stay here,' she whispered, staring at Edwin over the top of the package. 'Frances knows.'

Edwin sat down next to her and smoothed her hair from her face. She stared at him, biting her full pink lips. Edwin felt his groin tighten at the sight of her. Was there time to have her now? Here? He took his pocket watch out and checked. Sadly, no. He had a train to catch. No matter.

'Darling girl,' he said. 'Frances knows nothing. She is in a world of her own and I fear her character is weak. She means you no harm.'

He kissed her softly on those full lips, breathing in her smell of paint and sweat, and wished there was a later train. Over Violet's shoulder he saw her gardener. He was making the pretence of cutting down a branch but Edwin knew he was watching them through the leaves. He lowered his voice so the surly chap wouldn't hear.

'You have stolen my heart, Miss Hargreaves,' he said. 'We will be together one day. For now, alas, I must take your paintings to London in place of you.'

He took the parcel from her arms and pulled her along the bench towards him, pressing her body against his. Could she feel how much he wanted her?

'Alas, I must go,' he said, his breath raspy. 'I will return next week. I have plans to meet with Mr Millais, and I will show him your work.'

Violet's defiance had left her. Edwin was pleased. He

seemed to have a way with women. He smoothed his hair with the palm of his hand and straightened his tie, preening like a peacock.

Violet picked the parcel up from the bench and handed it to him.

'Two paintings,' she said in a faltering voice. 'There is *King Canute*, and *Daniel in the Lions' Den*. I have another one, but I thought these were best … for now.'

'Very good,' said Edwin. He tucked the package under his arm and stood up.

'I didn't sign them,' Violet said suddenly. 'I thought, perhaps, you could show Mr Millais first and see if he likes them. Before you tell them they have been painted by …'

'By a woman,' finished Edwin. He dropped a kiss on the top of her head as she sat on the bench. 'That is a wise plan. I will follow your wishes.'

He didn't look back as he left the garden. In fact, he didn't think of Violet again until he was settled on the train. As it powered over the Sussex downs, he took the parcel of paintings down from the luggage rack, and unwrapped it. He propped both works on the seats opposite him and sat back to look at them.

'They're rather good,' said an elderly gentleman who was sharing his carriage. He put down his newspaper to look at them more closely.

'Are they yours?'

Edwin paused while the train rattled under a bridge. Then he looked at his fellow passenger.

'Yes,' he said. 'Yes they are.'

The gentleman smiled at him. 'You have a talent,' he said.

Edwin brushed off his compliments modestly. 'Oh I'm just a beginner,' he said. 'In fact, I have not even put my name to these paintings.'

'You must,' said the gentleman. 'Here, I have a pen.'

He rummaged in his bag and handed Edwin a fountain pen. 'There should be ink enough for a signature,' he said.

Edwin took the pen. Then, before he had time to change his mind, he etched his name on to the bottom of Violet's painting of King Canute.

'That's the ticket,' the man said. 'Now this one. Ah, it's a self-portrait, I see.'

Edwin nodded as he scratched his signature on to *Daniel in the Lions' Den*.

'There is a lack of models,' he admitted. 'I often have to paint myself.'

The lies came easily after that. He and his companion chatted about art and London, and Edwin found himself repeating things Violet had said as though he'd just thought of them.

By the time they reached London Bridge Station, Edwin almost believed himself to be an artist. He bade farewell to the gentleman with a cheery wave and set off to his club with a spring in his step. Life was good.

Chapter 34

Edwin's Hackney coach dropped him at the corner of Jermyn Street just as the sun was setting. He tipped the driver and sauntered along the road, then climbed the wide stairs to the imposing building that housed his club, to reserve himself a room for the week.

He had chosen this club because of its reputation for attracting men of worth in literary and artistic fields. Edwin hadn't been lying when he told Violet that he loved art. Just as he'd not been lying when he told Beatrice that he loved music.

He did love art; that was true. What he really loved, though, was the world of art. He had, in fact, met Millais but if he were truthful it was a brief introduction and he knew Millais would struggle to remember him. And he had not been lying when he told Violet he fancied himself to be an artist, though he lacked talent and perseverance. His chosen profession of the law suited him much better. He was a man of rules and regulations – and often of finding legal loopholes for his clients to slip through. He loved nothing more than tying someone up in an argument based on logic and trickery and he was very good at it.

He had made a decent living from the law, but he still wanted to be revered the way artists were revered. He came from a modest background and despite his humble beginnings, he'd worked hard, and – every now and then – lied and cheated his way to success. He was a good businessman, he knew that, and Frances's father had thought enough of him to leave him in charge of the family firm. But he still didn't feel appreciated and he didn't feel secure. Always lurking at the back of his mind was the worry that one day someone would point out that his parents weren't the respectable people he pretended they were, that his carefully constructed house of cards could come tumbling down.

He hadn't been to boarding school or received the good start in life enjoyed by his peers, and so he pretended. He'd taught himself to draw because other chaps had had art lessons at school or from their tutors and he wanted to be like them. And to his surprise, he found he enjoyed it, though he was sadly lacking in technique. He occasionally sketched seabirds and when he and Frances were first courting he drew her. Once, he drew her naked, which he'd found very erotic and she'd found terribly embarrassing.

He felt his good mood abating at the thought of his wife, so he paused at the entrance to the club, congratulating himself once more for winning membership there and letting the beautiful architecture soothe him. Then, with the parcel of paintings under his arm, he went inside.

'Edwin, dear fellow!'

Edwin turned from the desk, where he'd been signing the visitors' book, as a plump gentleman with a mop of white hair greeted him.

'Laurence,' he said, shaking him firmly by the hand. 'It has been a long time.'

Laurence Cole was an old client of Edwin's firm, a jovial man who was a well-known patron of the arts.

They exchanged pleasantries and Edwin was pleased when Laurence invited him to dine later.

'What do you have there?' he asked, nodding at Edwin's parcels as they walked along the hall to their rooms.

Edwin smiled in a fashion he hoped was self-effacing. 'Oh just a couple of paintings,' he said. 'I am merely dabbling, really …' He let his voice trail off and hoped Laurence would jump in. He didn't disappoint.

'May I?' he said.

Edwin protested, but not too loudly and not for too long. He invited Laurence into his room, and poured them both a drink. Then he unwrapped his parcel and propped the paintings up against the wall.

'The light in here is not so good,' he said as Laurence peered at the work, but Laurence brushed aside his worries.

'My dear boy,' he said. 'These are marvellous. Really something.' He sipped his whisky and settled himself into the leather chair at the side of the fireplace. 'I wonder …'

Edwin glanced at him. 'You wonder?'

'I have a friend, John Ruskin. He is an art critic. Do you know him?'

'Of course. Though we have never been formally introduced.'

'I should like to show him these, if I may. I think he would enjoy them. They're of a style I know he favours.'

'Oh no,' Edwin said. 'I am simply a beginner, still learning.'

'Dear boy, you do yourself a disservice. You have talent. I think this could be the start of something for you.'

Edwin smiled. And after some protestations – but not too many – he agreed to give Laurence the paintings to show Ruskin.

There followed two days of uncertainty. Edwin met with clients and got a lot of business done, but his mind was never far from Laurence; wondering whether he'd yet met with Ruskin.

He hadn't intended to pass the paintings off as his own. That had simply been a spontaneous act, inspired by the man on the train. He'd not really had a plan beyond seducing Violet though he had vaguely thought he might be able to sell the paintings and pocket the proceeds. But now he had claimed ownership of Violet's work, he was plotting. If he could somehow encourage Violet to keep painting and pass off her work as his own, he would become the toast of the art world.

He imagined a stream of men wanting to be just like him, and of beautiful women desperate to get closer to him. He'd be respected around town, and Violet need never find out. She hardly ever left Sussex, so the chances of her stumbling across one of 'his' paintings were very low.

He wasn't sure how much money these artists made – he had a vague idea most of the Pre-Raphaelites were men of means masquerading as starving for their art – but he fancied it could be a rather nice second income. Perhaps even enough to take some rooms in London permanently. That would certainly make entertaining easier, he thought. He drifted off into a lascivious daydream, as he walked downstairs towards the dining room for dinner.

'Edwin,' he realized someone was talking to him.

'Laurence, I'm sorry, I was miles away.'

'No matter,' Laurence said, falling into step beside him as they entered the dining room. 'Shall we sit together or do you have guests?'

'No, no guests,' Edwin said, thinking surely if Laurence wanted to dine with him, he must have good news.

They sat down and the waiter poured them wine.

Laurence took a sip. 'Excellent,' he said. 'So, Edwin, how is the law treating you?'

'Well, well,' Edwin said, wishing he'd get to the point. Laurence always had been full of hot air.

'That is a shame because I fancy the legal profession may soon have to do without you,' Laurence said, sitting back in his chair and looking very pleased with himself.

Edwin suppressed the urge to reach across the table, grip Laurence's tie, and smash his smug face on to his plate.

'How so?' he asked politely, imagining Laurence's mutton chops dripping with gravy.

'Because, my dear chap, I have sold your paintings.'

Edwin stopped with his wineglass halfway to his mouth. 'Sold them?'

'Well, with your agreement, of course,' Laurence said.

Edwin merely stared at him. He wasn't sure how one was supposed to react in these situations.

'Shut your mouth, boy,' Laurence said with a smile. 'You must know how good your work is?'

Edwin bowed his head in false modesty. 'So, who …' he began.

'I was unable to show them to Ruskin,' Laurence said. 'Because as it turns out, he is in Italy. But it was probably for the best, considering he has just paid out a large sum to Miss Siddal.'

Edwin scowled. He didn't altogether approve of Ruskin's patronage of Elizabeth Siddal, who he considered to be nothing more than a whore.

Laurence saw his expression. 'Quite,' he said. 'Anyway, I showed them instead to a friend of Mr Ruskin – a Mr Henry Hughes.'

Edwin didn't know the name.

Laurence understood his blank look. 'Factory owner,' he said with a wave of his hand that dismissed poor Mr Hughes and everyone like him. 'Extremely rich. Knows nothing about art.'

Edwin thought he could see where Laurence's story was going. 'So this Mr Hughes …'

'He buys whatever he likes,' Laurence said with a smile. 'He offered £300 for the Daniel painting.'

Edwin stared once more. He earned £600 a year and that bought him a very comfortable lifestyle indeed. And this Hughes was offering him half that amount for one painting?

'I don't know what to say,' he said.

'I know,' said Laurence. 'It's almost insulting, no? Anyway, I talked him up to £450.'

Edwin drained his glass. His hand was shaking. 'You talked him up to four hundred and fifty,' he breathed.

'Indeed,' said Laurence. 'And, as I did the negotiating, I thought I would take my commission in kind.'

'Of course,' Edwin stammered. 'Do you need legal advice?'

Laurence chuckled. 'No, Edwin,' he said. 'The other painting. I will take the other painting.'

Somewhere deep in Edwin's bewildered mind, an alarm bell rang. 'For nothing?' he said, his business brain finally catching up with events. 'That's one hundred per cent commission.'

Laurence had the grace to look ashamed. 'Ah, it was worth a try,' he said. 'I'll give you £100 for it.'

'Two hundred,' said Edwin, topping up both their glasses. His composure regained, he noticed with an approving glance that his hand wasn't even shaking the slightest amount.

'One hundred and fifty,' said Laurence.

'Done.'

They shook hands across the table. Edwin's mind was reeling. He had just made his annual salary in five minutes. For a moment he thought about what that money could do for Violet – pay for art lessons, buy her time to paint – then he dismissed the thought. Women and money were a dangerous mix.

He watched, incredulous, as Laurence got out a fat billfold and counted out £100 in cash.

'If you care to accompany me to the bank in the morning, I can get the rest for you,' Laurence said.

Edwin took the money and folded it into his pocket.

'Don't you want to know where they are?' Laurence asked.

Edwin looked surprised. He'd almost forgotten about the

actual paintings. 'Of course,' he said. 'Forgive me. It's been a whirlwind.'

Laurence patted his hand like a kindly father. 'It will sink in soon enough,' he said. 'Mr Hughes will hang *Daniel* in the office of his factory. And I rather thought I might hang mine in here.'

Edwin was pleased.

'It will get you noticed,' Laurence warned. 'Can you produce more?'

'Without a doubt,' Edwin said, thinking about how prolific Violet was. He sent up silent thanks to a god he didn't believe in that he'd moved to Sussex and met her. His whole life was about to change –and it was all because of Violet.

Chapter 35

Present day
Ella

It was strange being back in London. I'd not been away that long, and we'd been into Brighton a few times so we were hardly country mice, but already I'd got used to our slower pace of life in Sussex.

It was nice, though, to be on the train by myself. I read my book, drank a coffee, and stared out of the window.

George was coming to London for some lecture at one of the universities. He had booked himself on an earlier plane so we planned to go to the private members' club and see Violet's painting for ourselves. I'd brought all the sketches I'd found, and George was confident that he could determine if the same artist had created them and the painting in the club.

I got on the bus from Victoria, enjoying watching London slide past the windows, and jumped off at Piccadilly Circus. I was meeting George at the café in the big bookshop there but I knew he was bound to be late, so I settled down with an iced bun and another coffee and waited.

He rang me, ten minutes later, flustered and full of apologies. 'I'm stuck on the bloody train,' he said. 'I knew it was a mistake to fly into Luton. Where is Luton anyway?'

I giggled. 'Don't worry,' I said. 'I can wait.'

'No, darling, you go ahead and charm their socks off and I'll meet you there. I'll be about an hour max. The manager is a guy called Scott something – I'll forward you the email so you've got all the details. He's expecting us.'

I shrugged. 'Okay,' I said. 'Let me know if you're going to be any later, though. I need your expert eye.'

I waited for the email to arrive, then I drained my coffee, pulled on my cardigan – summer was definitely in its last gasps – and wandered out of the shop's back door on to Jermyn Street.

The club was in a white stone building, with steps leading up to the entrance, flanked either side with pillars, and a heavy, black front door.

'Crumbs,' I said. It was very imposing. I wondered if Violet had ever been here but I thought she probably hadn't. I imagined she stayed in Sussex most of the time, and I didn't think establishments like this were very welcoming to women back then.

Nor, I quickly discovered, were they welcoming to women now.

The front door was open, so I went straight in. Inside it looked a bit like a hotel reception, with a heavy wooden desk to my left where a youngish man sat at a computer screen. In front of me were two glass-panelled doors and through them I could see a dining room straight ahead, what looked like a bar to the right, and a large sweeping staircase on the left, lined with paintings. I felt a glimmer of excitement that I was going to see Violet's finished work in the flesh.

'Can I help you?' the man at the desk said.

I smiled at him. 'Hello. My name is Ella Daniels and I'm here to see Scott Simpson. He was going to show me some of your art.'

The man looked at me disdainfully. 'Are you alone?' he said.

'Pardon?'

'Are you here on your own?'

I was confused. 'Oh, yes,' I said. 'My friend George Griffiths made the appointment but he's been held up. So it's just me for now.'

The man flashed me a quick smile. 'I'm afraid we don't allow unaccompanied women into the Jermyn Club, so if you'd care to make another appointment at a more convenient time …'

I stared at him. 'I'm sorry?' I said.

'We don't allow unaccompanied women …' he began again.

I shook my head. 'I heard you,' I said. 'I just didn't understand.'

'It's club policy.'

'Could you get Mr Simpson?' I asked. 'I do have an appointment.'

'I'm Mr Simpson,' he said. 'I'm sorry I can't help you on this occasion.'

He turned his attention to his computer screen; obviously our conversation was over as far as he was concerned. But I wasn't giving up.

'Look,' I said, putting my hands on the desk. 'It's really important that you show me this painting – *King Canute*. It's research for a book.'

I paused as an elderly gentleman came through the glass door and handed Mr Simpson a key fob.

'Thank you, Scott,' he said.

Mr Simpson nodded. 'See you next week, Mr Litten, sir.'

'I'm a crime novelist,' I said, desperately. 'My name is Ella Daniels and I really, really need to see that painting ...'

The elderly man had stopped by the door to put on his jacket. He turned to me. 'Ella Daniels?' he said. 'As in E.J. Daniels?'

I looked at him in surprise. 'Yes,' I said. 'That's me.'

'I'm reading one of your books at the moment,' he said. 'My wife recommended it and I have to say, I'm enjoying it enormously.'

I grinned at him. I loved people telling me they'd read my books.

'And is this research for your next novel?' he said.

'Kind of,' I told him. 'It's actually a real-life mystery that I'm checking out. I'm supposed to be working on my new novel, but until I get to the bottom of this, I just can't concentrate.'

The man nodded. 'Scott,' he said. 'I'll sign Ms Daniels in.'

Mr Simpson sighed, but he tapped the keys on his computer a few times. 'Is it Mrs or Miss?' he asked.

'Ms is fine,' I said, giving the older man an amused glance as he scrawled his name on a temporary membership card for me.

He winked at me. 'It was very nice to meet you, Ms Daniels,' he said, emphasizing the 'Ms'.

'You too, Mr Litten,' I said. 'Thank you.'

'Aren't you staying?' Mr Simpson said, a look of horror on his face.

'Oh I think Ms Daniels will be quite all right on her own, don't you?' said Mr Litten. 'See you next week.'

I swallowed a giggle as Mr Simpson picked up the phone and asked a colleague to come and cover reception while he showed me round. How funny that Mr Litten, who had to be at least seventy, was the one to sign me in while young Mr Simpson was sticking to the old traditions.

'This way, please,' he said. He opened the glass doors and led me up the wide, curving stairs to a large, empty meeting room. At one end of the room, above the table, was Violet's painting.

'Oh,' I said in surprise. 'It's our beach.'

The picture showed a handsome, quite rugged young man, wearing a rich, red robe and a golden crown. He was standing, ankle-deep in the waves that sucked at the shingle of the beach at the bottom of the cliff path from our house. He held his arms out at shoulder height, palms facing the horizon, and he looked noble and strong. It was a glorious painting. The colours were bright and glowing. The water swirled round the man's ankles, and the clouds that gathered in the sky were so real I felt I could reach out and touch them.

And there, in the corner, was Edwin Forrest, written in a bold, flowing, blue ink.

'Gorgeous,' said a voice behind me.

'George,' I said, turning to hug him. 'You made it.'

Mr Simpson breathed an audible sigh of relief. 'I'll leave you to it,' he said. 'Please come to reception if you need anything.'

He turned and fled, leaving me giggling and George confused.

'What on earth was all that about?' he said.

I waved my hand. 'It's not important now,' I said, eager to get to work. 'Let's compare these pictures.'

We unrolled all of Violet's art that I'd found – the sketches of Edwin Forrest from the cupboard and the one I'd found in the book – artist unknown. I'd also brought the sketched self-portrait, and Violet's copy of the John Everett Millais painting called *Mariana*. Carefully, we laid them out on the large meeting-room table, beneath the painting that hung on the wall.

George snapped into art historian mode. He studied each work carefully, scribbling notes on a Moleskin notebook he produced from his bag. He peered closely at the sketches, then went right up to the painting hanging on the wall and peered at that, too.

I trailed around behind him trying to see what he was seeing. Actually, it wasn't too hard. I was no art expert, but even I could see that the style in the sketches we'd found and this finished work was the same. The storytelling quality that was woven among them shone out of the *King Canute* work. George had the finished *Daniel in the Lions' Den* on his iPad screen and he compared that with the sketches, too.

Eventually, he pushed his glasses up on top of his head, rubbed his nose, and gave me a wide smile.

'Well,' he said. 'I can't prove it, of course, but I'm prepared to bet that the same artist drew all of these works.'

'Violet,' I said.

George shrugged. 'Either Violet painted *Daniel* and *King Canute*, or Edwin made all these sketches,' he said. 'And given that the sketch titled *self-portrait* is of a young woman, I'd guess it was Violet.'

I hugged him. 'Thank you,' I said. 'I really appreciate your help and I will prove that Violet was the artist.'

'How are you going to do that?' George asked as we went back down the stairs in the club, to Mr Simpson's obvious relief.

'No idea,' I said. 'But I need to find out exactly what happened to Edwin and Violet first. I've made a new friend, called Priya. She's a detective and she's going to get me in to the police archives to see if I can read up about the crime.'

'Good plan,' said George. He looped his arm through mine.

'Now, I think you owe me a drink …'

Chapter 36

1855
Violet

'And so, my dear, I did everything I could.'

I stared into the sea and blinked back tears. Edwin was still talking, but I wasn't listening. He'd destroyed all my hopes and dreams in just a couple of sentences. Ruskin didn't like my work. He didn't want to see more and he didn't want to buy the paintings – or encourage anyone else to buy them. It was over.

'It's not over,' Edwin said, and I realized I'd spoken aloud. 'Not at all.'

He took my hand and pulled me down to sit on the sand next to him. We were in the shallow cave where we'd first kissed, hidden from the beach and the houses above.

'My darling,' Edwin said. 'I am a member of a club. It's not a fancy establishment, but it is frequented by artists, critics, writers, and so on.'

I wiped my eyes and gazed at him, willing him to have good news.

'I am fortunate enough to be friends with a couple of the committee members.'

I stared out to sea again. I wasn't interested in the politics of Edwin's club.

'Anyway,' Edwin said quickly, obviously sensing he was losing my interest, 'I persuaded Laurence, one of the committee, to hang your paintings in the dining room.'

I looked at him, a tiny bud of hope beginning to unfurl inside me.

'That way everyone who dines at the club – and their guests – will see it,' he said. 'It will be like your own, personal exhibition. And Laurence said if you can paint more, he'd see they were displayed also. I believe this could be the beginning of your art career.'

I flung myself at him, winding my arms round his neck and covering his face with kisses.

'Oh thank you, thank you, thank you,' I cried. 'Oh, Edwin, I love you.'

In horror, I realized I'd never said it before – though I'd thought it many times. But Edwin merely smiled.

'I know,' he said. Gently he kissed my skin where my dress ended, just above my breasts, and I shivered, half in pleasure and half in fear. I knew what he wanted. Slowly, I unbuttoned my dress and pulled it down to my waist. My skin was white in the bright sunlight, and dotted with freckles.

'Go on,' said Edwin. He stood up and pulled off his trousers. I averted my eyes. The sight of him still embarrassed me.

Closing my eyes, I unlaced my corset, exposing my breasts. I was ashamed of my actions but I felt more in control this way.

Edwin looked at me. I felt the heat of his gaze on my bare skin. Then he knelt down in between my legs.

'Good girl,' he said, as he pushed me backwards so I was lying on the sand. His hand was already burrowing up under my skirts. 'Good girl.'

Afterwards, Edwin shook the sand out of his trousers and kissed me briefly on the lips. 'Wait ten minutes,' he said. 'I will see you tomorrow.'

He left, without looking back, as I brushed my hair out with my fingertips and wound it up into a roll. Then I dressed slowly, noticing I had vivid bruises on my inner thighs. I judged it had been ten minutes since Edwin left, so I walked home, thinking all the time about my paintings.

The crushing disappointment I'd felt when Edwin told me Ruskin didn't like them had abated a little but I still felt deflated and sad. I'd spent so long dreaming of being an artist, telling myself that if only Ruskin could see my work he'd be won over, that I wasn't sure what to do next. But somewhere, deep inside myself, I felt the beginning of a plan. A burst of determination that, for the moment, I wasn't sure how to handle. I would go and look at my work, I thought. That might help to focus my mind and help me decide what to do for the best.

Chapter 37

1855
Edwin

Edwin hadn't unpacked his overnight bag yet, because he'd been eager to see Violet first and put the beginning of his plan into action. But now he dumped his clothes into the laundry hamper then reached into the side pocket of his bag and pulled out the money Laurence had given him. Sitting on the bed, he spread the notes out on the counterpane. In a burst of celebration he had bought drinks for everyone at the club and treated himself to a night at a very high-class brothel, but those expenses had barely made a dent in his windfall.

Frances, standing by the bedroom window, still and quiet as always, watched him.

'I just don't understand where it came from,' she said. Edwin regarded her with disdain; she sucked the joy out of every situation with her seriousness.

'It was a deal,' he said. 'A business deal. It's too complicated to explain to you.'

Frances looked at him in the unsettling way she had. It made him feel she was looking right into his soul.

'It's nothing illegal, is it?'

Edwin thought, briefly, of himself signing his name to

Violet's paintings. The law, normally so black and white, was shades of grey when it came to ownership of art. He was fairly certain his actions, while perhaps not within the spirit of the law, were well within the letter.

He tutted at Frances's questions. 'Of course not illegal,' he said. 'It's just the beginning of a new venture. Something big.'

Downstairs, the doorbell rang. Edwin tutted again. 'Are you expecting a caller?' he asked Frances. She shook her head.

Agnes stomped halfway up the stairs.

'Mr Forrest,' she bellowed. 'Someone to see you, sir. Fella from the village, wants help with a contract matter.'

Edwin grimaced at her rudeness. 'We have to get rid of her,' he said. He made for the door, waving at the money on the bed as he went. 'Pick all that up and put it in the safe in my study, will you?'

Chapter 38

1855
Frances

Frances waited until he was downstairs, then sat on the bed and counted the notes. There was well over £500. She was astonished. What had he done to come by such riches? She was positive it wasn't something he wanted her to know about. He often closed deals or won cases and couldn't wait to boast about them, whether or not he thought she'd understand. Which, of course, she usually did.

She stacked the banknotes neatly and took them into the study to put them into the safe. There was a moneybag in there, with more cash inside. As she added the new notes to the haul, she paused. Glancing behind her to make sure Edwin hadn't come upstairs without her hearing, she took a few notes, rolled them up and stuffed them up her sleeve. Then she took a few more and stuffed them up the other sleeve. She closed the safe and locked it, then went to her dressing room, shut the door, pulled a table in front of it, and lifted the loose floorboard.

Underneath was what she was beginning to think of as her 'running away package'. Wrapped in a piece of cloth she had her diary – in it she poured her heart out, giving details of her marriage to Edwin that she'd never dare to speak of in real life, and practised her new signature. She planned her life as Florence Bennett, widow of Alfred.

She also had the book about Scotland, her railway time-table and route, the money of course, and her most recent acquisition: some clothes. She'd gone into Brighton and bought a plain black dress with a high neck, and a little bonnet that tied under her chin. It was miles away from her usual clothes and made her look both more lower class than she was and every inch a wife in mourning – absolutely her intention.

She was confident that if she timed her departure right, while Edwin was in London, and left her 'Frances' clothes on the beach at high tide, as though she'd drowned, no one would be looking for her on the train.

She stroked her swelling belly. She would have to act fast – she estimated she could only stay a couple more weeks. She had resolved to go the next time Edwin went up to London and now she'd made up her mind, she was eager to leave. She wanted to start her new life, away from Edwin, and get ready for the birth of her baby.

And then, she thought, she would be safe. Once more she pushed away her worries for Violet Hargreaves. She couldn't save her, just like she couldn't have saved poor, tragic Beatrice Sanderson.

'It's not your responsibility,' she muttered to herself. 'That girl is not your responsibility.' But could she really leave, knowing how vicious Edwin could be? She would be safe, and her baby would be safe, but Violet would not be. Could Frances have that on her conscience?

Chapter 39

Present day
Ella

August slipped into September and the days at last began to cool off. Oscar started school and settled in straight away thanks in no small part to Amber. And Stanley toddled off to nursery without a backwards glance. Our days fell into a rhythm. Every morning I'd get the boys up and dressed and drop them at school – Ben sometimes came along too if he wasn't starting work early. Then I'd go home, take a pot of coffee up to the attic and struggle through another few chapters of Tessa's fake murder story.

It was finally coming together but I knew it wasn't as good as it could have been if my mind had been completely on the job. At lunchtime, I'd collect Stan from nursery, then Margaret would arrive and take over and I'd head back to work.

In the afternoons – if I'd hit my target number of words during the morning – I allowed myself to think about Violet Hargreaves. I had read reams about the Pre-Raphaelite Brotherhood and discovered that, as I suspected, women from nice families did not paint. There were a few women in their group but they were mostly models or shop girls turned artists like Dante Gabriel Rossetti's wife, Elizabeth Siddal. I couldn't imagine a girl from Violet's background fitting in with the Victorian art world, no matter how talented she had clearly been.

I had an appointment at the police archives but infuriatingly it wasn't for another week. Priya – who'd been signed off work altogether now and who was twitchy and restless – and I talked endlessly about the possible scenarios. Did Violet murder Edwin and attack his wife? Did the wife fake her injuries, kill her cheating husband and do away with poor Vi? We went round and round.

When Ben had a rare Saturday off because his team wasn't playing that weekend, Dad and Barb came to stay. I fretted a lot before they arrived, worried that Dad wouldn't like the house, that his worries about our move would be realized. But actually, and to my enormous relief, his visit went well.

We were sitting in the garden watching Ben playing football with the boys, and chatting.

'Ben's very happy here, isn't he?' Barb said.

I smiled. 'So happy,' I agreed. 'He loves his job – it's been his dream to work for a football club for so long and even the irregular hours don't bother him.'

'And you?' Dad said, looking at me intently.

'I'm really happy too,' I said truthfully. 'The boys are really settled, I've made a good friend, and the other mums at school seem nice too. The house is a bit old-fashioned but it's gorgeous and I love the location. I feel lighter and more relaxed than I've felt for years.'

Dad reached out and squeezed my hand. 'You made the right choice,' he said.

I squeezed back. 'I did. We did.'

'I'm sorry about being so negative.'

I gave his hand a little pat. 'You said exactly what I was thinking,' I said. 'I was so worried about taking the risk but …'

I gestured towards Ben and the boys, and the beach and the sea. 'Look, Dad. How could this be wrong?'

Dad nodded. 'I'm proud of you,' he said.

Embarrassed, I ducked my head and Dad chuckled.

'How is your writing going?'

I made a face. 'It's okay,' I said. 'I'm sort of doing two things at once.'

'Is that wise?' Dad said, his brow furrowed. 'Don't you have a deadline to meet and a contract to fulfil?'

'Dad,' I said, in a warning tone as Barb said: 'James' in the same tone. Dad smiled.

'Sorry,' he said. 'I just worry about you.'

'Come and see,' I said spontaneously. 'Come and see what I've been working on.'

I led him and Barb upstairs to the attic study, where Violet's self-portrait was pinned to the middle of the whiteboard with lots of scribbled notes round the side.

'This is Violet Hargreaves,' I said. 'She lived in our house about one hundred and fifty years ago and she went missing. No one knows what happened to her.'

Barb's eyes shone with interest. 'And you're trying to find out?'

I nodded. 'My new friend Priya is a detective,' I said. 'She's found out a bit, and I'm going to the police archives in Lewes next week to read the crime reports from the time.'

'How wonderful,' Dad said. 'Do you have any theories?'

'A few,' I said. 'She was an artist, and someone else put their name to her work.'

Briefly I explained about the painting in the club in London and how Edwin Forrest had signed it – and been murdered the same night Violet disappeared.

'Priya says it gives Violet a motive,' I said. 'And it does, of course. But Forrest's wife was beaten up the same night, and Priya also says it's unusual for a woman to attack like that.'

'Unusual,' said Dad. 'But it does happen.'

'S'pose,' I said. 'I can't see Violet as the villain in this though. I just feel that she was the victim, somehow.'

'But Forrest was the one who died,' Dad pointed out.

'True,' I agreed. 'And his poor wife was hurt too. Maybe Violet was the murderer, after all.'

'You might get more information from the archives,' Dad said. 'Though did they keep detailed records in those days?'

'Priya's not sure,' I said. 'It was the very early days of the police in Sussex, so maybe not. She's told the archivist what we want to look at, but it takes them a while to dig them out. They're not all on computer, not yet. And they're so old, they're really delicate so they have to be careful.'

'Are you going to write this?' Barb said, looking at the notes piled on my desk. 'It's a great story.'

I shrugged. 'Not sure,' I said. 'I keep coming back to it, and I can't seem to settle to Tessa. But it's all just my imagination at the moment.'

'What does your agent say?'

I grimaced. 'I've not mentioned it,' I admitted. 'I've sent her what I've done of Tessa so far, but I've not told her about this yet.'

'I think you should tell her,' Dad said. 'See what she thinks.'

'Really?' I said, surprised at his interest.

'Well, I'm intrigued,' said Dad. 'So I think your readers will be too. Now, take me through what you know again from the start.'

Chapter 40

1855
Violet

I sat on the attic floor and looked at my version of *Mariana*. I looked at it for a long time, studying the form and the colours, and the brushstrokes. Then I got up and collected together my other pictures and spread them out on the floor, sat back down, and looked at them too.

'I'm a good artist,' I said to myself. I knew that despite what Edwin had said, I had the talent and the determination to make a living from my art. After all, his club had said they would display my paintings – there was some comfort to be taken from that. I wondered if Edwin had perhaps said something wrong to Ruskin, something that had turned him against my work without seeing it properly. And he hadn't mentioned Millais, who I wanted so badly to see my paintings.

'If I could have gone with him,' I murmured. 'If I could have spoken with Millais …'

'Why don't you, then?' said a voice in my head. 'Go to London, speak to Millais yourself.'

But that was a foolish idea. Foolish and dangerous. I had been to London with my father, many times, but I'd never been alone. I'd never been anywhere alone – I'd never even been to Brighton without one of my many governesses or Father by my side.

'You know where to go,' the voice in my head said. 'You know where to stay and which train to get.'

'Someone would surely stop me,' I said aloud. 'Someone would ask me what I was doing and stop me.'

But what if they didn't?

With a burst of energy, I got up again and went to the cupboard in the corner where I kept all my cuttings. I leafed through my file until I found the piece I was thinking of. Last month, the *Illustrated London News* had published a detailed article about the PRB, written by a friend of the men. In it, he'd mentioned the places the artists went to enjoy their debates about the state of art in the modern world.

I ran my finger down the piece and found the name of a pub, the White Hawk Tavern. It was in Bloomsbury. It was not a part of town I was familiar with, but I thought I would easily find it with the help of a cab …

Money. I'd need money.

I had none of my own, of course, but I knew where Father kept his. Funny how this idea had become a firm plan all of a sudden.

I carefully rolled up my *Mariana* and a couple of sketches and tied them with string, then I ran downstairs to my bedroom and packed a small overnight bag. It was almost eleven o'clock now and I knew there was a train to London at half past twelve. I'd need to hurry. I bustled into the dining room and took down the mirror that hung over the fireplace. Behind it was a safe. Without pausing for thought, I spun the dial – the combination was my birthday – and opened the stiff door. Inside was my mother's jewellery, some documents, a bag of coins, and some piles of notes.

'So now I'm a thief as well as a liar,' I said. But I reached inside, took a handful of change from the bag, and a bundle of notes. I stuffed them into the side pocket of my bag and fastened it tightly. Then I shut the safe again and went to find Philips.

'I need you to take me to Brighton urgently,' I told him. 'My old governess has been taken ill and she needs me.'

More lies.

Philips, who was pulling up carrots in the garden, raised an eyebrow.

'Telegram,' I said desperately. 'I got a telegram.'

Philips straightened up. 'Are you in trouble, Violet?' he said, staring right into my eyes. 'Do you need help?'

I caught his hand, which was muddy from his gardening.

'I'm not,' I said. 'I'm quite safe and I'm not in any trouble but I don't want to tell you what I'm doing in case you get into trouble. It's better that you don't know.'

Philips looked at me for so long I started to become uncomfortable and shifted from foot to foot in unease.

'Please,' I said.

'Brighton?' Philips said.

I nodded. 'Yes, just Brighton,' I said. 'Not far.'

More lies.

'Fine,' Philips said. 'Be round the front in five minutes.'

I nearly fell over with relief. If we left in five minutes, I'd make the train easily. And I did. I asked Philips to drop me off in a road near the station, saying that was where my governess lived – that wasn't a lie, actually, I had once had a governess who'd lived in that road. Whether she was still there was another matter but I felt smug that I had told at least one truth.

'I can collect you later,' he said, as I clambered out of the trap.

'No need,' I said. 'Miss Mason has arranged for me to stay the night, and she'll make sure I get home tomorrow.'

Philips looked like he was going to argue, but the horse was getting restless and instead he just nodded and drove away.

I waited for him to turn at the end of the street, then I hoisted my bag up my arm, picked up my skirts, and ran to the station.

Inside it was dim and smoky, but I had been here with Father enough times to feel confident that I knew what I was doing. I went straight to the ticket office.

'A first class return to London, please,' I said in a clear voice.

Then I bit my lip waiting for the clerk to question why I was on my own, where I was going, what I was doing …

Instead he handed over the ticket and took my money without a word.

'Thank you,' I said.

'Platform two,' he said, without looking up. 'You'd better hurry.'

Obediently, I bustled along the platform to the first class carriage. The porter helped me up the step and lifted my small bag into the train for me.

'There you go, Miss,' he said.

I smiled at him as though I travelled to London by myself every day.

'Thank you so much,' I said.

The train was quiet and I was alone in the carriage, much to my relief. No sooner had I settled down than the train shuddered and began to pull out of the station.

I watched the south downs out of the window, feeling a bit shaky and still not completely sure about what it was I was doing. But deep down I knew I was doing the right thing. My desire to be an artist burned so strong that I couldn't ignore it any longer – and if Edwin couldn't help me, then I'd just have to help myself.

Chapter 41

London Bridge station was crowded when I arrived but with my new-found determination and courage, I simply picked up my bags and negotiated my way through the people without any trouble.

It was only once I got outside that my courage deserted me and for a minute I paused, thinking I might simply go back into the station and find the next train back to Brighton.

A burst of laughter nearby made me look round. Two young women were walking past, arm in arm. They were both dressed in stiff skirts like Frances wore and both had their hair neatly rolled up at the back. But despite their respectable appearance, the women were beside themselves with giggles at some unheard joke. As I watched, one of them doubled over.

'Don't,' she said to her friend. 'Don't make me laugh any more, I promise I shall be sick.'

The other woman looked solemn. 'That would never do,' she said.

There was a pause, then they both burst into chuckles again. I watched as they walked on, one dragging the other who was weak from laughing. They were a similar age to me, those girls, but how different their lives must be, to have the confidence to walk the streets of London, to be so happy, to wear such beautiful clothes – for a minute I wanted to throw myself on to the pavement and beat my fists on the ground and wail at the sheer injustice of it all. But as the women walked on, ignoring a vagrant who sat on a wall further along the road, I pulled myself together.

'I am one of the fortunate ones,' I whispered to myself. 'I have money in my purse, and a hat on my head, and food in my belly.'

I patted my bag where my paintings stayed safely tucked away. 'And I have my talent.'

Feeling more confident, I started walking. I had little idea of where to go, but I thought I would follow the river west, until I saw Westminster Bridge. That would take me in the right direction, I assumed.

It was a warm day, and the sun shone defiantly through the smoke round the station. My back was soon damp with sweat and my legs ached as my bag bumped against them. But eventually, I crossed Westminster Bridge and then I was in a more familiar part of town.

Finton's hotel where I stayed when I was with Father was nearby – close to Piccadilly where the Royal Academy was – and I hoped I'd be able to stay there alone. It was known as a family hotel, and I had an idea it had women-only rooms, so I was quite confident it would be fine – but there was still that element of the unknown that made me nervous.

As I approached Regent Street, my steps got quicker and I soon found myself at the hotel entrance. Without pausing

– because that would give me time to change my mind – I climbed the steps and pushed open the door.

The man behind the desk was someone I recognized – he had attended to me and my father many times. He smiled at me.

'Miss Hargreaves,' he said. 'We weren't expecting you.'

I took a breath, marvelling again at how easily I lied nowadays. 'I am so pleased to see you,' I said. 'I assume you received my father's telegram?'

The man looked apologetic. 'I'm not aware of any telegram …' he said.

I gave a heavy sigh. 'I feared this might happen,' I lied. 'My father is stuck in Manchester and needs me to deliver something for him here in London. He was supposed to telegram you and arrange for me to have a room for the night, but he obviously forgot. You know how distracted he can be.'

My father could be nothing of the sort but I stared straight into the man's kind face, daring him to argue.

'Certainly, Miss,' said the man, whose name I remembered now was Robert. He leafed through the large, leather-bound guest book, and smiled. 'We do have a vacancy on our women-only floor though it's not as large as your usual suite.'

I dismissed his concerns with a careless sweep of my hands.

'No matter,' I said. 'I will be busy this evening anyway.'

Robert raised an eyebrow but he didn't question my plans.

I signed the book that he pushed towards me, told him to charge the room to my father's account, and then followed the porter as he took my bag upstairs to my room. My legs were shaking so violently I thought I wouldn't make it to the top of the stairs, but somehow I managed.

As soon as the porter put my bag down, and left the room I locked the door behind him and began to strip off. I was dirty and sweaty from the journey and I was desperate for a wash. I poured water into the bowl and sponged myself all over. Then, still in my underwear, I collapsed on to the bed, my heart pounding. I'd done it. I was in London and I was going to find Millais and persuade him that I was worth his interest.

I kicked my feet against the counterpane in excitement. Then I sat up, pulled my bag towards me, and carefully removed my rolled-up artwork, and my folder of cuttings about the Pre-Raphaelite Brotherhood.

I knew there was a chance they wouldn't all be there, or indeed that none of them would be there. I knew Mr Ruskin definitely wouldn't be there – he wasn't the kind of man who went to those sorts of places (I dismissed the thought that I wasn't the kind of woman who went to those sorts of places, either). But this was my only chance. I had to seize it.

I dressed carefully in my favourite dress. It was white with a print of tiny sprigs of blue flowers. I'd had it made by the dressmaker in the village and I had given it a high neck, puffed sleeves, a nipped-in waist, and a long loose skirt. I never wore the crinolines that some women – Frances for example – trussed themselves up in.

I unwound my hair and brushed it then let it flow across my shoulders. I pulled my bonnet on, picked up my gloves and my artwork, and I was ready.

Robert was still behind the desk when I went downstairs.

'Miss Hargreaves,' he said, standing up. 'Can I help you?'

I took a breath. 'I have an appointment in Bloomsbury,' I said. 'Could you get me a cab?'

'Certainly, Miss,' he said.

It was so easy, I thought. Why had I never done this before?

Robert went outside the hotel and I waited, clutching my gloves tightly until he poked his head back round the door and told me the cab was outside.

He tipped his hat to me as I climbed into the carriage and I smiled. 'Many thanks,' I said.

'Whereabouts in Bloomsbury are you going?' the driver asked as the horse began to trip-trap up towards Piccadilly.

'I am visiting a friend in Giles Street,' I said. It wasn't an out-and-out lie. The White Hawk Tavern was indeed in Giles Street. 'Number three.'

Surely all streets had a number three?

The cabbie didn't answer but drove the horse on. I sat back in the seat and watched London through the window, trying to contain my growing excitement.

'Here we are, Miss,' the cabbie said.

I clambered out, less gracefully than I'd have liked, and handed over some money. To my relief the cabbie drove off immediately.

I glanced round. I was indeed standing outside number three Giles Street, but just a little way down the road I could see the sign that swung outside the White Hawk Tavern.

It was growing late now – after seven o'clock – but it was sti—ll light and there was still a lot of warmth in the day. I took a deep breath, tucked my artwork under my arm, and without hesitating, I walked down the road to the pub and pushed open the door.

Chapter 42

I wasn't a drinker but I'd been past the Albion Inn in our village many times and knew what kind of men went there. Labourers, farm hands – Philips when he had a day off – until he'd got that in that fight and avoided it ever since. Not my father, and not Edwin.

The White Hawk Tavern wasn't like that – to my relief. It seemed to be a more upmarket establishment and its customers were generally well-dressed men – in the front of the inn at least. I heard some shouts from the area behind the bar that suggested perhaps it wasn't quite so well heeled.

The pub itself was clad in wood. The bar, in front of me, was dark, shining mahogany with gleaming brass fittings and the floor was tiled: black and white. Around me were wooden chairs and tables and the walls were clad in the same wood. It smelled of beeswax and cigar smoke and malt, which was unfamiliar to me but not unpleasant.

Despite the welcoming décor, however, and the fact that the customers were far less rough than I'd expected, it was clear from the moment I stepped inside that I was out of my depth.

I was, I noted, dressed in a similar way to the few women

in the pub, though their dresses were cut lower across their busts than mine. One woman, walking across the floor with two cups of ale, paused as she reached me.

'Lost?' she said. There was a mocking tone to her voice.

'No,' I said carefully. 'I am exactly where I intended to be.'

The woman put the cups on a nearby table, where two men in waistcoats hunched over a game of cards. They ignored her and she sighed.

'Looking for someone then,' she said to me. 'And I reckon I know who.'

I shifted my paintings under my arm and looked at the woman. 'Who?'

'Nice girl like you? Red hair?' the woman began. She nodded at my bundle. 'Drawings?'

I bit my lip, feeling like a silly schoolgirl.

'He's over there,' the woman said, pointing to the corner of the inn. 'Usual place.'

'Who?' I said again, hoping it was Millais but not daring to look.

'Who she says, who,' the woman laughed. She looked sympathetic. 'Gabriel,' she said. 'But don't expect nothing from him. He's silver-tongued when he wants to be but he don't give his heart easily. Least not to anyone but Lizzie.'

I smiled, a thrill coursing through me. Dante Gabriel Rossetti was here. Here. In the same room as I was. And if Millais wasn't with him, then he'd know where I could find him.

'Thank you for your help,' I said to the woman. 'My heart belongs to another.'

The woman gave a disbelieving snort and stood aside to

let me past. I walked over to the table that was crowded with young men and a few women. I tried to look as though I did this all the time. I scanned the group for any sign of Millais – I'd studied pictures of him so closely that I was confident I'd recognize him – but I couldn't see him.

Gabriel, or at least the man the barmaid had pointed out so I assumed it was Gabriel, had his back to me. He was wearing a velvet jacket and he was arguing furiously with the man next to him about money.

'It seems wrong to let it go for the sake of £5,' he was saying.

The other man laughed. 'Well that's fine for you to say, Gabriel,' he said. 'But I don't have £5 …'

I cleared my throat. 'Excuse me,' I said.

No one heard.

'Excuse me,' I said again, louder this time. 'Mr Rossetti.'

The man next to Gabriel gave him a violent nudge. 'Gabriel,' he said. 'Gabriel.'

Gabriel stopped talking and turned to look at me. At the same time, I noticed that while he was talking to the man on his left, his right hand rested on the upper thigh of the woman to his other side, casually caressing the inside of her leg. She was carefully ignoring him and talking to the woman she sat next to, though I could see her chest heaving as she took deep breaths in time to Gabriel's caresses.

Tearing my eyes away from Gabriel's fingers, and blushing furiously, I met the artist's gaze.

'I was wondering, sir, if you knew of the whereabouts of Mr Millais?'

Gabriel grinned. His eyes were crossing slightly and though I had little experience of such things, I thought he was drunk.

'Millais?' he said, thoughtfully. 'Millais …'

I waited patiently.

'I might know,' he said. 'But why should I tell you?'

The women on his right giggled and I felt myself blush even more.

'I have some paintings to show him,' I said. My voice quivered and I hated myself for it.

'Your paintings?' Gabriel asked.

I bit my lip, reluctant to admit they were mine. But I nodded eventually.

Gabriel looked me up and down. 'Show me,' he said. He was very handsome but I was scared of his flashing eyes and sharp tone.

'I'd rather show Mr Millais, sir,' I said boldly. 'Do you know where he is?'

'No idea,' Gabriel said.

'You are a pig,' said a voice behind me. I turned round and saw Millais himself standing behind me. He was looking at Gabriel with a disappointed, yet tolerant, expression.

'No wonder you annoy everyone,' he said to Gabriel. 'You're always so rude.'

Gabriel sat back on his bench, and grinned his wolfish grin again. 'Everyone loves me,' he said with the arrogance of one who knows he is right. 'It doesn't matter how rude I am, they love me all the same.'

Millais shrugged. 'One day, Gabriel, your luck will run out,' he said. He glanced at me for the first time and I felt my face redden again. Inwardly I cursed my fair skin. 'Who are you?'

'She is an artist,' Gabriel said, laughing. 'An artist who wants to show you her paintings.'

He made the words *artist* and *paintings* sound like insults and I flinched.

'She wants to show the great, the wonderful, the famous John Everett Millais how good she is at drawing,' he went on.

I looked at my feet. This was not going the way I'd hoped.

Gabriel put on a shrill voice. 'Oh, Mr Millais, let me show you what I can do,' he said. He hoicked an imaginary bosom and thrust it towards Millais. 'Let me show you what I can do for you in exchange for your oh-so-clever advice on how to draw a pretty picture ...'

'Gabriel,' warned a man on the other side of the table. He had blond curls and I thought he might be William Holman Hunt, another member of the Brotherhood and someone I'd have ordinarily been excited to meet, but everything was ruined now and I found I didn't really care any more. 'Enough, Gabriel.'

'Are you an artist?' Millais asked me.

I nodded numbly.

'May I?'

Millais gently tugged at the rolled-up paintings under my arm. Suddenly it was all too much for me. My confidence – already more affected than genuine – deserted me all at once. I knew – I absolutely knew – that there was no way I could stand there while Millais looked at my work. So I pushed my artwork towards him, then I spun round on my heels and fled.

Chapter 43

I didn't know exactly where I was going. I marched down the road in the direction I'd come in, feeling angry, upset, embarrassed – a mixture of emotions – and wishing that I'd never come up with this harebrained idea to come to London. I would go back to the hotel, I thought, then rise early and get the first train back to Sussex. And I would stay there.

I reached the corner of the street and, unsure of which direction to take, paused to catch my breath. It was getting dark now and soon the lamplighter would be out. I peered through the gloomy twilight, hoping to see something I recognized that would tell me which way to walk.

A shout behind me made me start.

'Miss!'

My stomach lurched in fear. How foolish I'd been to risk coming to an unfamiliar, quiet part of town, late in the evening. I began to turn away from the voice, but it followed.

'Miss, wait,' it called. 'I just want to speak to you about your work.'

My work? I stopped and turned to see Millais himself hurrying out of the mist towards me.

'In a hurry?' he said as he reached me.

I shrugged. I eyed him cautiously, afraid I was going to be mocked again.

'Would you join me for a cup of coffee?'

He nodded a little way down the road, where I could see the illuminated windows of a coffee house.

'Please?' he said.

I nodded and he led the way inside.

We settled at a table and I took off my gloves and bonnet and shook out my hair. I tried my best to look as though I always took coffee with famous artists, but I felt very young and ill at ease as Millais laughed with the waitress and ordered coffee and cake on my behalf.

'Forgive me,' Millais said, as the waitress disappeared through the doors to the kitchen. 'I don't even know your name.'

'Violet,' I said. 'Violet Hargreaves.'

Millais nodded to me politely. 'Pleased to meet you,' he said. 'I am John.'

I gave a small smile.

'I know,' I said.

John put my rolled-up work on the table between us and touched it gently with his long fingers. 'This is very good,' he said. 'It's yours, I trust?'

I trembled with disbelief. He thought my work was good?

'It is,' I said. 'Except for the *Mariana*. That's yours.'

John smiled at me. 'With your own touch,' he added.

I smiled back. I played with the raffia mat on the table, trying to think of how best to explain my connection to Mariana.

'I do a lot of waiting,' I said.

John nodded in understanding. 'I know all about waiting,' he said, with a faraway look in his eye. 'As does my wife.'

He paused, then gathered himself.

'So why did you come to me?'

Distracted momentarily by thoughts of his wife – I remembered reading reports of his marriage but couldn't remember the details – I blinked at him.

'Why did you come to me?' he repeated.

'Because I want to be an artist,' I said simply. 'And my friend Edwin said you or Mr Ruskin could help me.'

John looked confused. 'Edwin?'

'Edwin Forrest,' I said. 'I believe he is a friend of yours.'

I told him about meeting Edwin on the beach, about his links to the art world, and his friendship with Mr Ruskin. I mentioned how he'd come back from London with disappointing news from Mr Ruskin but hadn't managed to meet with John, so I'd decided to come myself. I left out, of course, any mention of my relationship with Edwin.

'Edwin Forrest?' John said when I paused for breath. His brow was furrowed. 'Forrest?' He took a sip of coffee. 'Tall chap? Blond? Pleased with himself?'

I smiled at his succinct summing up of Edwin. 'Yes,' I said.

John nodded. 'Met him once,' he said. 'At some do at the Academy. Haven't seen him since, though. And Ruskin's in Venice so I doubt he's seen him either – though we're not really talking at the moment ...'

With a start I remembered what was newsworthy about John's marriage – his bride was Effie Ruskin, who'd been married to the critic for many years before they divorced. No wonder he looked tired – his personal life was the talk of London and Effie had suffered all sorts of degrading and intrusive tests before her divorce was allowed.

'He's spinning you a yarn,' said John.

I shook my head. 'No, not Edwin,' I said. 'He told me he'd seen Ruskin and he couldn't be a patron for me because he spent too much money on Lizzie Siddal.'

John gave a bark of laughter. 'Well that's true enough,' he said. 'Perhaps this Edwin has been to Venice after all.'

'Or perhaps you are mistaken and Mr Ruskin is in London,' I said, knowing very well that Edwin had only been away for two or three days.

John shrugged. 'So you want me to be your patron?' he said, getting to the point.

I flushed. 'I thought if you saw my work, then you'd want to help,' I said. 'Support me, teach me …'

John studied me and I lowered my eyes in embarrassment.

'You have confidence in your work,' he said. 'I like that. You should be confident.'

'My father wants me to get married,' I said. 'Then my confidence will all be for nothing.'

There was a pause. I was painfully, acutely aware that whatever John said next would change my life.

'If you'd come to me last year, or two years ago, then I could have helped,' John said. He looked genuinely sorry. 'I could have taught you, and introduced you to Ruskin. But now …'

'Now …' I said. My voice shook.

'Now I have no spare money with which to help you, and no leverage with Ruskin,' John said. 'And my reputation is shaky to say the least. I can't help you.'

I closed my eyes briefly. Then I forced myself to smile. 'Perhaps Mr Holman Hunt?'

But John was shaking his head. 'He is off to the Holy Land again soon. He may be away for some time.'

'Mr Rossetti?' I couldn't imagine working with Rossetti but needs must.

John shook his head again.

'Any money he has pays debts and supports Lizzie,' he said, his mouth twisting slightly in disapproval.

'Lizzie,' I repeated in disgust. My heart contracted in pure brilliant envy of the woman who had somehow got the life I wanted.

John reached out and touched my hand briefly. 'Lizzie lives a chaotic life,' he said. 'Not one you should wish to copy.'

I felt ashamed. I gathered my things and pulled on my bonnet. 'I must go,' I said. 'Thank you for your time.'

John stopped me with a hand on my arm. 'Keep in touch,' he said. He pulled a pencil out from his jacket pocket and wrote an address on the back of one of my sketches. 'Send me drawings, write to me of your work. And maybe in a year or two from now, things will change.'

'Really?' I said, my mood swinging violently from desolation to delight.

'Really,' he said. 'Wait like Mariana.'

'Mariana waited in vain,' I pointed out.

John smiled. 'Your time will come.'

Chapter 44

Present day
Ella

'I think everything you need is here,' said the police archivist. She was young and pretty with bright red hair and a ring through her nose, and looked absolutely nothing like I had expected. She handed me a pair of cotton gloves and slipped a similar pair on her hands. She had chunky silver rings on both her thumbs. I smiled at her, grateful she was being so helpful.

'Thanks for getting all this out for me, Lainey,' I said. We were sitting at a large table in the cool airy new police archives building in Lewes, a large box of books and files in front of us. It was all fairly intimidating even though I was no stranger to research, so I was very pleased Lainey was so enthusiastic about it. Priya had wanted to come with me, but Amber was sick so she'd reluctantly stayed behind.

Lainey heaved one of the leather books out of the box and opened it at a marked page.

'This is my bread and butter,' she said, her eyes sparkling. 'I love this kind of stuff. Now look.' She ran her finger down a handwritten list of numbers. 'We're going right back to the early days of Sussex police here, but their record-keeping was brilliant.'

I squinted at the writing, but I couldn't make head or tail of it.

'Each crime was given a number,' Lainey explained. 'And the name next to it is the policeman who investigated – for yours it's Inspector Croft. You'll get the hang of reading the writing.'

She pointed to a row of tight script. 'Then here, is the type of crime it was, and next to it, the names of the victims. This is your one.'

I pulled the book back towards myself. 'Murder,' I read aloud. 'Attempted murder. And, erm, what's that last one?'

'Missing person,' Lainey said.

'And the names.' I looked carefully at the tiny writing. 'Edwin Forrest, Frances Forrest, William Philips, Violet Hargreaves.'

The hairs on the back of my neck stood up. This was it.

'That's them,' I told Lainey. 'Is there any more?'

She looked thrilled to be asked. 'Oh yes.' She stood up and pulled another, even larger, book out of the box, her skinny, sinewy arms straining.

Again the right pages were marked – she'd got everything ready for me, bless her. She opened the book using both hands to turn the heavy pages.

'Crime reports,' she said in a triumphant manner. 'Everything they recorded about it – it's all here.'

I couldn't believe it. I checked the name of the investigating officer on the report and sent a silent prayer of thanks to the long-dead Inspector Croft who'd written everything down in such detail.

'I'll leave you to it,' Lainey said. 'Give me a shout if you need a hand.' She looked stern for a minute. 'And no food or drink in here. It's all too precious.'

I'd been about to ask where I could get a cup of tea, but instead I nodded meekly. Then I turned my attention to the book.

I resisted the temptation to read ahead, instead making notes on the crimes diligently. Then when I'd copied it all into my notebook, I turned to the witness statements. They were disappointing to say the least.

The housekeeper – Agnes Hobb – had seen nothing, heard nothing, knew nothing. Frances merely said she, her husband, and Violet had been chatting in front of her house when someone attacked them from behind. She'd been knocked unconscious, she said, and could remember nothing. And the Hargreaves family's gardener – William Philips – died. In Inspector Croft's writing, it said Philips expired three days after the attack.

I sat back in my chair, feeling unaccountably sad for the gardener, who'd not even merited a mention before now. And of course I felt awful about Edwin and Frances who were the other victims of the brutal attack. But where was Violet?

I leafed through the reports, skimming to see if Inspector Croft had found another body, but I could see nothing. 'Some post-mortem reports would be nice,' I muttered, missing the brilliant bureaucracy of the modern police.

'There's a doctor's report,' Lainey said from behind me. I hadn't noticed her approach. She leaned over and rifled through the pages. She smelled like joss sticks and made me think of my university days.

'Here it is.' She stuck her finger in the right page and

pushed the heavy book back to me. 'Also, I thought you might want this.' She held out a Post-it Note. 'It's our login for the newspaper archive,' she explained. 'Probably worth checking what was reported at the time.'

'Brilliant,' I said. 'I'm going to get a cup of tea – in the canteen,' I added as I saw her disapproving face. 'Then I'll be back.'

I spent all afternoon in Lewes. I read the doctor's report on Edwin Forrest and William Philips. The doctor wrote that Edwin died due to a blow to the head, at the bottom of the stairs. His wife, Frances, was found at the top of the stairs so he concluded the pair had fled their attacker, Edwin had tried to stop his wife from being hurt, and become a victim himself. William Philips had been found unconscious outside the house and died, the doctor thought, from bleeding on his brain.

'From the bruises around his jaw,' he wrote. 'I surmised he had been struck violently, throwing his head back and knocking him unconscious. His brain, no doubt, continued to swell until he expired.' But there was still no mention of Violet – until I logged on to the newspaper archive.

'So there was just no trace of her?' Ben asked later, spreading the printouts I had made across the table.

'They found her hat,' I said. 'Near the beach. So they thought she might have drowned. But they didn't find anything else.'

I picked up one page that Lainey had printed out for me and handed it to him. 'The paper went really big on it. Look, here they're asking for local people to report any sightings of her.'

'Sussex woman missing after violent attack,' Ben read aloud.

'Sussex woman still missing,' I read from another page. 'That's a week later.'

Ben picked up another story and scanned it. 'Ah so her dad was away when it happened,' he said. 'Look, here it says he's returned and is organizing search parties. That's so sad.'

'It is sad,' I agreed with a shudder. 'Imagine always looking for your child and never finding her.'

'How long did he look for?' Ben asked.

'Months, I think,' I said. 'Years, even. But he moved to Brighton and did it all from there. I read somewhere that he closed the house up as soon as he returned and found Violet gone.'

I imagined Violet's father, alone in this big family house, his footsteps echoing through the empty rooms where his wife and daughter had once been, and decided I didn't blame him one bit for leaving.

'What about Frances?' Ben said suddenly. 'She was the only one who survived. Did she know anything?'

I shook my head. 'Nothing.' I showed him the notes I'd made from Frances's witness statement and he looked deflated.

'Annoying,' he said. He got up and went to the fridge.

'More?' he asked, waving the wine bottle at me.

I nodded but I didn't look up. Him mentioning Frances had given me another idea. I leafed through my notes again until I found the doctor's report.

'Ah ha,' I said. 'Frances was pregnant!'

Ben looked interested. He topped up my glass and sat

down again. 'Frances was pregnant?' he repeated. 'So what happened? Did she come back here to have the baby?'

I shrugged. 'It didn't say. But …'

'If she had a baby, then perhaps she's got relatives,' Ben finished for me. 'Relatives you can find.'

'Exactly.'

I grinned at him. 'So I thought I'll phone Barb,' I said. 'She works in probate – she's always tracing people.'

Ben chinked his glass against mine. 'We're getting somewhere,' he said.

***

'It's not really me you need to speak to,' Barb said the next day when I called her at her office.

'Is there a colleague of yours who could help?' I asked.

Barb's laughter pealed down the line. 'No, darling,' she said. 'Ring your dad. Once you know if this Frances has any living relatives I can find them, for sure, but for now it's your dad who can help.'

I was genuinely flummoxed. 'Dad?'

'He's been doing his family tree, hasn't he? He loves all that *Who Do You Think You Are?* stuff.'

'He does?'

'Yes, he's got quite far back – you know all this. He told you.'

I vaguely remembered my dad waffling on about something that had happened during the First World War, and me ignoring him. I felt guilty suddenly.

'I'll call him,' I told Barb.

'Please do, sweetheart,' Barb said. 'He would love to help.'

'I will,' I said.

I ended the call and dialled my dad's number. He sounded so pleased to hear from me I grinned.

I told him all about what I learned at the archives and he asked a lot of questions.

'Funny how one doesn't imagine such terrible crimes happening back then,' he said as I outlined the facts of the case. 'Ridiculous really.' He paused. 'So what can I do to help?'

'Well,' I said, 'the woman from next door – Frances – she was married to Edwin, the guy who was killed. Frances was hurt but she didn't die. And she was pregnant.'

'Ah,' said Dad. 'Brilliant. Family. No wonder you're intrigued. Hold on, let me get some paper.'

I heard the phone being put down, and my dad rummaging through his desk. Then he came back on the line.

'Fire away,' he said. 'Tell me everything you know about her.'

Chapter 45

1855
Violet

The next day, invigorated by my new-found friendship with John (John Everett Millais likes my work, I kept saying to myself. My work.), a good night's sleep, and a hearty breakfast, I left the hotel intending to head straight to London Bridge and the train back to Sussex.

I knew I could pick up a cab at Piccadilly Circus so I started to walk the short distance from the hotel, but as I crossed Jermyn Street I paused. This was where Edwin's club was. The club where he'd said my pictures could hang.

'He lied about knowing John,' a nagging voice in my head said. 'He lied about meeting Ruskin …'

But then again he hadn't lied altogether, had he? John knew Edwin – albeit only slightly – and even he had conceded Edwin could have spoken to Ruskin. I was no longer sure what to think or what to believe.

'Go and see,' the voice in my head said. 'Go and see if your paintings are in the club.'

I stood on the corner of Jermyn Street for a moment, wondering if I should listen to the voice, or to trust Edwin. Then I slowly but deliberately, began walking away from Piccadilly Circus, down Jermyn Street.

I found the club without too much trouble at all. It was a tall, white building with two stone pillars. Without pausing to think about what I was doing, I climbed the stairs and pushed open the heavy door.

Inside, a man sat at a large wooden table, writing in a ledger. He looked up when I entered.

'Miss?' he said, questioning my very presence in this cathedral of men.

I pulled off my bonnet. 'Good day,' I said, assuming my fake confidence once more. 'My name is Violet Hargreaves. I am the daughter of Marcus Hargreaves.'

Vague recognition glimmered in the man's eyes but he said nothing.

'My father and I are close friends of Edwin Forrest, who I believe you count among your members.'

Now there was proper recognition in the man's face, but still he didn't speak.

'Mr Forrest tells me he has recently gifted some paintings to this club,' I said. I smiled a little. 'Wonderful paintings.'

The man nodded.

Encouraged, I went on. 'I wondered if I may see them?'

'You?' the man said.

'Yes.'

'No.'

I thought about how my father behaved when someone told him something wasn't possible. I fixed the man with a steely glare.

'No?'

'No.'

The man picked up his pen again and began writing in the ledger once more. I was irritated by his disdain.

'I'm afraid you have misunderstood me,' I said, speaking slowly and clearly as though I were talking to a child. 'My friend Edwin Forrest recently gifted some paintings to this club. These paintings are especially close to my heart because they were created by …'

'One painting,' said a voice behind me. I turned round to see an elderly gentleman with fluffy white mutton chops. 'Well, there were two originally, but the other one has been packaged up now and …' He pulled a pocket watch out and peered at it. 'It's well on its way to Manchester.'

I blinked at him in surprise.

'Laurence Cole,' he said, offering his hand to be shaken. 'I know all about the paintings.'

'You do?'

'Indeed I do,' he said, nodding. 'Don't mind Mr Trevor here. Some of the members are a bit odd about the presence of women – he's just looking out for their interests.'

I snorted. 'Well he doesn't have to be so rude while he's doing so,' I said.

The man, Laurence, chuckled. 'You have spirit, Miss …'

'Hargreaves,' I said. 'Violet Hargreaves.'

Laurence regarded me. 'Related to Marcus?' he asked.

I hesitated for a second, wondering if he would tell Father he'd met me, then I nodded. 'He's my father.'

Laurence smiled. 'Wonderful,' he said. 'Wonderful. Marcus Hargreaves is a great man.'

I smiled back, wishing he'd get to the point.

'And Edwin?' he said. 'How do you know Edwin?'

Just the mention of his name made colour rush to my cheeks. 'He's our neighbour in Sussex,' I said. 'And a friend.'

'Another fine man,' said Laurence. 'And so talented.'

'Indeed,' I said, not remotely interested in Edwin's skills as a lawyer.

'His paintings are quite remarkable,' Laurence went on. 'Immature, of course, but he shows great promise.'

His paintings? Edwin hadn't mentioned showing his own work to anyone. He'd never even shown me anything he'd drawn. I stared at Laurence.

'I'll show you,' he said.

He looked past me to where the man still wrote in the ledger.

'I am accompanying Miss Hargreaves to the boardroom,' he said. 'We will be a quarter of an hour – no longer. No need to panic.'

The man didn't look up. 'I will come to find you if you're not back here by half past,' he warned.

'Very well,' said Laurence, making a face at me and making me smile. 'Come along, Miss Hargreaves. Come and see Edwin's painting.'

Laurence offered me his arm and together we walked up the wide sweeping staircase to the second floor of the club and into a long room with a large table. On the wall at one end was King Canute turning back the tide.

I gasped. 'But …' I said, in shock. It was my painting. Mine. Why did this man believe Edwin had painted it?

'Marvellous, isn't it?' said Laurence. 'Edwin is very modest. He told me he'd only put his name to this work on the train on his way into town.'

'On the train,' I repeated softly. My mind was racing. I walked closer to the painting and saw Edwin's signature etched on to the canvas at the bottom.

'I don't understand,' I said. I sank on to a chair and gazed up at the painting, noting with a mixture of dismay and pride that it looked wonderful framed and hanging in a room.

Laurence smiled at me. 'You didn't realize Edwin was so accomplished, I gather,' he said. 'I was taken aback too, I must confess.'

He sat down next to me. 'He was reluctant to show me his work at first,' he said. 'But I talked him into it. And when he discovered I could sell it, well, he was very surprised.'

'I'm sure,' I muttered.

'I sold one to a contact in Manchester, an industrialist called Hughes. He's planning to hang it in his office at his factory.'

The name was familiar to me as someone my father occasionally worked with. I couldn't comprehend that perhaps Father would see my painting hanging in an office and not know his daughter was the artist.

'And this one?' I asked. 'Edwin gifted this one to the club?'

Laurence chuckled again.

'Good heavens, no,' he said. 'I bought this one – at a reduced rate of course.'

'Of course.'

'I have lent this to the club. They're making a small plaque to say that it's from my collection and Edwin has promised to let me see his next work.'

I looked at my painting and then at Laurence. 'You believe you could sell more?' I stuttered. 'More of these paintings?'

'Certainly,' Laurence said with a smile. 'Talent as great as Edwin's will have its rewards. I believe I can sell everything he can create. These paintings are going to make him very wealthy.'

I stood up suddenly. 'I must go,' I said. 'I have a train to catch.'

I picked up my bag and, watched by a startled Laurence, I fled down the stairs and back out into the street.

It was only when I was in a cab, speeding through the streets towards London Bridge, that I realized I hadn't asked how much the paintings had sold for.

Chapter 46

The train journey back to Brighton was warm and uncomfortable. I tried to doze but my slumbers were interrupted by the whirlwind of my thoughts. I kept picturing Millais saying I should keep in touch, Laurence admiring the painting, then Edwin telling me – lying to me – that he'd arranged for my work to be exhibited at the club, and the shock of seeing his name at the bottom of my art.

By the time I reached Sussex, I was hot, tired, and absolutely furious. I came out of the station and thought for a moment. I was desperate to see Edwin, to find out what he was thinking when he put his name to my artwork but I knew he wouldn't be home. It was a weekday so Edwin would be at work – in Brighton. I knew where his office was – well, I knew the name of the road at least. Would it be madness to go and see him there?

Before I'd even made up mind fully, my legs were carrying me down the hill towards the sea and the street where I knew Edwin worked.

It wasn't hard to find. It was a white, double-fronted building with a brass plaque bearing his name. I pushed open the door, marvelling at how bold I'd become in the last two days, and went inside.

'I have an appointment with Edwin Forrest,' I told the clerk at the desk. He went to open the leather-bound book in front of him and I stopped him by placing my hand on his.

'Just tell him Violet Hargreaves is here,' I said.

The man glanced at me. Then he nodded in what seemed to be recognition though I had never met him before. He stood up and disappeared into a nearby room. I was amazed at how he had done exactly what I'd asked him to do.

Then he reappeared and gestured to me to go into the room he'd just come from. 'He's in there,' he said.

I took a breath and went into the office. Edwin was standing by the door and as soon as I entered, he shut it behind me and grabbed hold of my wrist.

'What are you doing here?' he hissed. 'How dare you come to my office and risk my livelihood.'

I pulled my wrist away and glared at him. 'Your livelihood?' I said, not bothering to lower my voice. 'What about mine? How much money have you made from my paintings, Edwin? How much?'

Edwin paled. 'Ah,' he said.

'Ah,' I repeated.

With a sigh, Edwin went to his desk and sat down. 'Sit,' he said.

Obediently, I did so.

Edwin rubbed his forehead and sighed again.

'How did you find out?' he asked.

'I met your friend Laurence,' I said. 'He showed me my

painting – with your name at the bottom. And he told me you'd sold them both.'

'But he didn't tell you how much?' Edwin asked.

I shook my head. 'He said you were going to be rich,' I said, spitting out the words.

Edwin smiled. 'Not me, my darling. You. You're going to be rich.'

I felt the same disconcerting confusion I'd felt when I'd seen the painting. I stared at Edwin.

He opened his desk drawer and took out a bundle of papers tied with a blue cord. 'I was going to wait to tell you until I'd drawn up all the contracts,' he said. He waved the papers in my face. 'I'm only halfway through.'

I didn't speak.

'When I arrived in London, I got the paintings out in my room,' Edwin said. 'I spread them out on the bed, just as Laurence knocked on my door – he'd seen my signature in the guest book and had come to say hello.'

'Go on,' I said coldly.

'He assumed the paintings were mine and I didn't correct him fast enough,' Edwin said. 'Almost straight away he said how good they were and how he thought he could sell them. I couldn't shut him up, he was so excited.'

'And?'

'Then the next day he said he had a buyer. I thought of what that money could do for you – and how important it was that this all happened. And I thought about how he would react if I said a young girl from Sussex was the artist ...'

I stared right at him.

'And I lied,' Edwin said. 'And when he asked me to sign

them, I did. But I did it for you, Violet. I thought we could do a deal – you paint and I'll be the face of your art. Then, when you're established, you can show yourself and we'll tell the art world the truth. You'll have made enough money by then to support yourself.'

He waved the papers again. 'I was going to draw up a contract,' he said. 'Make it all legal. Make sure you knew I was acting in your best interests.'

'Laurence said you signed the paintings on the train,' I said, remembering his story. 'Before you'd even got to London.'

Edwin smiled. 'Laurence is fond of a drink,' he said. 'He must have misunderstood.'

I felt myself softening. 'You think I could make enough money to support myself?' I said.

'I know so,' said Edwin.

'How much were my paintings sold for?'

Edwin paused.

'I understand money, Edwin,' I said, his hesitation annoying me. 'I'm not some stupid little girl, whatever you might think.'

'One hundred,' Edwin said. 'They sold for £100.'

I gasped. 'Altogether?'

Edwin's eyes flickered slightly, then he smiled.

'No, my darling,' he said. 'They sold for £100 each.'

I was light-headed. 'Two hundred,' I breathed.

Edwin was suddenly all business. 'What I'm proposing is this,' he said. 'I will act as your agent. I will take your paintings to Laurence and other buyers, and sell them. I will tell the buyers that I am the artist but I will give you the money we make.'

I nodded slowly. 'All of the money?'

Edwin ducked his head.

'That was my intention initially, but on drawing up these contracts it became clear that the amount of work involved does mean I will have to take a small commission …'

'How small?'

'Twenty per cent.'

I pursed my lips. 'Fine,' I said. My voice was steady, but my heart was beating fast and my head was spinning. This was it. This was my way out. I could paint, carrying on as I had been up until now. I could even go along with Father's plans to marry me off, if it came to it, as long as I could delay the actual wedding for a year or so. Then I could sell my work, build up some savings and, when the time was right, reveal myself to the art world.

'And this would all be legal?' I said.

Edwin nodded. 'I'll make sure the contracts are all in order,' he said.

I held my hand out across the desk. 'Then we have a deal,' I said.

Edwin shook my hand efficiently. Then still holding my fingers he came round the desk and pulled me close to him. He pressed his lips to mine.

'Darling girl,' he said. 'We are going to make a perfect team.'

Chapter 47

I was exhausted when I finally got home. I had shared Edwin's carriage back from Brighton, which was a relief. He said he would tell Frances he'd seen me at the station and offered to accompany me home. If she asked, which she probably wouldn't, he'd said. Frances showed little interest in his comings and goings these days, he told me.

I said a polite farewell to Edwin at the gate of his house, and walked the short distance home. I was eager to get back, strip off my dusty travelling clothes, and rest. I had a lot to consider. Edwin's offer sounded wonderful. It sounded like the best chance I had to become an artist.

But something made me cautious. Had Laurence really misunderstood what Edwin told him about signing the paintings, or was Edwin – as Millais had said – spinning me a yarn? Plus, painting under someone else's name wasn't quite how I'd pictured my career and I wanted to be sure I was doing the right thing. Although, I thought, I didn't really have many options.

The house was quiet when I arrived, with no sign of Mabel or Philips. I unpinned my hat and hung up my cape, then I went to go up the stairs to my room and stopped in horror as I noticed Father's bags at the bottom of the staircase.

Father was home? When had he arrived? Did he know I'd been away all night? Had Philips told him my lie about my former governess?

Feeling sick with dread, I crept into the lounge, ready to face the music. But Father wasn't there. He wasn't in his study either. This was strange. Perhaps he'd been called away again, and not realized I was gone. I hoped that was the case.

'Father?' I called. 'Father?'

Nothing.

Dizzy with relief, I went upstairs with my bag and threw it on my bed. I changed my clothes, washed my face, and climbed the stairs to the attic.

It was getting late, and I was tired and hungry, but I had an idea for a painting showing a scene from *Romeo and Juliet* and I was eager to get on with sketching out my plans while they were still fresh in my mind.

I reached up to loosen my hair from its tight roll and gasped in surprise as I noticed Father sitting, straight upright, in the middle of the chaise.

'I should have married again,' he said, as though my arrival had merely interrupted his train of thought. 'I should have found myself a good woman, perhaps had more children. It would have done you good to have siblings.'

I took a step towards him. 'Father,' I said.

'Where have you been?' he asked.

I paused, wondering whether to lie. 'London,' I admitted. 'To talk to an artist about my work.'

I braced myself for his outrage. Father was a good man,

but he did have a temper when he was crossed. I was rarely on the receiving end of his rage, so when I was, I felt it keenly.

Father nodded. He looked up at me and with shock I realized he had tears in his eyes.

'I'm sorry, Violet,' he said. 'I fear I have left you alone too long, let you run wild. My absence has allowed you to construct a fantasy world with your drawing.' He glanced at the wall where my sketches and paintings were pinned. 'No more.'

I was thrown. When I'd imagined Father discovering my art, I had never expected him to react in this way, so sadly.

'I missed your mother,' he continued. 'I missed her so much. And work was a release. And by the time I'd stopped missing her so badly, you were grown and I thought you no longer needed a father.'

I let out a sob. I may barely remember my mother but I missed her greatly and I'd never really considered that Father had been bereaved too. I sat down next to Father and took his hand.

'Father,' I said. 'I may be grown but I still need you.'

'No more,' he repeated. He looked at me as if he was seeing me for the first time. 'There is still time to save this,' he said. 'To make amends.'

'Father,' I said. 'You have no need to make amends, you …'

'Not me,' he said. 'You. You must make amends for this shameful pastime. This flight of fancy. These ideas of art must end, now.'

'Father,' I said, urgently. 'No, you don't understand. This is special. This is what I want to do with my life. What I must do with my life.'

Suddenly Edwin's idea seemed like my only way out. It wasn't perfect, but I could make it work.

'I have a plan to paint,' I began. But Father held up his hand to stop me talking.

'No,' he said firmly. 'No more. What you must do, Violet, is stop painting altogether. You must marry, and you must give up this ridiculous notion.'

He got up and walked to the wall of paintings. With a sudden burst of anger, he pulled down one of my King Canute sketches. I winced as though he'd hit me.

'I will ask Philips to come and return this room to its former purpose,' he said, pulling more pictures down and throwing them on to the chaise beside me. 'I forbid you to come up here.'

My sadness turned to anger. I was incensed.

'This room was full of junk and old furniture,' I cried. 'That was its only purpose.'

Father didn't reply. He was staring at my sketches for Daniel – the drawings of Edwin without a shirt.

'What is this?' he asked. He turned round to face me, his face pale and a vein in his temple bulging. 'What in the name of God is this?'

'Daddy,' I said. I hadn't called him Daddy for years. My mind raced. What should I say? That Edwin was a patron of the arts, who volunteered to pose for me? That he was my sponsor. That we were in love?

Father pushed the picture into my face and I shrank back.

'You have brought such shame on me – and worse than that, you have brought shame on the memory of your late mother,' he said. 'How could you do such things?'

245

His eyes were wild. 'Who else has seen these pictures,' he said. He didn't wait for me to answer. 'The servants,' he said. 'They cannot be trusted. I must warn Mr Forrest.'

I was confused. 'Warn him?' I said.

'I must tell him the truth about your disgusting fantasies,' Father almost spat out the words. 'I must confess that my daughter has been drawing filthy pictures of a respectable married man. What a sinful imagination you have.'

Sitting on the chaise where that respectable married man had forced himself upon me many times, I would have laughed had anything about the situation been remotely funny.

'He is a man of the law,' Father said. 'An educated man. God knows what he will think when I tell him.'

With my spirit utterly broken, I let myself fall back on to the cushions of the chaise. I couldn't look at Father, couldn't bring myself to think about my shattered dreams, or Edwin's shattered reputation – there would be no way he could act as my patron now. It was over. It was all over. I wondered how Edwin would react when Father told him and I feared his temper.

'Here is what will happen,' Father was saying. 'I will go next door and tell Mr Forrest the truth about the drawings – better he hears it from me than some salacious rumour from a servant. In the meantime, I will ask Philips to destroy all this filth, and restore the room. Tomorrow I will travel to London where I will throw myself on the mercy of John Wallace and ask him if he would consider taking you as a wife. I will tell him the truth but explain you are remorseful and determined to live a good life. I trust that marrying into the business will be of enough benefit to him to allow him to overlook this …' he gave me a look of such disgust that I felt sick '… this misdemeanour.'

I didn't speak. It was clear to me, as it had never been clear before, that my life was not my own to live as I pleased but rather my father's and, one day, my husband's. For a second I envied Mariana, waiting for a husband who never came. At least she was beholden to no one.

'And what am I to do?' I said, unable to keep the venom from my voice. 'While you are organizing everything?'

Father threw down another picture. 'You will stay here,' he said. 'You will stay in the house and you will read, and sew and walk in the garden. You will talk to no one but the servants. You will trouble no one.'

He gathered up the sketches of Edwin. 'I cannot look at you,' he said. 'Go to your room and stay there. I am going to call on Mr Forrest.'

Chapter 48

Present day
Ella

I was wandering round the house aimlessly. 'Pootling' Barb called it. Wasting time was what it was really. I was waiting for Dad to email me the information he'd found on Frances's living relatives, and knowing him it was going to take a while; he wasn't the most savvy chap when it came to technology.

It had taken Dad just two days to find Frances and Edwin's marriage certificate, and the birth certificate of their son, Charles, from March 1856. It took him a week more to trace Charles's offspring. He had three children, and the youngest – who was also called Frances – had one son. The son – our Frances's grandson – had four children himself who were all still alive.

'Dad,' I said when he told me. 'You are incredible.'

'Oh, it's nothing,' he said, but he had sounded pleased. It was funny, I couldn't help thinking, that I had been interested in Violet in the first place because her family background was so like mine, and now researching her story had helped to bring me and my dad back together.

We'd not talked about my outburst at the pub, but we were speaking regularly. I feared we were just papering over the cracks and maybe we were, but Dad was – I thought

– genuinely interested in Violet. I wondered if Violet's dad had been interested in her work, or what their relationship had been like. He must have loved his daughter very much to search for her the way he had.

Along with thinking about Violet, I'd had plenty of other work to occupy myself with while I was waiting for Dad to do his family tree thing. My agent had got back to me with feedback on my new Tessa story. She liked it – ish – but she said it felt like my heart wasn't in it. She was right. After all, I was still spending all my time thinking and wondering about what had happened to Violet. Or talking to Priya about it.

'It's always someone close,' Priya told me after I'd filled her in on the details of the crime. 'People think strangers are the scary ones but they're not. It's the people you're closest to you should be frightened of.'

I shuddered. 'There was no one else,' I said. 'Just Violet's dad. But he was away when it happened and then he spent his life trying to find his daughter. He can't have been the attacker.'

'Perhaps it was a stranger then,' Priya admitted. 'It's not as common, but it does happen of course. Just a burglar who was disturbed. Or someone who was mentally ill, perhaps? Edwin was involved in the law, right? People bear grudges. Perhaps he'd done something wrong and someone was angry about it.'

It was frustrating going round and round in circles but it had all happened such a long time ago there was no easy way to discover any more about it.

So now I was waiting to hear from Dad about where Frances's living relatives were, and I was getting impatient.

Gripping my phone tightly, in case a message pinged

through, I trailed through the house and up to the study. It was quiet. The boys were at school and nursery, and Ben was at work. I perched on the windowsill and looked out to sea, watching a tiny speedboat bounce soundlessly across the waves. I checked my phone again. Nothing.

'We've found Frances,' I said out loud, imagining I was talking to Violet and completely aware how ridiculous that was. 'Dad's just emailing me.' I waved my phone in the air, as a thought occurred to me. 'Do you know what email is, Violet?'

There was silence. Of course. I slid off the window ledge and went to look at my whiteboard. Alongside the self-portrait of Violet, I'd written the names of the victims – Violet Hargreaves, Frances Forrest, Edwin Forrest, William Philips – and what had happened to them – missing, injured, murdered, murdered. But staring at the names didn't help me at all.

I sighed and walked over to the cupboard where I'd found the pictures, and flung open the door. I'd cleared it out now – there had been nothing else there that belonged to Violet as far as I could see – and the shelves were now filled with my things.

In my left hand, my phone buzzed. Surprised, I jumped and dropped it. It bounced once off the carpet lining the cupboard floor, and disappeared into the furthest corner, where the sloping ceiling met the floor.

'Sake,' I muttered, getting on my hands and knees. It was very dusty down here; I really had to bring the hoover up.

I felt for my phone in the dark shadows, and then as my fingers closed around it, I felt something else tucked under the carpet. I pulled my phone out and then wriggled on to my stomach and reached inside the cupboard further. I pulled back the carpet and revealed a leather-bound notebook. It was fastened with a clip and had pieces of paper tucked inside.

Intrigued, I picked it up and sat back on my haunches, brushing the dust from my knees. I turned the book over in my hands. Its pages were yellowed round the edges but I couldn't open it to see what was inside.

Getting up with a grunt – exactly as Dad did, I noticed with dismay – I took the book over to my desk and found a paperclip. I straightened it out, stuck it into the clasp and wiggled it about, grinning as it released and sprang open. It was a diary; that was clear. It was filled with neat writing at the front and scribbled notes, rows of numbers, and lists of names at the back.

'Is this your diary, Violet?' I asked. I really was losing my marbles, talking to someone who'd been dead for more than one hundred and fifty years. The room stayed quiet, but my heart beat faster just the same – maybe this diary contained all the answers to the mystery.

I leaned back in my chair, opened the diary, and began to read.

And that's where Ben found me, hours later, when the shadows were growing longer and the boys were laughing with Margaret downstairs.

I jumped when he came in, because I was so involved in the diary.

Ben looked at me with concern. 'Are you crying?'

I put my hand to my eyes and found my cheeks were damp. I hadn't even realized that I'd been sobbing as I read. 'Oh, Ben,' I wailed. 'It's so sad.'

Ben perched on the desk next to where I sat and took my hand. 'What's happened?' he said. 'Is it your dad? Is he okay?'

I blinked at him. 'It's not me who's sad,' I said. 'I found Frances's diary.'

Ben's jaw dropped. 'Here?' he said in disbelief. 'Why would it be here?'

'I have no idea,' I said. I didn't care, really. The only important thing was that I'd found it and I'd read it.

'Ben, you must read it,' I told him. 'Edwin Forrest was a horrible, violent man.'

'Tell me,' he said.

'Edwin had been hitting Frances for years,' I said. 'He made her miscarry her baby.'

Ben breathed out. 'So Frances wasn't pregnant?' he said. 'I thought you read that in the police report? So who are these relatives your dad's found?'

'Oh no, she was pregnant,' I said, realizing I'd not yet read Dad's email. The one that had buzzed on my phone and made me find the diary. 'Frances had lost a baby before because of Edwin. So, as far as I can tell, when she realized she was pregnant again, she planned to leave without telling him. She had it all sorted out.'

'Brave woman,' Ben pointed out. 'Can't have been easy to be a single mum in those days. Nigh on impossible I imagine.'

'She was amazing,' I said. 'Look at this.' I opened the diary at the end, and showed him the scribbled notes.

'There's a whole backstory here for her new life – her new name and everything. She's even practised her new signature. There are train times, maps – looks like she was going to Scotland.'

Ben leafed through the pages, shaking his head in awe at the details they contained. 'It must have been really bad for her to plan to do all this.'

'She had a baby to think about,' I said. It seemed straight-forward to me. I knew I would do anything to make sure my boys were okay. 'She had to keep her child safe.'

'But she didn't go to Scotland, she stayed in Sussex after her husband died,' Ben pointed out. 'And where does Violet fit in to all this?'

'It's pretty sleazy,' I warned him.

Ben's eyes gleamed. 'Tell me.'

'Edwin seems to have been a right old philanderer – pros-titutes, women in London when he went on business.' I paused. 'And Violet.'

'Ah ha,' Ben said in triumph. 'As I predicted.'

I frowned at him. 'I think I was the one who predicted that,' I said. 'But I thought it was a bit boring.'

'Sometimes life is boring,' Ben said. 'So Frances knew about the affair then?'

'Sort of,' I said. 'Frances wasn't sure what was happening between Violet and her husband, but she really cared.'

'Was she angry?'

'No, I mean she cared about Violet,' I said. 'She was wor-ried about her. She was older than Violet, who was only eighteen at the time and she seems to have felt a bit maternal towards her.'

'Sweet,' said Ben.

I was thinking. 'If I was writing this, the two spurned women would team up to kill Edwin and make it look like an accident …' I said.

'Do you think that's what happened?'

I shrugged. 'I don't think Frances would kill anyone. She just seems so …' I searched for the right word. 'Nice.'

Ben had turned to the end of the diary entries. 'Have you read all of it?' he asked, rubbing his nose in concentration.

I shook my head. 'Didn't get that far,' I said. 'Why?'

'Frances thought her baby had died,' he said. 'That's why she didn't leave – she thought she wasn't pregnant any more.'

'But the baby survived the beating,' I said. 'Little Charles survived.'

I leaned over to see what he was reading. A thought struck me. 'Or maybe Violet was pregnant,' I said. 'Maybe Frances gave her the escape plan and that's why it's here in our house – in Violet's house. Maybe Violet got away. We should be looking for her relatives – well, relatives of this Florence Bennett.'

I paused. 'Oh no, hang on. Dad's found Frances Forrest's relatives. This is confusing.'

Ben looked at me. 'If you were writing this – if it was a Tessa story – what would you do?'

I thought and then I spoke slowly, because I was still working it out as I talked.

'If this was my story, I'd have Frances go – run to Scotland – just before the murder,' I said, staring at my whiteboard without really seeing it. 'Then Violet – who knew Frances had gone and taken a fake name – could see her chance and steal her identity after the attack. Maybe she was pregnant. If she became Frances Forrest, respectable widow, she would be able to keep her baby without any shame. Maybe that's why Violet disappeared.'

Ben looked at me, impressed. 'You're good at this,' he said.

I laughed. 'Could you have a word with my agent?'

'Any time,' Ben said, kissing me. 'So Violet and Frances were in cahoots.'

'Good word.'

Ben ignored me. 'They were in cahoots, Frances escaped, and in all the confusion of the attack, Violet told everyone she was Frances?'

'That's how I'd write it. Although I'm not sure how I'd get round Violet telling her own dad she was Frances …'

Ben screwed his face up. 'So if your theory is correct, these relatives your dad found should actually be Violet's descendants – not Frances's?'

'Exactly,' I said, scrolling through my phone to find Dad's email.

'Brilliant,' Ben said. 'Mystery solved. Let's go and get a glass of wine.'

Laughing, I followed him down the stairs.

Chapter 49

From: ggriffiths@unimail.com
To: elladaniels@writemail.com

So, last night I was at a dinner with lots of other dusty old academics (would you believe, these things are always much more fun than they sound?) where I got chatting to a historian, who is an expert in nineteenth-century industrialists. She was interested when I told her what you were up to. She knows about Marcus Hargreaves and she said to pass on her details and she'll see if she can help, so I'm doing just that.

Gx

'It's so kind of you to spare the time to meet me,' I said, as George's new friend, Louisa, led me along the corridor to her office. 'I really appreciate it.'

'My pleasure,' she said, showing me inside and pulling out a chair for me to sit on. 'I must admit, it's not entirely kindness on my part. I've always wondered about Hargreaves's story.'

I sat down on the chair and looked round. Her office was in a modern part of the university building in Canterbury. It was lined with bookshelves and a huge wooden desk with a pile of papers on one side, where Louisa sat.

'Marcus Hargreaves is an interesting character,' she went on. 'He was among the first generation to come of age in post-Industrial-Revolution Britain. He made a fortune selling equipment to the colonies – the Caribbean mostly – and to factories here too.'

I nodded. I knew all of this, but I liked hearing Louisa tell it. She had an easy, interesting way of speaking that made me think her lectures would be popular among her students.

'He used his money to do a lot of good work,' she said. 'Orphanages, hospitals, that sort of thing.'

'I found a school he'd set up.'

'Exactly.' Louisa smiled at me, and I felt like her favourite pupil.

'But then things went wrong,' she said.

'Because his daughter disappeared?'

'Well, before that really,' she said. She got up and went to one of the shelves where she pulled out a book.

'His personal life isn't written about much, because most historians from the time focus on his factory work, or his philanthropy,' she said. 'But every now and then I have come across a mention of it.'

She had a pair of glasses perched on top of her head. Now she pulled them down on to her nose and looked at the page she'd found in the book.

'Here's one,' she said. She handed it to me.

'His wife died,' I said, scanning the pages until I found a

mention of her name. 'I found the record of her death. And then he sent his daughter, Violet, away.'

Louisa nodded, pulling out another book. 'But he didn't want to send her away,' she said.

I blinked at her. 'He didn't?'

'This book has quite a detailed account of his wife's death,' said Louisa. 'Take it away with you if you like.'

'Thank you,' I said, genuinely pleased that she trusted me with her own books, but not able to wait until I read it to find out what happened. 'Where did Violet go?'

'She went to her mother's sister,' Louisa told me, sitting back down at her desk and resting her chin on her hand. 'Marcus wanted to keep her with him, but apparently he was told it wouldn't work, that a girl needed to be brought up by a woman, and that he couldn't care for her on his own. There are letters between him and other family members, telling him how wrong it would be for him to keep his daughter with him.'

'So he sent her to her aunt,' I said, marvelling once more at how similar our lives were, more than a century apart. 'But she came back?'

'She came back because her aunt's husband went to work in India,' Louisa told me. 'The family all went to live there and according to records, they were more than willing to take Violet with them. She's listed on the initial travel documents.'

'India,' I breathed. 'Why didn't she go?'

'Marcus didn't want her to,' Louisa said. 'He brought her home to Sussex and engaged a governess to look after her.'

'Because he wanted her with him,' I said. 'So there was some happiness for them at least.'

Louisa smiled at me. 'I'm not sure,' she said. 'It must have been a lonely existence for Violet. Marcus travelled a lot and he would have been away from home for weeks at a time. She must have been quite isolated and I imagine rather bored.'

'She painted,' I said, suddenly realizing why Violet had thrown herself into her artwork so passionately. 'It must have been her only pleasure really. Poor Violet. And poor Marcus.'

I thought about Violet and Edwin Forrest – an older man, certainly handsome from the look of the pictures Violet had drawn, perhaps charming and funny. No wonder she had fallen in love with him. Daddy issues, much? She must have been vulnerable and lonely. Thank goodness I'd met my lovely Ben, or perhaps I'd have gone the same way.

'What do you know about Violet's disappearance?' I asked Louisa.

'Actually, not much,' she said. 'It's referred to in some of the mentions of Marcus Hargreaves but not in a lot of detail so I've often wondered about it. You probably know more than me.'

'Violet went missing one evening in 1855,' I began. 'The night she disappeared, her neighbour who I think was possibly her lover, Edwin Forrest, was murdered. So was a man called William Philips who worked for the Hargreaves family. Edwin's wife, Frances, was also attacked. And Violet vanished.'

'Goodness,' said Louisa. 'I hadn't realized there were other people involved.'

I shrugged. 'There's no proof that it was all connected,' I admitted. 'But it has to be. Such awful tragedies all happening on the same day? I actually have a feeling it was something to do with Forrest. He doesn't seem to have been the most trustworthy chap.'

'Do you have any theories about what happened to Violet?' Louisa asked.

I shook my head. 'Nothing concrete,' I said. 'At the time they thought she might have drowned – they found her hat on the beach – but I'm wondering if she perhaps faked her own death and ran away.'

Louisa made a face. 'Would she do that to her father?' she said. 'It's one thing being bored at home, but breaking his heart like that?'

'You think it's too cruel?'

'I know Marcus spent a lot of time looking for Violet,' Louisa said. 'He organized search parties and spent a lot of time and money trying to track her down. He never really got over losing her.'

'That's sad,' I said. I'd not thought much about Marcus before now, other than as a heartless uncaring father who'd sent his daughter away. Now my opinion was shifting.

'He organized reconstructions of the crime to see if they sparked anyone's memory – they were among the first ever recorded, I believe – every year,' said Louisa. 'But as time passed, people lost interest.'

Ridiculously I suddenly found myself close to tears. This story was so sad. 'He really loved her,' I said. 'He was a good dad.'

'I like to think so,' said Louisa. 'Distant, perhaps. But not cruel.'

I blinked furiously, trying to stop myself from crying.

'Frances Forrest was pregnant,' I said, in a voice that

quavered much more than I wanted it to. 'I've been tracing her descendants. It's a bit complicated but she was planning to leave her husband, so I wondered if maybe Frances had left before the attack, then Violet had taken her identity.'

'So Frances could be the missing person, not Violet?'

'It's a crazy theory but you never know,' I said.

'Keep me posted,' Louisa said. 'I'm intrigued.'

After I'd thanked her profusely for making Marcus a real person in my head, and promised to keep her informed of every lead I followed, I headed back to my car. I couldn't stop thinking about Marcus, who'd stopped his daughter leaving the country and had devoted his life to finding her when she vanished.

'He didn't want to send her away,' I said to myself as I sat in the driving seat. 'He just thought he ought to.'

On a whim, I pulled out my phone and scrolled through the numbers until I found my Aunt Sally.

'Sal?' I said when she answered. 'It's Ella. I wondered if I could pop in?'

Chapter 50

Sally lived not far from where I'd grown up with Dad. Sort of halfway between his house and our new place. It was an easy drive from Canterbury and I felt when I said I was passing I wasn't even lying.

'It's lovely to see you, Ella,' Sal said when I arrived. 'I want to hear all about your new house.'

She handed me a cup of tea and paused to look at me. 'You're so like your mum,' she said, as she always did when I saw her.

'I'm older than she was now,' I pointed out. It was a strange fact that made me feel a bit funny.

Sally gave my arm a squeeze. 'She'd have been proud of you,' she said.

Sally was my dad's older sister and she looked a lot like him, or rather he looked like her. I had older twin cousins – Stephen and Simon – who'd both grown up to be scientists, and who I didn't have a lot in common with. Though I loved Sally and my Uncle Bill, I couldn't imagine growing up with them all.

'Actually,' I said as we settled in the lounge after I'd admired photos of Simon's new baby girl and showed Sal some pictures of the house and of my boys, 'it was Mum I wanted to talk about. Sort of.'

Sally frowned. 'What about her?'

I took a breath. 'About her funeral, really.'

'Go on.'

'I might be remembering things wrong,' I began. 'Because I was very small, and very sad, but there was something I overheard and I wanted to talk to you about it.'

Sally looked worried. 'Oh love,' she said. 'Did you hear your dad talking to me?'

I nodded, pressing my lips together tight.

'You heard him ask if I would look after you?'

I nodded again.

Sally sighed. 'Do you know, I always had a niggle that you were there, that day. You didn't let your dad out of your sight after the accident and I thought you'd be somewhere watching us. But I hoped you hadn't heard.'

'I was on the stairs,' I told her. 'I'd forgotten that I watched Dad. I was so scared when I went back to school in case he died too.'

Sally's eyes filled with tears and she took my hand. 'He was worried he wasn't enough for you,' she said. 'He thought he couldn't look after you and that you needed a mother figure. That's why he asked me to take you.'

'And you said no?' I was on the verge of tears myself.

'I did say no,' Sally admitted. 'But not because I didn't want you. I'd have taken you in a heartbeat. You were an adorable little girl and I loved you so much.' She smiled at me. 'Still do.'

'So, then why?'

'Because your dad wanted you, sweetheart. He was just worried about how to look after a little girl. He was lonely without your mum and he was heartbroken and he didn't know what to do for the best. Of course he wanted you.'

'I was so scared he would send me away,' I said, beginning to cry properly now. 'I was so scared if I did anything wrong he would get rid of me.'

Sally pulled me into a hug and I sobbed on her shoulder.

'He'd never have sent you away, you silly thing,' she said.

When I'd recovered enough to finish my tea and eat the biscuits she offered me, Sally looked at me.

'I heard you and your dad fell out,' she said.

I rolled my eyes. 'Barb?' I asked. She and Sally were good friends.

Sal nodded. 'I have a feeling it's all rooted in what you told me,' she said. She patted me on the knee. 'You need to speak to him, lovey. You can't just pretend it never happened and hope everything's going to be okay. Tell him what you heard that day. He'll want to know.'

She was right; I knew that. I had to talk to Dad. I didn't want to have tension between us. I thought about Marcus Hargreaves looking for Violet for so long, and how much she must have missed him when he was away at work, and I thanked my lucky stars that I'd been born all those decades later when Dad was encouraged to look after me, and had Sally's help to juggle childcare with work, and my grandparents, and later Barb. How different Violet's life could have been. And how different mine had been.

Chapter 51

I looked at the fading photograph of a petite woman with neat grey-black hair and felt completely deflated. Whoever this was, it wasn't Violet.

I looked over at my dad and gave a tiny shake of my head.

'Is she not the person you're looking for?' asked Winnie Flood, Frances's great-granddaughter.

I smiled at her. 'She's exactly who we're looking for,' I said, aware I sounded a bit odd. 'It's more that I was hoping she wouldn't be.'

I'd been confident in our theory about Violet stealing Frances's identity when I'd explained it to my dad. He'd been excited about tracking down Frances's relatives, and I still wanted to talk to him about Mum's funeral, so I'd impulsively invited him along to meet Winnie Flood, who was a seventy-four-year-old widow living in Eastbourne. I imagined a little old lady sitting on the prom, wearing a winter coat in the middle of summer.

'You seem very involved in all this,' Dad had said as we left the quiet streets of Heron Green and headed towards Brighton, Dad easing his Audi (a retirement present to himself) into the heavier traffic.

I glanced at him, wondering if he was criticizing me, but he was smiling. He loved driving.

'Do you think you might write this story, like Barb suggested?'

'I've been trying not to,' I admitted. 'I've been doing my best to write what I should be writing, but this story just keeps getting in the way.'

'Tell me the latest.'

'Violet was in love with Edwin Forrest,' I said. 'He's the man who put his name to her work, of course. But I don't know if he did it with her consent or without.'

'Surely without her knowing? Because why would she consent to that?' Dad asked.

'As a way to make a living from art,' I said. 'Or as a way to trick the establishment? A statement on a woman's place in the world? All sorts of reasons.'

'Or he was taking advantage of her, exploiting her talent for his own financial gain,' said Dad.

'When did you get to be so cynical?' I said.

Dad paused as he swung the car round the roundabout and on to the Eastbourne road.

'It's sad,' he said. 'If she couldn't claim credit for her own work – whatever the reason. It must be hard to have a passion for something and be prevented from doing it. It's easy to forget how hemmed in people were in the past, by their social class, or their gender, or their financial situation. We have a lot of freedom nowadays.'

I nodded, impressed with his insight into Violet's world. We stayed quiet for a while as we sped through the downs, past the university and the sweeping curves of the new football stadium, where Ben's team played. I wasn't sure whether to tell Dad that there was more about Violet that interested me than just the mystery.

'Violet's mum died,' I said eventually. 'When Violet was five years old. She died giving birth to her baby brother, and he died too. I think that's another reason I feel so involved in her story. I just can't ignore the similarities between our lives, even though she was born so long ago.'

'Ah,' said my dad. I waited for him to carry on, but he didn't. So I leant my head back and watched the landscape rushing by in my wing mirror.

'Do you miss her,' I asked. I'd never asked that before, strange as it sounded.

Dad was silent for so long I thought he wasn't going to answer.

'At first,' he said. 'I missed her every hour of every day. Then eventually I got used to her being gone, but it still hurt. I just arranged my life around her not being here.'

He overtook a camper van.

'Imagine you had a beautiful garden and someone dug a hole right in the middle of it,' he said. 'Eventually you might learn to walk round the hole, but you wouldn't like it. Then I met Barb and things were different. Of course I still miss your mum, and I wonder what she'd be like now, and I think about how much she'd have loved seeing you with Ben and the boys. But Barb has helped me build a bridge over the hole that she and Billy left.'

Dad kept his eyes fixed firmly on the road, but I could see a glitter of unshed tears.

'I miss her too,' I said. Dad, still looking at the traffic

ahead, reached out and took my hand briefly and I smiled. We were approaching Eastbourne now, pretty villages giving way to wide fields and large roundabouts.

'Dad,' I said, staring straight ahead. 'When Violet's mother died, her father sent her to live with relatives.'

'Poor git,' Dad said. 'He must have missed her.'

I took a breath. 'When Mummy died – at the funeral – I heard you ask Sally to take me,' I said.

My father inhaled sharply. 'I remember,' he said. 'I begged her. God, what a mess I was.'

I wasn't sure I could speak.

'And you heard me say it? Hells bells, Ells.'

I smiled, despite myself, at the expletive he'd used so often during my teenage years.

'Have you got the directions?'

I pulled out the map I'd printed off. 'Winnie said to follow the signs to the Marina,' I said. 'It's left at the next roundabout.'

Dad indicated left and I felt annoyed that I'd missed this opportunity to talk about what he'd said. But I'd misjudged him.

'I don't remember much about that time,' he carried on. 'I barely remember the funeral. I was falling apart. I thought I couldn't look after you. You were this wonderful little girl with a broken heart and I didn't know how to put you back together – I couldn't put myself back together. So I asked Sally if she'd take you.'

'She said no,' I said. 'But not because she didn't want me.'

Dad laughed. He actually laughed. 'Of course not because

she didn't want you,' he said. 'She knew I was yours and she knew I would realize that soon enough.'

More than that, she knew I needed you. What would I have done without you, eh? You were all I had.'

I closed my eyes.

'About three weeks after she died, I woke up,' Dad said. 'I wasn't numb any more, which was terrible because suddenly I missed your mum and the baby with a crippling pain. But it was also good because I realized how much I loved you.'

'Straight over at this junction,' I said. I felt a tear trickle down my cheek.

'One day you came to me; your hair was all tangly,' Dad said. 'You gave me your hairbrush and a bobble, then you sat down and waited for me to sort it out – just like your mum would have. I didn't know where to begin. I nearly told you to go away. But then I looked at you, just sitting there, trusting me to make it better, and I knew I had to try.'

'Left here,' I said. 'It's number 56.'

Dad slowed down to turn the corner. 'I even got a book out of the library,' he said. 'This is number 40, so I'll just stop here.'

He undid his seatbelt and deftly reversed the Audi into a tiny space.

'A book?' I said in a shaky voice. I bent down to pick up my bag from the footwell and wiped away a tear before Dad noticed it.

'A book about how to do hair.' He chuckled. 'I never did get to grips with plaits.'

'Dad,' I said. 'The whole time I was growing up, I thought you'd send me away if I was naughty.'

Dad looked at me, his brow knotted with worry.

'I never got into trouble,' I pointed out. 'Never. Because I was too scared.'

'Oh, Ella,' Dad said. 'That's what you meant in the pub.'

I gave him a weak smile. 'That's what I meant. I thought if I did something you didn't approve of, you'd not want me any more. I knew moving to Sussex was a bit risky, and I knew you'd worry, and I thought if I did it anyway you'd be cross and then you'd – I don't know – cut me off or something.'

Dad paused for a moment, then he turned in his seat and took hold of both my hands. 'Ella,' he said. 'Nothing you can do will stop me loving you. I admit, I'm a cautious bugger and I realize that's because of my own issues about what happened with your mum. I see dangers everywhere and I know you do too, and that's the way we are.'

I gave him a rueful smile, but he'd not finished yet.

'If you decided to climb Mount Everest, or start a new career as a trapeze artist, or move to Australia, I'd worry of course but I'd still be your dad. You can't get rid of me that easily.'

Once more I couldn't speak. Dad had just got rid of worries I'd held on to for thirty years.

'I'm scared of spiders,' I managed to say eventually. 'So Australia's out. And I'm not great with heights. I think I'll stick to writing in Sussex for now.'

Dad and I smiled at each other for a second, then he turned off the engine.

'Shall we go and solve this mystery of yours, then?' he said.

'Let's do it.'

As Dad got out of the car and came to stand next to me on the pavement, I gave him a hug. He ruffled my hair like he'd done a thousand times before and I ducked away like I'd done a thousand times before. I realized that all the while I'd been worrying my dad wouldn't love me, he'd simply been getting on with it. Loving me in his own way.

'We didn't do so bad, did we?' he said.

'We didn't do so bad at all,' I agreed. I looked down at the address in my hand in surprise.

'This is it,' I said. 'I think …'

It was nothing like I'd imagined Winnie Flood's house to be. We were standing outside a newly built, glass-fronted apartment block. To the side and in front of us was the Marina, where rows of beautiful yachts bobbed gently.

'God it's like Saint bloody Tropez,' said Dad. 'This isn't how I remember Eastbourne.'

I grinned and pushed the buzzer for number 56.

If Winnie Flood's house was nothing like I'd expected, then Winnie herself was even more of a surprise. She was no little old lady. Instead she had silver-blonde hair in a neat bob and she was wearing a striped Breton T-shirt, cropped chinos, and – I blinked in surprise – Converse.

'My husband and I did a lot of sailing,' she said as she made us all tea. 'When he died three years ago, I found I no longer wanted to be at sea, but I did want to be near the water. So I sold our house and the boat and bought this flat.'

Despite her downsizing, Winnie had a wealth of family history. She'd brought out a large hatbox full of papers and photographs and laid them out on her glass dining table.

'I have three older brothers,' she said. 'One is local but the other two live in Australia. They weren't interested in all this stuff.'

That was when Winnie passed me the photograph of Frances and I realized our theory had been wrong.

'So Frances was my great-grandmother,' Winnie was saying. 'I never met her, of course, or my grandfather Charles. I was a very late baby for my mother – I think I took her by surprise.'

Dad took the photograph from me. 'Do you know anything about her?'

'A bit,' Winnie said. 'There are some papers she left. I know her husband died before Charles was born.'

Feeling slightly awkward about revealing how Winnie's great-grandfather had met his end, I explained about the attack and that Violet had gone missing at the same time. Then I got out Frances's diary.

'I found this,' I said. 'It belonged to Frances. It explains that she was planning to leave.'

Briefly I filled Winnie in on what I'd read – about Edwin's abuse and Frances's pregnancy.

'Because Frances was so sure she'd lost the baby, we wondered if Violet had somehow stolen her identity,' I said. 'Once Frances had gone to Scotland.'

Winnie looked thoughtful. 'I'm sure someone went to Scotland.' She began to rummage through the hatbox.

'Ah yes.' She pulled out a sheaf of letters, bound together with yellowing string.

'I knew I'd seen Scotland written somewhere,' she said. 'Frances was writing to someone there.'

I was excited but I managed to resist the urge to punch the air. 'So Violet got away,' I said. 'Frances gave her the idea – and the diary – and she went. I'm so pleased …'

But Dad was shaking his head. Winnie had untied the string and he was leafing through the letters.

'They've all been returned,' he said. 'They're letters from Frances, not to her. They're only addressed to Florence Bennett, North Berwick – so she was obviously only guessing as to an address.

'And so they never got to where they were going,' I said. I was very disappointed. It seemed every time I thought I'd found Violet, she eluded me once more. I took a letter from the pile and opened the envelope.

Dear Florence, the letter read.

I do not know where you are. I trust you have made your way to North Berwick while I was unwell and are now settled. Please respond by return.

Your sister, Polly.

'Polly?' I said.

'Maybe another fake name,' Winnie pointed out. 'Like Florence. It's definitely Frances – it's the same writing as in the diary.'

'And perhaps Frances planned to pose as Violet's sister,' I said. 'Those clever, brave women.'

'But it doesn't look like Violet made it to North Berwick,' Dad said. 'There are dozens of letters here – all returned.'

'Read them,' Winnie urged. 'Go ahead.'

So Dad and I sat in Winnie's stylish apartment, with its huge windows and tiled floors, and revisited Frances's life.

She had written to Violet – Florence – for more than a decade. At first she explained she'd stay in Sussex until Violet wrote to confirm she was in North Berwick. Eventually her letters became more chatty, concentrating less on arrangements and instead sharing news of 'the gentleman next door, who misses his daughter so dreadfully' that he had shut up their house and moved away.

'That's Violet's dad,' I said. 'Frances obviously wanted Violet to know what had happened to him. I think that proves Florence is Violet.'

'I agree,' said Dad. 'At least, it proves that Frances believed Florence to be Violet. Look, in this letter she tells her that she can't keep quiet any longer and says she is going to share Florence's whereabouts with the gentleman next door.'

'Frances must have felt awful, watching Marcus search and knowing there was a chance Violet was in Scotland,' I said. 'Though she obviously wasn't there.'

I read through some more letters until I found one that referred to Marcus visiting North Berwick.

'Listen,' I said to Dad, reading out loud. 'It seems you have not settled in North Berwick after all. The gentleman from next door visited last month and though I asked him to look out for you, he neither saw nor heard talk of you …'

I sighed. This was hopeless.

Meanwhile, Dad had found a letter detailing Violet's father's death.

'This is all terribly sad,' he said. 'It looks to me like Violet definitely didn't end up in North Berwick. It's a small place as I recall, and though Frances didn't have the exact address, one of her letters would have reached her eventually.'

'So we keep looking,' I said, wondering where on earth we went from here.

'I think we do.'

Chapter 52

1855
Edwin

Edwin was on the stairs, looking out the window at the beach when he heard the doorbell and muffled conversation below.

He ignored the voices. Frances was downstairs; she could deal with any visitors. He turned to go up to his bedroom, but Frances called up to him through the bannister.

'Mr Hargreaves is here,' she said. 'He asked for you.'

Edwin sighed inwardly. He couldn't be bothered with fake friendship at the moment. But nevertheless, he had to maintain good relations with his neighbours. Heavy-footed, he went downstairs.

Agnes, sullen-faced and silent, showed Edwin into the drawing room. Mr Hargreaves was standing by the fireplace, his hat in his hand.

'Edwin,' he said, in an overly jolly voice.

'Marcus,' Edwin said, shaking his hand. 'Sit down. What brings you here?'

Marcus paused and Edwin noticed his fingers were gripping the brim of his hat very tightly. A slight shudder of anxiety passed through him. Had Marcus realized Edwin and Violet had been enjoying a closer relationship than was proper?

'I'm afraid I have something rather unsavoury to tell you.'

Edwin took a breath. 'Go on.'

'It would seem my daughter, Violet, has developed an, erm, attraction to you.'

Edwin breathed out again. He smiled. 'Oh just a young girl with a harmless fancy.'

Marcus frowned. 'I wish it were harmless,' he said. He turned his hat round in his hands. 'She has an interest in art, you know: Violet.'

'Yes, she told me,' Edwin said.

'To my shame, I have discovered she is pursuing this interest rather more vigorously than is appropriate.'

'Go on.'

Marcus looked wretched. 'She has been drawing you,' he said. 'I found sketches of you, that she had drawn.' He lowered his voice. 'Sketches of you almost naked. Without a shirt.'

Edwin arranged his face into a shocked expression. 'Heavens,' he said. 'What a vivid imagination she must have.' He shook his head. 'Marcus, dear fellow,' he said. 'Please don't allow this to upset you, or spoil our friendship.'

Marcus looked very tired suddenly. He pinched the bridge of his nose. 'Ah, Edwin,' he said. 'I am at a loss. I feel this is all my fault. I should have remarried. A girl needs a mother. I was often away, and Violet was left unchecked. Her imagination has run riot.'

'Marcus, please,' Edwin said. He was beginning to feel uncomfortable. He didn't like shows of emotion, especially from men. 'You must calm yourself. Where are these pictures now?'

'I have asked Philips, our gardener, to destroy them. The ones of you and indeed all her artwork. I want to nip this in the bud before it gets too out of control.'

Edwin felt a rush of horror. 'Are there many pictures?'

'Indeed,' Marcus said. 'None as lascivious as those of you. But she has obviously been spending her time painting. Time that could have been much better spent.'

'Marcus,' Edwin said. 'Do not worry yourself. I bear no ill will towards you or Violet. I must confess, this is not the first time a young woman has developed an attraction towards me. Frances will tell you that. I fear I am naive and sometimes my endeavours to help young people can backfire. Alas, I continue to do my best.'

Marcus gave Edwin an uncertain smile.

He carried on. 'Frances, and I, and all who know me, know I do nothing to encourage such behaviour. Your Violet is just a girl with an overactive imagination and too much time on her hands. There is no harm done.'

He smiled at Marcus in what he hoped was a reassuring manner, but inwardly his mind was racing. Could he get his hands on more of Violet's pictures? Could he reach this Philips before he destroyed them? He had to get rid of Marcus somehow. 'I have but one worry,' he said. 'Can this Philips be trusted?'

'In what way?' Marcus asked.

'At the moment, it is just you, Violet, and myself who know of these pictures, yes?' Edwin lied, thinking of Laurence, the old man on the train, the buyer in Yorkshire …

'Yes,' Marcus said. 'And Philips, of course. Though he hasn't seen them yet.'

'I am just slightly fearful he might talk,' Edwin said. 'You know how servants can be. I am a man of some standing in the local area and I worry about the damage such idle chatter could cause to my reputation.'

Marcus paled. 'Indeed,' he said. 'I hadn't thought.'

'No matter,' Edwin said. He stood up. 'I have a thought. Stay here, friend. I will ask Frances to come and sit with you. Please, help yourself to a drink to steady your nerves. Meantime, I will go to your house and speak to this Philips. I will impress upon him the importance of keeping this quiet.'

Marcus looked relieved that someone else was taking charge. 'That sounds like a good idea,' he said. 'If you do not mind?'

Edwin patted him on the shoulder. 'Of course not,' he said. 'Now, make yourself comfortable. I shall not be long.'

He found Frances in the kitchen, chatting to Agnes.

'Marcus is upset,' he said. He filled her in, briefly, on what had happened, ignoring her resigned look as he explained about the pictures of him.

'I am going to his house to try to sort out a few things. Could you sit with him and calm him down?'

'Of course,' Frances said with a sigh. She didn't seem as upset as he'd imagined, however. Perhaps, he thought, she had finally realized he was simply a man with needs and that as long as he came home to her, she was in a good position.

Smiling to himself, he set off to the Hargreaves' house, hoping he wouldn't see Violet.

He was in luck. He skirted the edge of the house, and went into the garden, thinking Philips was bound to be there. He was. He was digging one of the vegetable beds, sweat beading his forehead.

Edwin picked his way across the grass delicately – he didn't want stains on his trousers – and approached him. 'Hello there,' he said in a jovial voice.

Philips stopped digging and stood upright. He leaned on his spade and wiped his brow, but he didn't speak.

'It would seem we find ourselves in a situation,' Edwin continued in the same tone. 'Mr Hargreaves has explained to me that he found some …' he paused '… inappropriate sketches of me in his daughter's possession.' He gave a small cough. 'He also told me he'd asked you to destroy them – and all of Vi … Miss Hargreaves's paintings.'

Philips nodded.

'My dear boy,' Edwin said. 'I wondered if I could ask you to put a couple of paintings aside for me. I'd particularly like the …'

'Mr Hargreaves asked me to destroy them,' Philips said. He started digging again.

His insolence enraged Edwin. He reached out and grabbed his arm, his fingers pushing into the solid muscle of his bicep.

'Take your hand off me,' Philips hissed through clenched teeth.

Edwin didn't let go. Philips twisted his arm and in one swift move wrapped his strong fingers round Edwin's wrist.

'I know what you've been doing to Violet,' he said. 'And I am going to make you pay.'

For a moment they stared at each other. Philips was shorter than Edwin though he was undoubtedly the stronger man, but Edwin knew striking out was a risk he wouldn't take. He would lose his job, his home, and Edwin had an inkling he had designs on Violet himself – he would certainly not risk losing her.

'You are scum,' Philips said, releasing Edwin's wrist. 'And you are too late. The paintings have been destroyed. They are all gone. And I am glad.' He stared at Edwin in defiance and then he spat in his face.

Quick as a flash, Edwin lashed out and swiped him across the face with the back of his hand. Philips didn't even flinch. He simply wiped the blood from his nose, turned his back on Edwin, and started to dig once more.

Chapter 53

1855
Frances

Frances stood at the front door, watching Mr Hargreaves walk towards the church. He needed forgiveness, he'd told her, though he hadn't said why. Edwin wasn't back yet. She wondered what he was doing and to her relief discovered she no longer cared. It was time to go, she thought. Time to start her new life away from here. She watched a flock of starlings perch on the roof of Marcus Hargreaves's house and then, as one, they swooped into the sky and landed once more on the roof.

'They're practising leaving,' she said out loud, realization dawning. 'That's what I should do.' She decided to have one rehearsal of her flight, when she would work out times and places and check she had everything she needed, and then she would be ready to go.

The front door slammed and she jumped, as she heard Edwin's heavy tread stamp into the drawing room.

'Frances!' he bellowed. 'Get down here.'

Frances began to shake as she recognized the fire in his voice. Perhaps she did care after all. Every step she took down the stairs felt like it took an hour and yet it didn't take long enough.

Edwin was pouring himself a whisky. His eyes glittered as Frances came in the room and she felt icy cold fingers of dread walk down her spine.

'The thing I don't understand,' Edwin said in a falsely friendly tone, as though they were in the middle of a conversation. 'What I keep asking myself, is why the woman I love would do such a despicable thing to me.'

For a moment Frances didn't know who he was talking about when he said the woman he loved. Did he mean Violet? Then, with a shock, she realized he was talking about her. She wove her fingers together to keep them from shaking.

'Why would you make up such a story about me?' Edwin continued. 'Why would you spread such scurrilous lies?'

'Edwin,' Frances said, working hard to keep her voice calm. 'Dear. I have no idea what you are talking about.'

Edwin swallowed his whisky and took a step towards her. Frances felt herself cower and hated herself – and him – for it. She thought of her baby and tried to work out how to calm Edwin down, but her mind was blank.

'Mr Hargreaves is under the impression that his daughter and I have had improper relations,' he said.

Frances was surprised. Mr Hargreaves had looked contrite and ashamed, and she'd heard no raised voices when he'd been talking with Edwin – not the behaviour she'd expect from a father avenging his daughter's dishonour.

'Did you tell him?' In a swift move Edwin slapped her

across the face, then he reached out and gripped her wrist. She knew better than to pull away, despite the pain.

'I do not know what you are talking about,' Frances repeated in a soft voice. She felt blood begin to trickle from her nose but she didn't wipe it away.

'Did. You. Tell. Him?' Edwin pulled her towards him roughly and she felt her wrist click. She bit her cheek to stop herself crying out.

Edwin felt it too. He gave a strange smile, and twisted her arm again. Hard. This time she couldn't help giving a cry as she felt the bone break. Her vision went black and she thought she was going to faint. But then Edwin let go, and she slumped heavily to the floor, cradling her wrist. Edwin looked down at her in disgust.

'Is it any wonder I go elsewhere for my pleasure when you are so disloyal.'

So it was true. Frances reeled at the injustice of it all, but she knew better than to argue.

'I have no clue why I married you,' Edwin said. He sat down on one of the tapestry chairs by the fire and glared at her as she sat, undignified, on the floor. Her wrist was swollen and turning dark blue with bruising.

'My life would improve immeasurably if you were not in it,' he said.

Frances awkwardly pushed herself up to standing using her one good hand.

'Mine likewise,' she said.

Edwin looked startled. In ten years of marriage Frances had never talked back to him, not once.

'And you married me,' she went on, her voice laced with

the venom she normally kept hidden, 'so you could take over my father's firm when he retired because I have no brothers. You married me because without me, without my family money and my father's approval, you would always have been a lowly clerk in someone else's law practice.'

She had gone too far; she knew that. But somehow, she couldn't still her tongue. It was as though a dam had broken. Edwin was standing in front of her, his face purple with anger. Frances lifted her chin and looked into his eyes.

'You married me because I was the first woman who was foolish enough to say yes.'

Edwin hit her, hard, with the back of his hand, across her cheekbone. She staggered backwards and catching her foot on the rug fell to the floor. She cried out in pain as her broken wrist hit the hearth. Edwin stood over her, a half-smile on his handsome face.

He twisted the signet ring on his pinkie – a ring Frances suspected he'd picked up in a pawnshop because he had no family to pass it down to him, and which had cut her face as he'd hit her.

'I'm going out,' he said. 'I will send the doctor to set your wrist and we should move that rug; it's clearly a hazard.'

Frances tried to sit up but found she couldn't. She took a deep breath and tried again, successfully this time. The room swam and she lay on her side on the floor, feeling blood trickling down her face but lacking the strength to wipe it away. Edwin saw it too. He turned to go, then changed his mind.

'Clean yourself up,' he said. 'You're a disgrace. And, Frances? Never speak to me in that manner again.'

He kicked her, sharply, in the stomach, and walked out of the door without looking back.

Alone in the room, sprawled on the floor, Frances felt cramps grip her belly, and she started to cry.

Chapter 54

1855
Violet

I lay on my bed staring up at the ceiling. Since Father had found my artwork two days ago I hadn't spoken to anyone. I'd simply gone to bed, and stayed there. I could not summon up enough energy to get dressed or go downstairs, and I wondered if I ever would again.

A knock on my door made me jump.

'Go away,' I said turning my head into the pillow.

Mabel came into the room with a tray of boiled egg and toast.

'I said, go away,' I said.

'Nonsense,' Mabel said. She put the tray down at the end of the bed, then swept over to the window and flung open the drapes. I hid my eyes from the bright sunlight that flooded in.

'Your father has gone to Brighton,' Mabel said. 'And Philips would like to see you upstairs in the attic.'

I sat up and eyed the tray. I realized I was actually very hungry. 'I don't want to go upstairs,' I said.

'Now, Miss,' Mabel said, flinging open the doors to my wardrobe and pulling out a dress. 'Do you think Philips wants to upset you?'

I reached out for a piece of toast and shook my head.

'Well. Get up and go and see what he wants.'

Mabel laid the dress on the bed. 'I'll be back in fifteen minutes,' she said.

I was ready in ten. Nervous about what I might find, I climbed the stairs to the attic.

The room was very different from how I'd left it. The wall at the far end was covered in a deep-red wallpaper. My easel was dismantled and in a pile by the door, there was no sign of any of my paintings, and the chaise was under the window where the easel had once stood. I groaned in dismay and Philips, who was on his hands and knees finishing the edge of the wallpaper, looked round.

He jumped to his feet and grinned.

'I don't know why you're looking so happy,' I said rudely.

'You'll see,' Philips said.

He took my hand and led me over to the wall. It smelled of wallpaper paste.

'What's different?' he said.

'All my paintings are gone.'

'No. Well, yes. But something else. Look carefully.'

I looked at the wall. Then I looked at the windows. Then I looked at the wall again. I was totally confused.

'What have you done with the little window?' I said. 'Where's it gone?'

Philips looked like he was about to burst with excitement.

'It's behind the wall,' he said. He patted the wallpaper. 'It's behind here.'

I shrugged. 'And?'

'And,' Philips said, 'so are all your paintings.'

I began to smile; finally I understood. 'You've built a new wall?' I said.

'At first,' Philips said, 'I thought I might just brick up the alcove and leave your paintings behind there, so you'd be able to get them out one day.'

I nodded.

'And then,' he carried on, 'I thought it might be useful to have a hideaway.'

He touched his lip and for the first time I noticed his mouth was swollen and his nose had been bleeding.

I reached out, but he shook me off.

'It's fine,' he said. 'Look.' He pushed the chaise away from the wall, and bent down.

'There's a little door, here.' He felt across the wall and found it. 'You need to push it in and it should pop out.'

He gently pushed and suddenly a door opened. It was small, no more than a foot square, and just off the floor.

'I can fit inside,' he said. 'So you'll be able to. Go on.'

I looked at him and he nodded. 'Go on,' he said again.

I knelt down and wriggled through the small gap. I was in a tiny room – a cupboard really. It was about six feet long, possibly a fraction more, and narrow. I tried to stretch my arms out fully but couldn't. It was perhaps three feet wide. The ceiling was normal height, though, and I could stand up comfortably. And at one end, was the small window.

'What do you think?' Philips was wiggling through the gap, twisting his broad shoulders so he could get in.

He stood up and brushed dust from his thighs. We were very close together because there was not enough room to be apart.

'It's wonderful,' I said. 'And confusing. Was this really part of my room?'

Philips grinned. 'All I've done is brick up the alcove,' he said. 'But it looks right, you see. The alcove on the other side is already boxed in – I think there are some pipes behind there – and because I've changed the colour of the wall – well, that's why it looks different.'

I looked round me in amazement. 'So it's a hidden room. Like a priest-hole.'

Philips looked at me. 'I know there's been a bit of trouble,' he said. 'And I know Mr Forrest has a temper on him.' He touched his lip again.

I was shocked. 'Did Edwin do this?' I asked.

'I'd rather he hit me than you,' Philips said. 'Do you think he beats his wife?'

The thought had never crossed my mind, but I immediately feared Philips was right.

'Oh I don't think so,' I said. Irrationally, I felt I had to defend Edwin to Philips. 'It was only once and I think he had a bad day, and then I irritated him …'

Philips looked doubtful and I trailed off.

'Anyway,' I said. 'That's of no importance. Look at this room.'

But Philips kept looking at me. 'Like I said, at first I just wanted to hide your artwork so you could find it again one day. But then I thought you might need somewhere to disappear to.'

I felt uncomfortable under his astute gaze.

'So my art …'

'Is there.' Philips pointed to the corner. 'I remembered

you said to roll it up with the paint on the outside,' he said. 'And I've put it away from the window so it doesn't fade – the sun doesn't reach that spot, I've checked. And your paints are here too.'

In the opposite corner, neatly stacked, were my palette, brushes, and paints.

I breathed out. All my work was there – everything but my version of *Mariana* and a few sketches of Edwin that I'd already hidden in the cupboard on the other side of the room. I decided not to mention those for now.

'I'm going to burn some of the frames and your easel,' Philips went on. 'So your father thinks I've destroyed everything. And I told Mr Forrest I'd already done it. He wanted some of your paintings for himself.'

'Did he?' I said. I wondered if he'd wanted them for the gallery at the club. Perhaps it was his way of helping me – like Philips had done.

'So he hasn't got any.'

'No,' Philips said. 'I didn't want him getting his hands on your stuff.'

I felt a tiny prickle of annoyance that Philips had made that decision for me.

'So anyway, that's that,' he was saying. 'I don't think you should come in here, though.'

'Why not?'

'I just think you should only come in if you really need it. If you come too much, people might realize it's here. And the hinges on the door will start to show if you open it too often.'

'You've really thought about this,' I said. 'You've done all this for me?'

Philips looked at his feet. 'I don't know much about art,' he said. 'But I know your stuff is good and I know the way your face looks when you're painting. It's just not fair, that's all.' He looked up at me and grinned again. 'I hate it when things aren't fair.'

I took a step towards him and took his hand. 'Thank you,' I said.

He smiled at me.

'Philips,' I said. 'I don't know what I'd have done, without you. You've been a good friend to me.'

He nudged me with his elbow in an embarrassed fashion, and I reached up and kissed him on the cheek. Then, thinking of the way Edwin always wanted me to show my appreciation, I snaked my hand round his neck and pulled his head down so his lips met mine. For a second, Philips responded but then he jerked his head away.

'No, Violet,' he said. 'I am not like him. I didn't do this for you so you'd …' He looked away from me. I felt my cheeks burn in shame. 'I just did it because you deserve it.'

'Sorry,' I whispered.

Philips shook his head. 'Don't apologize,' he said. 'Not to me. Never to me.'

'About Edwin,' I began, feeling like I had to explain things to this man, this good man who had been so nice to me when no one else had seen me.

Philips screwed his face up. 'He's not right,' he said. 'Violet, I know you think you love him or something, but he's not the one for you.'

'He's not as bad as you think he is,' I said, but even as I said the words, I realized they were hollow. Philips was absolutely right in what he thought of Edwin. He hit me, and he forced himself on me, and he probably did it to Frances, too.

I leaned against the wall, then I slid down to the floor where I sat, with my head in my hands. 'Oh I have been such a fool,' I wailed. 'A selfish, silly fool.'

Philips sat next to me. 'He reeled you in,' he said. 'He's got the gift of the gab, and it seems to me he doesn't like it when people say no to him. You had no chance.'

'He has a wife,' I said in despair. 'He has a wife, and she warned me to stay away and I didn't.'

'Violet, this isn't your fault,' Philips said.

I grimaced. 'Some of it is my fault,' I said. 'I was just so desperate to be an artist that I went along with everything he said.'

'Some of it,' Philips conceded. 'But not all.'

'He signed my paintings,' I told him. 'He signed them and he sold them.'

Philips looked shocked. 'And he told you?'

'I found out.'

'What are you going to do?' Philips asked.

I shook my head. 'I have no idea,' I admitted. 'Avoid Edwin? Apologize to Frances? Get married?'

'Don't stop painting,' he said. 'Promise me that?'

I smiled at him. 'I promise.'

He nudged me gently with his elbow again. 'I know you think you're alone in this world and there is no one looking out for you,' he said. 'But you're wrong.'

I could marry Philips and we could start a new life miles from here, I thought. But I knew it wouldn't work, not really.

'I will be grateful to you for this as long as I live,' I said. 'Probably longer.'

Philips slung his arm around my shoulder and dropped a kiss on my temple.

'Come on then,' he said. 'Let's get out of here.'

Chapter 55

1855
Frances

15th Sep 1855

Edwin has been in London for a week and I have heard nothing from him. I am not sorry, nor do I miss him. I have stayed indoors these past days, waiting for my bruises to fade and my swollen lip to go down. Agnes has been tending to me with such care and gentleness that at first I could hardly bear it. It has been so long since anyone touched me with anything other than anger that her kindly attention almost hurt.

I have had no bleeding and the cramps in my belly have ceased. But in my heart I know my baby is no more. Edwin has taken that from me also. Agnes asked me how far along I was and when I told her, she looked grim-faced. I know she thinks I should have felt movements by now. She also thinks my baby is dead, though she has not said so much …

Frances looked up from her diary as the doorbell rang; its loud chime clanging through the quiet house. She heard Agnes march to the door and low voices. Then there was a knock on the door of the drawing room where she sat.

'It is Miss Hargreaves, Madam,' Agnes said. 'I told her you weren't receiving visitors but she was very persistent.'

Frances stood up – it was still quite painful to move even after a week of recovery – and forced a smile. Her heart was thumping. 'Of course, Agnes,' she said.

Violet came in, slinking round the door like the kitchen cat. She looked at Frances, her eyes wide with shock and a tear trickled down her cheek.

'I have come to apologize,' she said. She looked thin and pale and even her vibrant hair seemed muted. 'I have been foolish and made unforgiveable choices and I am so ashamed.' Her voice shook and Frances felt a rush of sympathy.

'Sit down,' she said, pointing to the sofa. Violet sat and Frances lowered herself down next to her, more gently, and offered Violet a handkerchief. Violet patted her eyes. There was a brief, awkward silence as Frances thought about what to say.

'If I know Edwin,' she said eventually. 'Believe me, I do. I imagine that you had very little choice, foolish or otherwise.'

Violet reached out and very, very softly, touched the bruise on Frances's jaw. 'He did this,' she said. It wasn't a question.

They stared at each other for a moment, then Frances pulled back her sleeve and showed Violet her bandaged wrist.

'I answered back,' she said. 'He did not like it.'

Violet shook her head. 'I thought,' she said. 'Edwin said … I was wrong.'

Frances watched as Violet finally put all the pieces of the puzzle together.

'You tried to warn me,' she said. 'I thought you were telling me to stay away from your husband, but you were worried about me. You tried to tell me and I ignored you.'

Frances took her hand. 'I should have been clearer,' she said. 'But I was scared.'

Violet nodded in understanding.

'I was so focused on myself, I didn't allow myself to hear what you were saying.'

Frances stood up, wincing slightly, and went to the door. 'No matter,' she said. 'I shall ask Agnes to bring tea.'

She felt, strange as it was, almost happy that Violet had come to call. She realized how much courage it had surely taken. Despite such a strange beginning, she wondered if they could be friends. It was unlikely – who knew what would happen now. Frances doubted if Mr Hargreaves would allow Violet to continue her strange half-wild existence. And, truth be told, Frances had not yet decided what to do. Her need to get away was less urgent now there was no baby, but she still quailed at the thought of staying. She asked Agnes for tea, then returned to the drawing room and sat next to Violet once more.

'Where is your father?' Frances asked.

Violet bit her lip. 'Manchester,' she said. 'But I have had no word from him.' She looked straight at Frances, her grey eyes clear and bright. 'Does it make you angry?' she asked. 'Having no power?'

Frances thought for a moment. 'What makes me very angry,' she said. 'Is not being allowed to be angry.'

Violet smiled a small smile. 'Since Father went, I've been going out into the garden and screaming,' she confessed.

'Screaming?' Frances said.

'Loudly.'

'And does it make you feel better?'

Violet let the smallest of giggles escape her lips. 'Not at all,' she said.

Frances chuckled. She liked this girl, despite the odd circumstances that had thrown them together.

'Look at us,' she said. 'Both beholden to men. I am forced to await the return of a husband who beats me, and you are waiting for your father.'

'Like Mariana,' Violet said.

Frances was confused. 'Who is she?'

'She's a character in *Measure for Measure*,' Violet explained. 'And there's a poem by Tennyson. She was waiting to be married but the boat carrying her dowry sank, so she waited and waited …'

She looked embarrassed for a second. 'There's a painting of her, by Millais,' she said. 'I copied it, but changed her face. Instead of painting hers, I painted my own.'

'Your own?' Frances said.

Violet nodded.

'How clever,' Frances said. She meant it. She envied Violet's creativity. 'Your talent could free you.'

But Violet shook her head. 'Father is making me a marriage,' she said. 'He's talking to one of his employees about marrying me. I know he'll agree. The business is worth marrying, even if I am not.' Her voice had grown harsh and bitter. 'And I will agree to the match, as soon as possible. Because …' She paused and looked away from Frances, colour rising in her pale cheeks.

'Because …' Frances prompted, but she already knew what Violet was going to say.

'Because I think I am expecting a baby,' she said.

Frances felt at once bereft and exhilarated. 'When God closes one door, he opens another,' she murmured.

Violet looked blank. 'The doors are all closed,' she said, in a shrill voice. 'I will marry John Wallace, and lie about the father of my baby, and I will never paint again.'

But Frances was barely listening. 'Violet,' she said. 'Could you pass me my diary? It's there on the writing desk.'

Violet gave her an odd look, but she stood up and handed Frances the diary. Frances held it in her lap, smoothing the brown leather cover. Then she looked up at Violet.

'I have been planning to leave,' she said.

Violet put her hand to her mouth. 'Leave?' she said. 'Where would you go?'

Frances smiled. 'Scotland,' she said. 'I imagined that would be far enough.'

Violet still looked confused, so Frances continued.

'I have money. Quite a lot of it, actually,' she said. 'And in this diary are all my plans. Train times, maps, a story to tell …'

'You've done all this,' Violet said.

Frances nodded. She handed the diary to Violet. 'Have a look – it's all at the back, mostly. There's a train timetable, and I've worked out when you'd have to leave here in order to catch the right train from Brighton.'

'When I'd have to leave?' Violet repeated, realization dawning on her pale, pretty face. 'Oh no, Mrs Forrest, this is your plan.'

'But it is you who needs it most,' Frances said. 'You have to think about your future. And your child.' Her voice cracked a little as she talked about the baby, but she thought Violet – who was leafing through the diary – hadn't noticed.

'I cannot bear to think of you living in an unhappy marriage,' Frances said fiercely. 'Your creativity stifled, your talent hidden. It will not do.'

Violet looked up. 'Come with me,' she said.

Frances shook her head. 'Two women travelling together alone would attract attention.'

'Then come later.' There was a gleam of life in Violet's grey eyes once more as she plotted. 'I could go – I could go soon, in the next few days perhaps – and get settled,' she said, her words tumbling over each other. 'I will tell my story – your story – and find a home. Then I will send you word and you can join me – you can be there for when the baby arrives.'

She looked at Frances, her eyes wide with fear. 'I'm so scared,' she said. 'I'm so frightened of being alone. I need you.'

Frances felt enormous relief. This could work. She needn't see out her days with Edwin, fearing his fists and his cold words. She could build a new life; forge a family from the ruins of her old one.

'You could be my sister, come to help with the baby,' Violet added.

'Sisters?' Frances said doubtfully, looking down at her neat figure and then at Violet's rangy, long-limbed beauty.

'Different mothers,' Violet said, in a matter-of-fact fashion. 'Should anyone be so rude as to ask.'

Frances laughed. 'You see how easily the lies come,' she

300

said. Then she paused. 'I have no family. No one who would miss me, or who I would miss. But you have your father, Violet. What about your father?'

Violet chewed her lip. Frances thought she looked very young.

'Do you know when your father is due back?' she asked.

Violet shook her head. 'It could be weeks,' she said. 'He often stays in Manchester for a month. He says the journey is so ghastly he needs time to recover.'

'Then you have time to decide,' Frances said. 'Take the diary and read all my plans, see what you think. And, Violet, think about what it means to leave your father.'

Violet nodded. She closed the diary carefully. 'I will look after this,' she said as she stood up. 'Thank you, Mrs Forrest.'

Frances stood up too, more slowly. 'Please,' she said. 'Call me Frances. If we are to be sisters …'

Violet smiled at her, then pulled her close in an awkward embrace, much to Frances's surprise.

The younger woman spoke into Frances's hair. 'Thank you,' she said.

Chapter 56

1855
Violet

Over the next day or two, I read Frances's diary again and again. I wrote lists about leaving and lists about staying, then I burned them. I wrote a letter to my father explaining how I felt I'd lost both my parents the day my mother died, then I burned that too. I wept for Frances, reading her accounts of Edwin's beatings, and felt guilty that by taking her money and her plans I would be leaving her at Edwin's mercy. Eventually, I went to find Philips. He was in the pantry, fixing a shelf.

'Are you busy?' I asked.

'Yes,' he said. He was holding nails in his mouth, so his voice was muffled.

I stayed where I was, scuffing my toe on a mark on the floor.

'Still here?' Philips said.

'Yes,' I mimicked.

Philips took the nails from his mouth and gave me a resigned smile. Then he went out of the back door into the garden and I followed him to a tree at the far end of the lawn. I went to throw myself down on the grass next to him, then paused. I wasn't sure how I felt about this baby, if indeed there was a baby, but I didn't want to harm it. I sat down in a more sedate fashion than I was used to.

'I'm in a bit of trouble,' I said to Philips.

'When are you ever not in trouble,' he said with affection. I shook my head slowly and his eyes grew wide.

'Trouble,' he repeated. 'I see.'

There was a pause.

'What are you going to do?'

'Well,' I said. 'I could marry John Wallace and pretend the baby is his, and live a respectable life.'

'Marry me,' Philips said in a rush. 'Don't marry Wallace, marry me.'

I was tempted. But Father wouldn't be pleased about that either, and knowing the contempt Philips felt for Edwin I wasn't sure he would be able to love his baby as a father should.

I took his hands in mine. 'William,' I said. 'Lovely William. I wish I could marry you, but I can't. You know that.'

'I do know that,' he said. 'But we could make a life together.'

I shook my head. 'I love you for asking,' I said. 'But no.'

He shrugged his shoulders. 'So what will you do,' he said. 'If you don't marry?'

I took a breath. 'I could run.'

Philips snorted. 'Where would you go? What would you do?'

I felt a rush of pride for Frances's hard work and preparation. 'I have some money and a place to go,' I said. 'I just don't know how to leave Father. I'm all he's got.'

Philips was frowning. 'Then don't go,' he said. 'This is madness. A woman out in the world on her own? With a littl'un to think about?' He trailed off. 'This would break your father's heart, Violet.'

He was right, of course, I thought later. Father was prickly and set in his ways, but he loved me. Clutching Frances's precious diary, I climbed the stairs to my former studio and put the diary in the cupboard where I'd hidden my version of *Mariana*. Then I stood for a moment in the middle of the room, imagining a life without art.

I couldn't. I couldn't imagine a life where I didn't draw. And that gave me hope. I could marry John Wallace and still draw – of course I could. And as for the baby, well there might not even be a baby. I still wasn't sure and probably wouldn't be for weeks.

I went to bed that night determined to stay. I would repair my relationship with Father, I thought as I put on my nightdress, and I would make my marriage work. I would be a dutiful, loyal wife, and if I had to paint in secret then so be it. As I drifted off to sleep I felt calm and relieved. Everything was going to be fine.

Two things happened to change my mind. The first was the sickness. I woke the next morning and lay for a second, enjoying the low autumn sun that shone through my bedroom window. Then, as I sat up, I was hit by a wave of dreadful nausea. I scrabbled under my bed for my chamber pot, then vomited violently several times.

Mabel found me, quarter of an hour later, still hunched over the pot, pale and sweating, and I thought I'd never been so pleased to see anyone.

'Oh, Mabel,' I said.

Mabel took the pot from me and smoothed back the hair that was stuck to my clammy forehead. 'Ginger,' she said. 'My sister swears by it. She suffers terrible when she's …'

She stopped abruptly, and I was grateful she hadn't voiced what we were both thinking.

'Can you manage to get dressed?' she said. I nodded. I found myself to be suddenly and inexplicably ravenous.

'Breakfast is ready,' Mabel said. She paused. 'And there is a letter from your father.'

That was the second thing.

My dear Violet, the letter read.

I am writing with good news. I have spoken at length with John Wallace and he has agreed to marry you. Violet, I know this is not what you wanted but I fear we must be practical. Without a good marriage you will have no security, and my business will eventually have to be sold. This way, I know you will be cared for when I am gone.

Wallace is a good man and a kind one, and I know will he care for you.

There was more, about his business deals in Manchester, and then …

We are to leave Manchester tomorrow and hope to be with you in Sussex within a week. I have written to Rev. Mapplethorpe to ask him if your marriage can take place the following weekend. I feel under the circumstances it is best to get things arranged as soon as possible.

I felt sick again. I was sitting alone at the long dining table, where I'd eaten many meals facing Father in silence. I imagined sitting here in twenty years' time, facing John Wallace, and knew without a shadow of a doubt that I couldn't do it.

I drained my coffee cup and stood up. I would go and find Frances straight away to put our plans into action. I swept out into the hall, without even pausing to pick up my hat and gloves.

Philips was in the front garden.

'Don't do it, Violet,' he said as I passed. I ignored him. I walked up Frances's path and knocked, loudly, on the door, feeling Philips watching me the whole time. Agnes opened the door and showed me out into the sunny terrace where Frances was eating breakfast. She stood up when I approached, her face full of hope.

I took her hand. 'I have decided,' I said. 'I will go.'

Chapter 57

1855
Frances

Violet and Frances were laughing as they walked to the front door.

'I'm just not sure I am a Florence,' Violet was saying.

'I will call you Flo,' Frances said, giggling like a girl.

'I may not answer,' Violet said. She linked her arm through Frances's. 'I think we make fine sisters,' she said. 'Florence and Polly.'

Frances felt like her whole life had shifted from despair to hope. She was still terribly sad about the baby but her friendship with Violet had given her a future to plan. They met every day to go over the details of Violet's escape and how Frances would follow as soon as she could, and they were almost ready to put it into practice.

Frances opened the front door to let Violet out.

'Heavens,' she said. 'It is dark. I had not realized it was so late.'

'That is because you do not stop talking,' Violet teased.

They laughed again, then Frances gasped as a figure loomed out of the darkness.

'Well, this is nice,' a voice said.

Frances's blood ran cold. Beside her, she felt Violet freeze.

Edwin.

He swayed up the garden path with his overnight bag in his hand, and dropped it at Frances's feet. 'What is she doing here?' he hissed in her face.

Frances recoiled from the smell of whisky on his breath. 'Miss Hargreaves just called by,' she stammered.

'Whores,' Edwin said coldly. 'Are you plotting against me?'

Frances tried to fake a laugh. 'Plotting?' she said lightly. 'Oh, Edwin, why in heaven's name would I plot against you? Anyway, you know me. I couldn't plot against you even if I wanted to – my mind isn't half as quick as yours.'

She saw Violet shoot her a quick questioning glance and hoped she would understand she was trying to calm things down.

'You are right,' Edwin snarled. 'You are one of the most stupid women I've ever met.'

Frances lowered her eyes, accepting his insults, but he wasn't finished.

'Stupid,' he said. 'Stupid enough to believe anything you're told.'

Frances forced a smile. 'Edwin, you are the only person whose opinion I value.'

Violet was looking terrified and angry in equal measure. A dangerous combination, Frances thought.

'Don't speak to her like that,' Violet said.

'Hush,' Frances said frantically, too late. Edwin swung his gaze on to Violet.

'I will talk to my wife as I please,' he said. 'Who are you to tell me what to do?'

Violet went to speak and Frances grabbed her arm to stop her making things worse.

'Go,' she said to Violet. 'Go home.'

She watched as Violet tried to edge past Edwin and, quick as a flash, he reached out and grabbed her by her long hair.

Violet cried out as Edwin wound her hair round his fist. He pulled her towards him roughly. Violet's head jerked back until her back rested on Edwin's arm.

'What have you told her?' he growled into her ear.

'Nothing,' Violet said. 'I have told her nothing.' She began to cry.

Frances felt helpless. She longed to help Violet but she was so scared of Edwin that she was paralysed. 'Edwin,' she said, her voice trembling. 'Let go of Miss Hargreaves's hair.'

Edwin pulled Violet again. This time both she and Frances cried out.

'Let her go.' Philips came striding down the path.

'Oh look, Violet,' Edwin sang. 'Here's your knight in shining armour, come to protect your honour. Bit late for that.' But he let go of Violet's hair.

Frances, still shaking with fear, opened her arms and Violet ran to her. Her hairline was beaded with blood. Frances kissed her temple.

'There, there,' she cooed. 'Philips will put this whole sorry mess to rights.'

But she was not as sure as she sounded. Frances recognized the spark in Edwin's eyes that told her he'd gone past the point where he cared about the consequences of his actions, and she feared for Philips.

'It's late,' Philips said. 'We're all tired. Will you not go inside and we can talk about this in the morning?'

Frances cradled Violet closer and winced. Edwin did not like being told what to do in the best of circumstances.

Edwin looked at Philips with contempt. Frances found herself sizing them up. Philips was smaller than Edwin but younger and stronger. She thought he would have the edge in a fight.

Edwin obviously had the same thought. 'You are right,' he said. 'I am sorry. I have had a busy day and perhaps a glass of whisky too many. I apologize for my actions.'

He held out his hand to Philips, but as the other man relaxed and held out his own, Edwin struck. He punched Philips, upwards, under his jaw. Philips's head flew back, his eyes rolled, and his legs buckled. He slumped to the ground and a thin trickle of blood dripped from his nose.

Violet screamed. The noise split the quiet night.

Surely now someone will come, Frances thought in desperation. Surely someone will help us.

'You've killed him,' Violet wailed. 'You have killed him.'

Frances was suddenly filled with a calm resolve. She put her mouth to Violet's ear and spoke in urgent tones. 'Violet, listen to me. I can distract Edwin now. You must go – do you understand – you must go home and hide. If he knows your father is not there, Edwin could come to look for you. At first light, take the money and my diary and leave – as we planned. Send me word you are safe.'

Violet had stopped screaming but she clung to Frances still.

Edwin was standing over Philips but now he turned to the women.

'Whores,' he hissed again. 'Why do you torment me?'

'Go.' Frances pushed Violet so hard, the younger woman lost her footing and fell. Breathing heavily, Frances pulled her to her feet then pushed her again. 'Go,' she repeated. 'Go.' She could see blood on Violet's leg, but it did not look too bad.

'Go on,' Edwin said. 'Run home to Daddy.'

Violet staggered down the path and into the darkness. Frances braced herself as Edwin lurched towards her. She tried not to look at Philips's body.

'My darling wife,' Edwin said. 'Have you been sticking the knife further into my back? Spreading lies about me to the neighbours?' Spittle frothed at the edges of his mouth.

Frances looked into his eyes, which were filled with hatred, then she turned and fled back into the house. But Edwin was too fast. He gave chase as, gibbering with terror, Frances ran up the stairs. He grabbed her just as she reached the top, pulling her leg out from under her. She fell with a thump on to the landing and banged her head hard on the bannister.

Dazed, she lay still for a second. Edwin loomed over her, blocking out the light from downstairs like an evil creature from a frightening fairy tale. Frances tried to pull herself along the landing but Edwin stamped on her leg.

'Stay here, wife,' he said. He began to unbuckle his belt. 'You belong to me and it would serve you well to remember that.'

Frances's leg was throbbing, her head ached, and she couldn't see out of her left eye. 'I will die here,' she thought, knowing with absolute clarity that no one would come to help her. Even if anyone heard noises, they would leave well alone, thinking that one should never interfere in business between a husband and his wife.

Edwin still stood over her and suddenly Frances was filled with anger. She had been afraid for too long.

As Edwin pushed his trousers down from his hips, Frances saw her chance. With her healthy leg she kicked out. It was a feeble attempt, all things considered. She had no strength left. Her foot did not even connect with Edwin. But her sudden movement took him by surprise. He stepped back – off the top step – and like an oak tree falling in the forest, he toppled backwards down the stairs.

Frances heard him land on the tiled floor of the hall. And then the shadows on the edge of her vision crowded in.

'I am so tired,' she thought. She closed her eyes, and went to sleep.

Chapter 58

1855
Violet

I ran and ran. I picked up my skirt and ran through the front garden. The wind pulled my hat from my head and sent it spinning into the night, but I didn't stop. I ran into the house and up the stairs. My leg was bleeding badly but it didn't stop me, so frightened was I.

The house was quiet and dark. Mabel had long since gone home and Philips … I gave a sob. I couldn't think of him now.

Exhausted, I crawled up the stairs to the attic room and lay for a second on the floor, catching my breath. A noise from outside made me jump. If Edwin wanted to find me, he knew where I'd be. I had to hide.

'Just in case you ever need to get away,' I remembered Philips saying.

Whimpering, I pulled myself to my feet, scuttled over to the corner of the room and slid behind the chaise.

I pushed it backwards with my behind to give myself more room, then panting slightly I felt for the concealed panel. My hands were shaking so badly I couldn't open it.

'Come on, Violet,' I said. Another noise downstairs made me gasp, just as I unlatched the panel. I thought briefly of Frances's diary, hidden in the cupboard on the other side of the room, but I could hear voices now outside and knew I had to get away.

I lay on my stomach and wriggled backwards through the space. I tried to pull the chaise back into the position it had been in but I couldn't shift it. No matter, I would be out of here again at first light.

I pushed myself backwards and dropped the panel back into place, hearing the latch catch with a click.

The room was very dark. All I could hear was my own breathing. As my eyes adjusted to the darkness I felt my way to the corner of the room and, exhausted, I curled up on the floor. I thought of Frances and hoped she was safe. Edwin had obviously been drinking; perhaps he had passed out before he could take his rage out on his wife.

'It's almost over,' I told myself, speaking aloud in the darkness. 'One more night and I will be free.'

I must have slept because I woke, a few hours later, aching and thirsty, with the cold grey light of dawn creeping through the tiny window.

My leg was hot and fiercely painful. I rolled down my stocking and examined it. It was an angry red around the wound and the skin was tight and shiny. I found I could not bear to roll my stocking back up, so I pulled it off, and the other, and threw them into the corner. Then I lay on my stomach and pushed the panel. Nothing happened.

'Odd,' I said aloud. I tried to remember how Philips had opened it from the inside but could not recall him doing it at all. Why hadn't I paid more attention?

'Think logically, Violet,' I said. There was a catch somewhere on the side. I had to push the panel in to release it. So from here I would have to pull it to open it … but the door was flush against the wall. I tried to get my fingernails into the edges but they split and after a few attempts my fingers began to bleed.

I started to sweat. I knew that to panic would not help but I could not help myself. Was I to stay here for ever? Only Philips and me even knew about the space. Father was not returning for a week, and Mabel would never think to look up here. I went to the tiny window. It was narrow – no wider than my face. I peered out. No one would see me up here. It was raining. I looked for a second at the water running down the outside of the glass.

'I could break that,' I thought. 'And call for help. Perhaps someone walking on the cliffs would hear.' I looked round. Philips had stacked all my art supplies neatly but none of them would do. Instead, I picked up my shoe, wrapped my discarded stocking round my hand to protect it, and hit the window. It was no use. The window was so narrow I could not break it.

I had nothing to do but wait. I shrugged off my shawl and fashioned it into a pillow. Then I lay down in the corner, and closed my eyes.

Chapter 59

1855
Frances

'Mrs Forrest.' The voice sounded a very long way away. 'Mrs Forrest.'

Frances opened her eyes, then shut them again as the light flooded in and made her wince.

'Mrs Forrest.' Someone took her hand. 'Can you hear me? Squeeze my fingers.'

Frances squeezed. Then she opened her eyes again. She was in her bed, at home. It was daytime, though the rain lashed against the windows. The person holding her hand was a doctor in a smart black suit. Behind him stood Agnes, a glass of water in her hand.

'Well, hello,' said the doctor. 'We thought you were going to leave us.'

Frances licked her dry lips and Agnes put the glass to her mouth. She drank eagerly.

'Careful now,' said Agnes. 'Don't make yourself sick.'

Frances closed her eyes again.

When she woke the doctor had gone, the rain had stopped, and the pain in her head had subsided. She lay still for a few minutes, checking her injuries. Her leg was bandaged and her eye swollen shut.

The door opened and Agnes came in, carrying a pile of linen. 'Oh you're awake,' she said, a rare smile on her face. She put the linen down and came to Frances's side.

'Sit,' Frances croaked. 'Please, tell me, what's happened?'

She meant since Edwin had returned and fallen, and killed Philips but Agnes misunderstood.

'Oh do you not remember? I said that to the doctor. I said she'll not remember, a nasty bump to her head like that.'

Frances began to correct her but somewhere, deep in the swollen recesses of her aching head, she thought it would be best if everyone believed she had lost her memory.

'There was an attack,' Agnes said. 'Someone broke in.' Her dark eyes searched Frances's face.

'Someone broke in,' Frances repeated.

'Madam, your husband ...' Agnes paused. She took Frances's hand. 'Mr Forrest had returned from London. I'm afraid the attacker pushed him down the stairs. He's dead, Madam.'

Frances blinked at her. 'Dead,' she said. She could not take it in.

Agnes pursed her lips. 'William Philips, the gardener from next door, was also attacked,' she said. 'In your garden. He is alive, but only just. Doctor does not expect him to last the night.'

Frances's eyes filled with tears. 'He is a good man,' she said.

'I have more bad news,' Agnes said. 'About Miss Hargreaves.'

Frances braced herself.

'She is missing. No one has seen her.'

Frances was thrilled. Well done, Violet, she thought. Aloud, she said: 'Goodness. Are they looking for her?'

'You have been asleep for two days,' Agnes said. 'They have searched the village and the beach. They found her hat on the cliff edge – it is thought she might have drowned. But there is no sign of her. The doctor has sent word to her father.'

'Poor Violet,' Frances murmured, but inwardly she was thinking how brave her friend had been.

There was a knock on the door, and the doctor put his head round. 'Ah,' he said with a smile. 'You look much better.'

He came in to the room and pulled up a chair next to Frances's bed. 'Has Agnes filled you in?' he asked, his brow furrowed.

Frances nodded.

'I am so sorry about your husband, my dear.'

Frances lowered her eyes.

'Still, he will live on,' the doctor continued.

Alarmed, Frances looked at him. Agnes took her hand again.

'She does not yet know,' she said to the doctor.

'Frances,' he said. 'I believe you are expecting a baby.'

Frances's head spun. 'I thought ... but I fell ...' she said.

'Your baby is obviously a hardy chap,' the doctor said. 'Congratulations, my dear.'

Frances was exhausted by all the news – good and bad. She put her hand to her belly and felt comforted.

'I am tired,' she said. 'I must sleep.'

Chapter 60

1855
Violet

I was painting. It was my third day in the room. The first day I had slept most of the afternoon and woken, disorientated and confused, in darkness. I decided I had to keep track of passing time, so I took a paintbrush from the piles in the corner and painted a line on the wall to mark my first day. I was confident Father would find me when he returned but I was not sure exactly when that would be.

Thoughtfully, I felt the end of the narrow brush. Could I lever open the panel using that? I got on to my knees and tried to stick the paintbrush in the edge of the panel, but narrow as it was, it was still too broad. I needed to file it down somehow. I spent a while rubbing it on the rough edge of the bricks around the window, grazing my knuckles in the process. But though the brush now slotted in to the edge of the panel, as soon as I put pressure on it, it snapped.

I sat on the floor with my back against the panel, exhausted. I had run out of ideas. I had tried every way I could think of to open the latch – and the window – and nothing worked. I would simply have to wait for Father to come. And that gave me another idea. I had my paints, and a large blank wall to paint on. I took a pencil from my supplies and began to sketch.

That had been two days ago, and now I had covered almost half the wall with a giant depiction of myself as Mariana. I had to paint from memory because I had nothing to copy, but that was no problem.

I had changed Mariana's room into the grey cell I was now trapped in. Mariana's large, leaded window was now a thin pane of glass, surrounded by bare brick, and instead of the sewing Mariana had thrown down, I added brushes and paint. Once more I planned to give my heroine my own rounded face and red hair.

My days and nights fell into a rhythm, uncomfortable and strange as it was. I had shed most of my outer clothes and now used them as bedding, wearing only my petticoat. Each day I marked another line on the wall by the window, where I'd also painted a sun and a moon.

I found I was no longer hungry, but I was weak and tired, and I could only paint for a short while before needing to rest. Increasingly, I spent most of the day sleeping, and after finding that shouting for help and banging the wall made me faint with exhaustion, I no longer did that either.

Father will come, I thought. But I could hear nothing in the house. No sound to reassure me of his arrival.

On the evening of my sixth day in the room, I finished my *Mariana*. It was enormous; I'd had to stand on the box holding my paints to reach the top. The colours glowed in the setting sun and I thought it was the best work I'd ever done, though I couldn't be certain – I found it hard to think now, feeling my mind dance from thought to thought – some real, some fanciful. Sometimes I didn't know if I was awake or asleep and dreaming.

Fatigue overwhelmed me once more and – for the first time surprisingly – a feeling of hopelessness. I was very weak and feared Father would not find me in time. I curled up in the corner of the room and slept.

I woke a few hours later but found myself not rejuvenated. Too weary to rise, I simply adjusted my piles of clothes, then I slept once more.

Later, when daylight filled the room, I woke again. This time I had enough energy to take a paintbrush in my trembling hand. Sitting on the floor – I still found I couldn't stand – I wrote *Violet Hargreaves* in shaky script on the wall above the useless panel – opposite to the *Mariana*.

Worn out from the effort I leaned my forehead on the cool brick for a moment and found I'd slept once more – just as I was. This time when I woke I lifted my brush and wrote *Edwin*. I couldn't think of the words to explain what he'd done so instead I scored out his name. Then I wrote *Frances*, and finally, the word *sorry*.

Still holding the brush, I crawled back across the floor to the nest I'd made myself from my clothes. I was so tired now. I lay down and curled up. My head ached and my eyes, though they were closed, burned.

And then, suddenly, the pain was gone. I felt arms around me and smelled a familiar smell – a fragrance I'd not smelled for many years.

'Mama,' I said. My mother kissed me, and stroked my hair like she'd done when I was small.

'Hush, my darling,' she said. 'Hush. You are safe now. Sleep.'

I was filled with joy. To think I had been waiting for Father and it was Mama who had come. I tried to see my mother, but she was surrounded by a blinding light.

'Hush,' Mama said again. 'Sleep now.'

And I slept.

Chapter 61

Present day
Ella

I was at a loss. All my efforts to track Violet down had come to nothing. She wasn't in Scotland, and she hadn't stolen Frances Forrest's identity. I was beginning to think she'd drowned after all and I'd even spent one whole afternoon staring at incomprehensible tidal patterns, trying to work out where a body that fell from our cliffs would wash up. It was impossible.

And yet, I couldn't shake off the feeling that I was meant to write this story. My Tessa mystery was with my editor but I knew deep down that it wasn't very good and how could it be, when I'd barely paid it any attention at all?

As autumn became winter and the weather worsened, I tried really hard to move on from my Cliff House Mystery, but it didn't work. Even Ben and I making the decision to put our house in London on the market and make our landlord a ridiculously small but eagerly accepted offer on our house in Sussex didn't distract me.

'I can't believe he didn't want more money for it,' I told Priya one day in November. I was visiting her at home – tomorrow she was going into hospital to have the twins and I was supposed to be helping her prepare. Instead we were sitting on the sofa, eating the chocolates out of one of the Advent calendars I'd bought for the boys.

'He said it had been a millstone round his neck, he'd had trouble renting it out for years, and we would be doing him a favour.'

'His loss,' Priya said, popping out the chocolate from door number 15. 'He'll be sorry when you do up that bathroom and lose the peach toilet.'

'Dunno,' I said. 'I've grown to like it.'

Priya gave me a disdainful look. 'Don't make jokes,' she said. 'I'm not in the mood to be funny.'

'Nervous about tomorrow?'

'Terrified,' she said. 'Tell me something to take my mind off the fact that these babies are coming out in a few hours' time.'

'I've been searching for information about unidentified bodies washed up on Sussex beaches,' I told her.

She frowned. 'Violet?' she said. 'Still?'

'I have to find her, Priya,' I said.

'Ella,' she said, in a world-weary tone. 'I've had a lot of cases that haven't been resolved the way I wanted them to be. I've seen people walk free who were definitely guilty. I've seen bereaved people never find out what happened to their loved ones. If you don't move on it can eat you up inside.'

'I can't forget about her,' I said.

'I know you feel a connection with her, and that's understandable,' Priya said. 'But her father spent his whole life searching and never found her. Maybe your search is just as fruitless.'

I leant my head back against the sofa and gestured for her

to pass me the Advent calendar. 'You're right,' I said. 'I know you're right. I just can't give up on her.'

Priya made an 'ooph' sound and cradled her bump as one of the babies kicked her. I put my hand on her stomach and grinned as I felt the wriggling inside.

'You're a writer, though,' Priya said. 'Why don't you write your own ending for Violet?'

'Make it up, you mean?'

'Why not? If you're never going to find out what happened to her, and you can't settle without knowing, why not create something?'

'I suppose,' I said, not convinced.

'You can't carry on like this,' Priya said. 'Searching and searching. It's going to start messing with your head – and your family life.'

I thought about how I'd missed out on a family trip to the beach the weekend before because I wanted to research unidentified bodies and tidal flows, and wondered to myself if perhaps Priya had a point.

'Okay,' I said. 'I'll make up my own ending.'

But even that didn't work because my fictional imaginings kept clashing with the evidence. I thought about how I'd want Violet's story to end. I imagined her leaving Heron Green and fleeing to London, changing her name and launching a successful career as an artist. But George had examined all sorts of lesser-known works by lesser-known artists influenced by the Pre-Raphaelites and none of them matched the pictures we knew Violet had drawn. She'd obviously stopped painting when she disappeared. Or if she'd continued, she'd not had any success as an artist.

I drummed my fingers on my desk. I was sitting in my study, a few days after Priya had her babies. One of the twins had surprised everyone by turning out to be a boy, much to Nik's delight, and the girls doted on their new siblings, Nina and Arun. She was home already and coping brilliantly. I was planning to pop round and see her later, but first I wanted to have a crack at writing a new ending for Violet's story.

Fed up with my lame attempts, I spun round in my chair and stared out of the window to the sea beyond. It was a gloomy day and the waves were deep grey.

'Where are you, Vi?' I said out loud.

Over by the wall, Dumbledore gave a little snore. As soon as he'd got big enough to get up and down the stairs by himself, he'd taken to sleeping in my study. I liked having him there when I was on my own during the day and I thought he liked the patch of sunlight that fell along the wall – the mystery wall as we jokingly called it – because that's where he always chose to curl up. In the end, I'd put a blanket there for him and even though the low winter sun didn't reach his spot now he still stayed there.

I smiled at him and turned back to my work. Maybe it wasn't a happy ending Violet needed after all. Despite my fondness for her and my desperate hope that perhaps it all worked out in the end, I couldn't ignore the fact that all the evidence pointed to a miserable outcome.

'I can work this out,' I muttered to myself. 'I've read enough crime novels, talked to enough police officers, and plotted enough stories to come up with a credible story about what happened.'

Filled with a new enthusiasm, I cleaned off my whiteboard

with a flourish. Time to start working out who was where, and when.

I knew Edwin Forrest was a nasty piece of work, prone to violence, and I knew that Frances and Violet seemed to be – unlikely as it sounded – allies of a sort. The handyman, William Philips, must have known Violet well as he'd worked for her father for years, so I thought perhaps he was protective of her.

I spent all day in my office, staring at the whiteboard, trying to make various scenarios work given what I knew about crimes, and domestic violence, and murders.

The one thing I kept coming back to was that William Philips was found outside the Forrests' house, while Edwin Forrest had been at the bottom of the stairs, inside, and Frances upstairs on the landing.

'Was it you?' I said, looking at a copy of the photo of Frances that Winnie had given me. 'Did you fight back? Shove him down the stairs just to make him stop?'

I couldn't blame her if she had. I even admired her in a way. But that still didn't explain what had happened to Violet.

I imagined the four people – Violet, Frances, William, and Edwin – outside the Forrests' home. It had been raining, so they wouldn't have been chatting and hanging out in the garden – they'd have to have been going in or out of the house. Perhaps Violet had been walking past when she had come across an argument or confrontation between Frances and Edwin. Maybe Frances was trying to get Edwin to leave?

Whatever the reason, I imagined Violet rushing up the path trying to stop the argument. Maybe William Philips got involved in the same way? Edwin was brutal; I knew that.

Maybe he'd lashed out at Violet and William Philips had charged to her aid?

I paced round the study, Dumbledore darting about my feet thinking it was all a game.

'So there's a big fight,' I said aloud. 'Violet is trying to calm things down and Edwin lashes out at her. What would she do? He's violent and angry presumably. Has he hit her before? Is she scared? Would she run away?'

I stared out of the window to the rough sea. 'Where? To the beach?'

I shook my head. She wouldn't go to the beach on a day like this, with the wind whipping the waves up the shingle.

'She'd go home,' I said to Dumbledore. 'She'd run home, where it was safe.'

He yapped at me in agreement. Or possibly just because he wanted to play. I bent down and rubbed his head and he ran around wildly for a few seconds then bounded back across to his blanket and curled up by the wall once more.

I stared at him.

'She'd want to be safe,' I said again, more slowly this time. 'Maybe she felt safe up here, where she painted her pictures.'

I looked round at the cupboard behind me. She could have squeezed in there if she'd had to. But she couldn't have stayed in there long – as soon as people started looking they'd have found her.

Then I looked again at the mystery wall. Wondering if the crazy way my mind was going could possibly be right.

Carefully, I pulled sleepy Dumbledore on his blanket away from the wall. Why did he choose to snooze there? I felt the patch where he curled up. It was warmer than the rest of the wall – could that mean something or did it just mean Dumbledore had warmed it up with his body heat?

Sitting on the floor, I ran my hand along the bottom of the bricks, where the wall met the floor, to see if I could feel anything different about Dumbledore's chosen spot. The whole wall was wallpapered but right at the bottom I could feel a slight difference. Parts of the wall were rough to the touch, while Dumbledore's bit was smoother.

'Mummy?'

I jumped in surprise as Oscar appeared beside me. I hadn't realized it was so late. 'Hello, darling,' I said. 'How was school?'

'I want the iPad,' he said. 'Can I have it?'

'Not just now,' I said, slightly annoyed at his interruption. 'After dinner.'

'I just need it for a minute,' he said, flashing me what he obviously thought was a winning smile. 'Why are you on the floor?'

'I was looking for something. Want to help?'

'Can I have the iPad after?'

'No, you can have it after dinner. Now are you going to help?'

Oscar gave me a look of sheer defiance. 'I am not going to help you unless I can have the iPad.'

'No,' I said again.

'But,' Oscar began.

'No.'

'You're not even letting me talk.'

'No.'

Infuriated, Oscar aimed a small kick at the wall next to

where I sat. 'I hate this house,' he said. 'It's stupid. Stupid house.'

He pulled his leg back, and with a strike worthy of David Beckham, kicked the wall with all his might. And his foot went right through.

'Mummy!' he said in terror, hopping on the foot that wasn't stuck.

'Oscar!' I said, grabbing him to steady him on his one foot.

'Sorry,' he wailed. 'Are you cross?'

Still hanging on to him, I clambered to my feet and dropped a kiss on his head. 'Actually, no,' I said. 'You've found what I was looking for, you clever boy.'

Oscar looked bewildered as I tried to pull his foot gently out of the wall. It was stuck fast thanks to his sturdy school shoe.

'Take your foot out of your shoe,' I said.

'I can't,' Oscar cried. 'Help me!'

I swallowed a laugh as I bent down. I reached into the hole he'd made and pulled the Velcro straps on his shoe. 'Wiggle your foot out,' I said.

Oscar did as I'd said. His foot came free, but his shoe stayed sticking half in and half out of the hole. He stood looking sheepish.

'Sorry, Mummy,' he said.

'You shouldn't kick walls,' I said, trying to look stern while a bubble of excitement was rising up inside me. 'But maybe you have solved the mystery.'

Chapter 62

Oscar still looked like he didn't really understand what on earth was going on. I gave him a cuddle.

'Is Daddy here?' I asked.

Oscar nodded. 'He's in the kitchen with Margaret.'

'Then can you run downstairs – take your other shoe off first I think – and tell Daddy what's happened? Tell him I need him up here.'

Oscar pulled his shoe off without undoing the straps and fled, no doubt thinking he'd got off lightly.

I pulled at his shoe, which was still stuck in the wall. It wouldn't shift. I pulled harder, then pushed it. It disappeared behind the wall in a puff of dust.

'What's going on?' Ben appeared behind me.

'Look,' I said. 'Oscar kicked the wall.'

'He did what?' Ben tutted.

'No, no, it's fine – look what happened.'

Ben crouched down next to me. 'I knew it was hollow,' he said in triumph.

'Oscar's shoe is inside the hole,' I said. 'Shall we bash the wall some more to get it out?'

I looked at him, desperately hoping he'd agree and we

would find out what was hidden behind the wall. I had a strong feeling whatever we found was going to reveal the truth about what had happened to Violet.

Ben stood up.

'Where are you going?' I said.

'We need a hammer,' he said with a wink.

He was back in a flash.

'The boys are watching *Elf*,' he said. 'I told Margaret we'd found something interesting in your study. She's making their tea.'

'Good stuff.'

Ben aimed the hammer at the edge of the hole Oscar's shoe had left, chipping away the edges, and I pulled off layers of the wallpaper as he worked.

Ben's efforts revealed a smallish square hole.

'I'd been wondering why Dumbledore always sleeps at the same patch,' I explained. 'I could feel it was different but I didn't know why. That's why I was sitting here when Oscar came upstairs.'

'I think the rest of the wall is brick,' Ben said. 'But this bit is wooden, which is probably why Dumbledore likes it. It's warmer no doubt. Look, it's a little hatch with hinges, and it's rotten, that's why Oscar's foot went through it. If Oscar had kicked a little way over, he would have just hurt his toes – he wouldn't have gone through.'

He reached into the now much bigger hole and picked up Oscar's shoe. I swept away the wood chips with my arm and together we crouched down and peered through the wall.

'What would you do if someone looked out at us,' I said,

only half joking. All the hairs on the back of my neck were standing up. Ben shuddered.

I blinked as I stared into the dim light of the recess, hardly believing what was beginning to show itself as my eyes got used to the gloom.

'I can see a painting,' I said. 'At least I think I can.' I could see an outline and faint colours.

Ben looked at me in disbelief. 'Where?'

'There.' I gestured through the hole. 'See the colours on the wall?'

'I can't see anything,' Ben said.

'I can fit through there,' I said, surprising myself with my boldness. 'I'm going inside.'

'No you are not,' said Ben. 'What if you can't get out again?'

'Scaredy cat,' I said.

He frowned. 'You've changed your tune,' he said. 'Seriously, though. What if it's not safe? What if the whole wall comes down?'

'It's been here for well over a century,' I pointed out. 'The house isn't suddenly going to fall down because a small boy kicked a wall. What if this is to do with Violet? What if it's the answer I've been searching for?'

Ben shuddered again. 'Fine,' he said. 'Just be careful.'

I got on my stomach and squeezed through the gap. It was a tight fit but with a bit of wriggling I made it. Then I got to my feet, rubbing the dust from my jeans.

'Oh. My. God,' I breathed. It was incredible. The space was tiny – simply the chimney alcove – but one whole wall, the wall opposite the hole I'd just wriggled through – was covered in the most wonderful painting. I was transfixed. It was Violet's work, there was no doubt about that, and it was another – enormous – copy of *Mariana*, but she'd changed the details again. Once more this painting was of Violet, but the room she waited in now was this tiny cell.

In the background, where a candle burned in the original *Mariana*, was a strange ethereal glow. I squinted. It was almost in the shape of a woman. And at Violet's feet, instead of leaves, were crumpled pieces of paper.

'Ella,' Ben called from outside. 'Ella?'

'Ben,' I said. 'You have got to see this.'

'I'll never get my shoulders through that gap,' he said.

I snorted. 'If I can get my arse through, your shoulders will be a breeze,' I said. 'Come on.'

There was a thump and a grunt and Ben's head appeared. He inched through, complaining and swearing the whole time, then he stood up, staring at the wall.

'Bloody hell,' he said. 'That's Violet.'

'It's Violet in here,' I said. 'Violet trapped in this tiny room. I've been thinking that she ran away from Edwin Forrest that night. Do you think she ran and hid here in this cell?'

Ben gazed around him. 'Maybe,' he said. 'Though I can't imagine anyone choosing to be in here.'

I went to the corner where I'd seen a few boxes and rolled-up canvases. 'These are art supplies,' I said, pulling out one of the paintings and examining the roll. 'I'm not going to unroll this because I think it will crack but it definitely looks like Violet's work. Perhaps this place wasn't a hiding place. Maybe it was just a kind of studio for her – a sanctuary.'

But Ben was shaking his head. 'I don't think so,' he said. 'Look.' He pointed at the wall opposite – above the hole we'd made – where, in wobbly writing, was painted *Violet Hargreaves*. There was also the name *Edwin*, with a thick black line scored through it, and finally, at the bottom, *Sorry Frances*.

I put my hand to my mouth. 'Oh God,' I said.

Ben had gone to the other corner, where a pile of rags lay, stiff and discoloured with age. He crouched down next to them and pulled the top layer back. I jumped myself as he recoiled violently, swore, and dropped the cloth.

'What is it?' I said, but I knew really. All my worst fears – my most awful theories – were coming true. 'Is it Violet? Is Violet here?'

Ben put his arms round me. I could feel him trembling. 'I think so,' he said.

'I want to see,' I said.

'No.'

'I want to see her.'

Ben knew when he was beaten. Together we went to the corner and crouched by the pile of cloth.

'Ready?' he asked.

I nodded, clenching my hands into fists to stop them shaking.

Ben pulled away the top rag. Underneath was just bones of course. They were surprisingly small and curled up in a foetal position.

'Oh,' I breathed. 'Oh, poor girl.'

'We mustn't touch,' Ben warned. 'I suppose this is a crime scene, of sorts.'

I put the cloth back over Violet's remains.

'We've found you,' I said to the room. 'And we are going to look after you.'

'Come on,' Ben said. 'Let's get out of here. And I think you'd better call Priya. She'll know what to do next.'

He squeezed back through the panel, and I followed.

'I can't believe she's been here this whole time,' I said with a shiver as we walked downstairs. 'Do you think she was trapped by mistake? She must have been. How utterly terrifying to be stuck in a tiny space like that and not be able to get out.'

'Maybe she couldn't get the little door open,' Ben said. He looked pale and shaky and I imagined I looked the same. 'Or maybe Edwin Forrest locked her up.'

I felt sick. 'Poor Violet,' I breathed. 'And poor Marcus. Why oh why didn't he check the house before he shut it up?'

'He probably did,' Ben said. 'But even if he looked in all the rooms for her, there was no reason for him to check inside cupboards. And if it was a few days – or even weeks – after she disappeared, she'd probably have been dead already.'

I grimaced. Real life was truly stranger – and crueller – than fiction ever could be. 'All that searching and she was right here all along,' I said.

The boys were eating their dinner in the kitchen with Margaret, who raised an eyebrow at our dusty appearance. I mouthed 'explain in a minute' over the kids' heads, then I picked up my phone and headed into the hall out of the range of little ears, scrolling through the numbers until I found Priya's.

'I've found her,' I said when she answered. 'I've found Violet.'

Chapter 63

I couldn't stop shaking, and I felt close to tears as I told Priya what we'd found. But I also felt a strange sense of satisfaction. It was awful to think that poor Violet had been lying there, just behind a wall, for one hundred and fifty years, but I was pleased and relieved that we'd found her.

'Bloody hell,' Priya said. 'Why couldn't you have found her before I'd had these two imps? I'm stuck to the sofa, here.'

I managed a brief chuckle. 'You'd never have fitted through the hole in the wall,' I said. 'Can you ring someone though? Do the police have to come?'

''Fraid so,' said Priya. 'Don't move anything yet. I'll sort it out and someone will be there soon.' She paused. 'Can you take some pictures?'

'You ghoul,' I said. 'But yes, we probably should. I'll send Ben to do it.'

Ben headed back upstairs and took lots of photos, while I filled Margaret in on what had happened.

'She was there the whole time?' she said in wonder. 'How awful.'

'I'm just so pleased we've found her now,' I said.

She took the boys into the lounge to finish watching their

film as Ben and I paced the kitchen and waited for the police to arrive.

'Okay?' he asked and I nodded.

'Surprisingly, yes,' I said. 'As long as I don't think about how scared she must have been.'

Ben made a face. 'So scared,' he agreed. 'I just hope she went in there of her own accord, and she wasn't locked in by Edwin.'

I thought about the writing on the wall of Violet's prison, the way she'd written *Edwin*, then crossed out his name, and I couldn't help thinking whoever had killed him – Frances, I thought for sure now – he'd probably deserved it.

I had been slightly nervous about how the police would deal with what we'd found. But as soon as they arrived, they put my mind at rest. There were two of them – and older man with greying hair and a twinkle in his eye, and a young enthusiastic PC called Joely.

'So you've lived here about ten minutes and you've solved a crime that locals have been wondering about for one hundred and fifty years,' the young one said, smiling over her shoulder at me as we climbed the stairs to the attic. 'Trev here has been filling me in on all the stories.'

'It was our son, Oscar, who found her really,' I said. 'Oscar and his bad temper.'

I showed them the hole in the wall and Trev nodded.

'Did you touch anything?'

'We just moved the rags covering the remains,' I said. 'We put them back.'

I found I didn't want to go into the cell again, so Ben

crawled through with the police officers behind him. They weren't there for long.

'Well it's obviously a very old body,' Joely said as she crawled backwards out of the hole in the wall. 'I don't think we need to take you in for questioning.'

Instead she phoned the coroner – an efficient, smartly dressed woman called Maeve Gregory, who arrived within an hour.

While we were waiting for Maeve to swing up the road in her white BMW, I phoned Dad and explained what had happened, Margaret went home for her own dinner, and Ben made tea for the police.

'Good heavens,' Dad said. 'She was there all along?'

'It's so sad,' I said. 'This whole time she was just the other side of the wall.'

'So is it chaos down there?' Dad said. 'Do you need help?'

'Oh would you?' I said. I felt as though detectives and coroners and bodies didn't mix with two small boys watching Christmas films.

Dad and Barb agreed to drive down to ours and take the boys back to their house for the night. I was pleased the kids would be away from the house soon. I didn't want them to be there when the police – would it be the police? Or an undertaker perhaps? – took Violet's body away. Stan was thrilled at the prospect of a night at Granddad's but Oscar was more subdued.

'Is this because of the lady in the picture?' he asked. I was startled and, not for the first time, impressed at just how much he paid attention to what was going on around him even though he gave the impression of not taking anything in at all.

'Sort of,' I admitted. 'But it's nothing to worry about. She used to live in our house a long time ago and she did some paintings on the walls.'

Oscar studied me carefully. 'Did something bad happen to her?'

I pulled him in for a cuddle and stroked his hair. 'She died,' I told him. 'And no one knew she'd died. They always wondered where she'd gone. But now we know and we are going to make sure that everyone knows about her now.'

Once the boys had gone, and Maeve had inspected the body, things happened very quickly.

'Can we knock the wall down a bit more?' one of the police officers asked.

I winced at the thought of the mess, but I knew it would make getting Violet – and her paintings – out of her cell much easier.

I cleared away my notebooks and computer so they wouldn't get covered in brick dust. More police officers arrived, along with some guys who weren't in uniform but who brought some big sledge hammers with them and we watched as they knocked a bigger hole in the wall so a specialist team from Sussex university – called by Maeve – could fit in.

When they eventually pulled up – as darkness was falling and I was drooping with tiredness – they turned out to be less of a team and more of a trio. A forensic anthropologist called Dr Davies, who was like Louis Theroux's younger, geekier, Welsher brother and two over-excited PHD students.

They were beside themselves at the discovery and spent

more than an hour in the cell, taking photographs and samples of the rags Violet was wrapped in. Eventually they gently put her on to a board, and put the board into a bag, and took her out through the hole and down the stairs.

'Be careful with her,' I said as they pushed the board into the back of their small van.

Dr Davies smiled at me, and pushed his floppy hair out of his eyes. 'We always are,' he said.

I believed him.

And suddenly there was just Ben and me in the house: no detectives, no children, and no Violet. Feeling a bit shell-shocked, we sat on the sofa and watched the news – I half expected to see our story reported but of course it wasn't.

'Not yet,' Ben said. 'But people will be interested. You have to write this story, Ella.'

So I did.

Chapter 64

Present day – six months later
Ella

I stared out to sea, enjoying the warmth of the spring sunshine on my shoulders after what seemed like months of winter. My hair blew in the breeze and I tucked a stray strand behind my ear, then smoothed my billowing dress over my stomach. I was getting quite a bump now halfway through my pregnancy and despite being very surprised when I first discovered I was unexpectedly expecting, I had quickly come round to the idea of us being a family of five. Just last week Ben and I had discovered our new arrival would be a little girl and I wanted to name her Violet.

I smiled to myself, as I felt the baby fluttering inside. 'Hello, little Violet,' I whispered. 'You will be named after a very special lady.'

I glanced at my watch. There were still a few minutes before we had to leave. Today was a celebration of sorts though it didn't seem that way on paper. Today we were laying Violet to rest in the village churchyard, next to where her parents, and her baby brother, were buried.

It had taken a while for the experts to confirm it was Violet who we'd found in the stony cell in our attic.

Dr Davies and his enthusiastic students had done lots of

tests on the remains. They tested the DNA and they tested the bones, and they agreed the age of the remains was consistent with Violet's disappearance in 1855. And nestled inside Violet's tummy they found tiny, tiny bones that told them Violet had been pregnant, as I'd suspected, but hoped wasn't the case. It made the whole story even sadder, I thought.

While Dr Davies was doing his thing, Dad got the bit between his teeth and traced some living relatives, several generations removed from Violet's aunt – the one who'd looked after her for a while when she first lost her mother. Then Barb got on the case, and tracked them down. It turned out Violet's closest relations were a family who were living in Australia.

Barb rang one of them, and I had breathed a sigh of relief when the relative turned out to be an enthusiastic schoolteacher called Karl Rivers, who had a love of everything British and a passion for history.

He'd agreed immediately to have his DNA tested and had gone to his local police station the very next day to give his sample. The Aussie police sent it to Priya, she passed it on to Dr Davies, and we waited. It took weeks for the results to come back, but eventually it had been confirmed that the body in the attic was Violet.

I had been worried that we would never have official word that it was Violet – even though Ben and I were convinced – so I was really grateful for everyone's efforts. I emailed Karl pictures of Violet's paintings and told him what we knew about the mystery of her disappearance. He'd emailed me a link to an article in the local paper, over in Darwin, all about his British ancestor and his part in her discovery. He couldn't make it to the UK for today's service as it was the middle of the school term in Oz, but I had promised to write and tell him all about it.

I felt the baby move again, stirring me from my daydreams. 'Come on then,' I said to my belly. 'Let's go.'

Violet's memorial service – could it be considered a funeral so long after her death? I thought so, because that's what it was – was both the end of the story and the beginning, I mused as I wandered back towards the house. Violet was gone, but her reputation as an artist was just beginning to grow.

The day after Dr Davies and his team had taken Violet away, Ben and I had sat in the attic room and carefully unrolled the paintings that had been left in the cell. There were many – not as wonderful as the huge *Mariana* – but each told its own story.

'You can see how much she improved, the more she painted,' I had pointed out to Ben. 'Think how amazing she would have been if she'd carried on.'

We went back into the cell, the entrance now much bigger, and gazed at the mural on the wall.

'It's breathtaking,' I said. 'What will happen to it?'

'It's nothing to do with the police,' Ben said. 'I guess it will just stay here.'

But I wanted it seen. I couldn't bear to think of Violet's work being ignored for a moment longer, having been hidden for so long. So I photographed the paintings, and the mural, then emailed them to George. He arrived on virtually the next plane, sweating with the effort of travelling and desperate to see.

'This is astonishing,' he said, as I proudly showed him Violet's work. 'Astonishing.'

He touched the wall, ever so gently. 'We've been fortunate with the conditions in the room,' he said. 'There's very little environmental damage.'

'What can we do with it?' I asked. 'Can we save it?'

George looked at me over his shoulder. 'I think we have to,' he said.

It hadn't been easy especially as I'd been feeling sick then, as we tried to work out how to get the painting out of the house, but I'd thought it was just the excitement and stress. It was another couple of weeks before I found out I was pregnant.

Meanwhile, from St Andrews, George was working hard. He was contacting every Victorian art specialist he knew, and reading everything he could about the Pre-Raphaelites and their followers. He wrote a feature on Violet for an art journal and the photographer came to the house and snapped away at the mural and the crumbling wall that still hadn't been touched. We were all amazed and thrilled at how well it was received.

Then the Curator of Victorian Art from an art gallery in London came to visit. She was much younger than I had imagined, with a neat dark bob and nice shoes. Her eyes shone when I took her upstairs.

'Oh,' she breathed. 'Oh my.'

I imagined she was seeing her future mapped out as the person who discovered Violet Hargreaves.

'Can we move it?' I said, more abruptly than I'd meant to. 'I want people to see. I want them to know about her.'

'We can,' the curator said. 'We most certainly can.'

It had taken a team of restoration experts, artists, and

builders working together a full week to carefully take down the wall. They wrapped it in thick cords, then winched it down to the ground with the help of a crane and strong cables. The boys watched, fascinated, as the lorry churned up the lawn and men in fluorescent jackets called to each other while the wall edged its way down from the top of the house, leaving the hole covered in a tarpaulin that flapped dolefully in the sea wind. Thankfully the Tate covered the cost of rebuilding the attic wall, or it would have been a very cold winter.

Violet's exhibition would open at the Tate in September. The BBC were already recording a documentary about her and they were coming down to Sussex next week to film in the house. I had been writing faster than I'd ever written before and I'd delivered my delighted agent the manuscript for my version of Violet's story. It was being rushed out to coincide with the opening of the exhibition and already there was talk of the book being adapted for television. It would rival *Downton*, my agent had said when he came to see the house.

'This is the big one, Ella,' he'd said, gazing at my photos of *Mariana*, then looking at the rebuilt attic wall. 'This is huge. We'll push for someone fabulous to play Violet. That redhead from *Doctor Who*, she'd be perfect.'

But really, I thought, even though the big advance was desperately needed, and the boost to my career most welcome, really it was all about me, Ben, the boys, the new baby, and Violet.

Ben's job was going brilliantly, the boys were settled and happy, I was nervous about the new baby after what happened with Stan, but I was being well looked after at the hospital in Brighton and my doctor had assured me I was in safe hands.

And as for Violet, she was going to get the recognition she'd always wanted, albeit more than one hundred and fifty years too late.

Predictably, Priya hadn't let the birth of her twins slow her down. She'd talked through all my theories about what happened to Violet and we'd agreed that there had been an altercation outside the house – possibly a fight between Edwin and the gardener, William Philips.

Priya thought Violet and Frances probably witnessed the fight and had run – in different directions – from the violence. Violet had gone home and hidden (we hoped; I still couldn't bear the idea that someone had deliberately imprisoned her) and Frances had fled into her house where Edwin attacked her.

Of course we still didn't know if she had pushed Edwin down the stairs, or if he'd fallen. I didn't really care. I thought Frances was a hero and I knew Edwin was the villain. I wanted Edwin's role in Violet's death, and the truth about how he stole Violet's work and beat Frances, to be exposed. And today Violet would finally be gently put into a real grave, with a headstone that people could visit and put flowers on.

I had continued to work in the attic – once the wall had been rebuilt. Some people asked me if it was creepy, knowing Violet's body had been there, that Violet had died there, but I didn't feel like that at all. It felt peaceful.

'Ready?' Ben slung his arm around my shoulders and I turned to kiss him.

'Ready,' I said. 'I just needed a minute.'

Ben nodded. 'I'm not surprised,' he said. 'It's been a hell of a year.'

Together we walked up the garden towards the house. The boys were standing at the kitchen door, smart in chinos and blue shirts, along with Barb and my dad.

'Winnie Flood is meeting us at the church,' Ben said. 'She's coming back to the house afterwards though. Her daughter's coming with her.'

'I'm so pleased she could come,' I said. 'This is Frances's story too so it's right that her family are involved.'

'Come on then, fatso,' Ben said. He waved to the boys and Stan barrelled towards him.

I paused and watched my family walk out of the garden gate. Then I looked up at the attic window where, all those months ago, I'd first thought I'd seen a figure. For a minute, I thought I could see someone standing there. But when I blinked, the figure was gone.

Loved *The Girl in the Picture*?
Then turn the page for an
exclusive extract from
THE FORGOTTEN GIRL

Chapter 1

2016

I was nervous. Not just a little bit wobbly. I was properly, squeaky-voiced, sweaty-palms, absolutely bloody terrified. And that was very unlike me.

The office was just up ahead – I could see it from where I stood, lurking behind my sunglasses in case anyone I knew spotted me and tried to speak to me. I wasn't ready for conversation yet. The building had a glass front, with huge blown-up magazine covers in its windows. In pride of place, right next to the revolving door, was the cover from the most recent issue of *Mode*.

I swallowed.

'It's fine,' I muttered to myself. 'They wouldn't have given you the job if they didn't think you were up to it. It's fine. You're fine. Better than fine. You're brilliant.'

I took a deep breath, straightened my back, threw back my shoulders and headed to the Starbucks opposite me.

I ordered an espresso and a soya latte, then I sat down to compose myself for a minute.

Today was my first day as editor of *Mode*. It was the job I'd wanted since I was a teenager. It had been my dream for so long, I could barely believe it was happening, and I was determined to make a success of it.

Except here I was, ready to get started, and I'd been floored by these nerves.

Shaking slightly, I downed my espresso in one like it was a shot of tequila and checked the time on my phone. I was early, but that was no bad thing. I had lots of good luck messages – mostly from people hoping I'll give them a job, I thought wryly. I couldn't help noticing, as I scrolled through and deleted them, that there was nothing from my best friend, Jen. She was obviously still upset about the way I'd behaved when I'd got the job. And if I was honest, she had every right to be upset, but I didn't have time to worry about that now. I was sure she'd come round.

I stood up and straightened my clothes. I'd played it safe this morning with black skinny trousers, a fitted black shirt and funky leopard-print pumps. My naturally curly blonde hair was straightened and pulled into a sleek ponytail and I wore a slash of red lipstick. I looked good. I just hoped it was good enough for the editor of *Mode*.

A surge of excitement bubbled up inside me. I was the editor of *Mode*. Me. Fearne Summers. I picked up my latte and looped my arm through my Marc Jacobs tote.

'Right, Fearne,' I said out loud. 'Let's do this.'

I wasn't expecting a welcoming committee or a cheerleading squad waiting for me in reception (well, I was a bit) but I did think that the bored woman behind the desk could have at least cracked a smile. Or she could have tried to look a tiny bit impressed that I was the new editor of *Mode*. Mind you, if this office was anything like my old place – and I was pretty sure all magazine companies were the same – there would be a never-ending stream of celebrities, models, and strange

PR stunts (last Christmas we'd had mince pies delivered by a llama wearing a Santa hat, and that was one of the more normal visitors). Perhaps a new editor was terribly run of the mill.

'Here's your pass,' she said, throwing it across the desk at me. 'The office is on the third floor, but you're to go up to fifth first of all to meet Lizzie.'

I was surprised. Lizzie was the chief-exec of Glam Media, the company that owned *Mode* along with lots of other magazines. I knew I'd have to catch up with her at some point today but I thought she'd give me time to meet my team, and find my office first.

Lizzie was waiting for me when I got out of the lift. The bored receptionist must have told her I was on my way.

She was in her early fifties, petite and stylishly dressed, with a cloud of dark hair. She was friendly and approachable, but she had a reputation of being ruthless in pursuit of profit for the company. She scared the bejesus out of me if I was honest, but she'd been very nice when I met her at one of the many interviews I'd done to get the job. Now she smiled at me and shook my hand.

'Great to have you on board, Fearne,' she said. 'This is a time of big change for *Mode*.'

'I've got loads of ideas,' I said, following her down the corridor to a meeting room. 'I can't wait to get started.'

She gave me a brief smile over her shoulder.

'Great,' she said again.

Except she didn't really mean great, I quickly discovered. She meant, *yeah good luck with that, Fearne.*

It turned out that Glam Media was worried about *Mode*.

Really worried. I'd looked at the sales, of course, and seen they weren't as good as they could be but I hadn't really grasped just how much trouble the magazine was in.

'The problem is the competition has really raised its game,' Lizzie explained as I stared out of the big window in her office and tried to take in everything she was saying.

'*Grace?*' I said. It had been a fairly boring, unadventurous magazine called *Home & Hearth* until it was bought by a new company and had loads of money pumped into it. Now it had a new name, it was exciting and fun, and it was stealing lots of *Mode's* readers.

'So the finance department have redone your budgets for this year,' said Lizzie. 'To reflect *Mode's* sales.'

She slid a piece of paper across her desk and I stared at the figures she'd put in front of me in horror.

'I can't run a glossy mag on this budget,' I said. 'How am I supposed to pay for fashion shoots? Or commission writers?'

Lizzie shrugged.

'Times are tough,' she said. 'That's all that's in the pot.'

'Can't I have some of the website budget?' I asked.

She shook her head.

'Digital budget is separate,' she said. 'The website's going very well. Advertising and readership are both up. It's the magazine that's in trouble.'

I looked at her, suddenly realising where this was going, and why my predecessor had been so keen to leave her job.

'Are you going to close *Mode?*' I asked.

She stared back at me.

'Nothing's decided yet.'

'But it's possible?'

Lizzie looked at a point somewhere past my ear.

'Print isn't working,' she said.

'But *Mode* is an iconic brand,' I said desperately. 'It's been going since the sixties. It was the first ever young women's glossy. You can't close it.'

Lizzie still didn't look me in the eye, but she did at least assume a slightly sympathetic expression.

'We'd still have the website,' she said. 'It's not ending, it's just changing. *Mode* will still exist – just in a different form.'

'A glossy mag is a treat,' I said. 'People will pay for that.'

She shrugged.

'Would people lose their jobs?' I asked, suddenly realising this didn't just affect me.

'That's also possible,' she said.

I put my head in my hands. This was a nightmare. My dream job was collapsing around my ears.

Lizzie took a breath.

'Fearne, we took you on for a reason,' she said. 'You're a great editor with a good reputation.'

I forced myself to raise my head and smile at her. That was nice to hear.

'But you're also known for being cut-throat,' she carried on. 'We all know you're single-minded and determined. That you don't let anything get in the way of success,'

I nodded slowly. I wasn't sure I'd use the word 'cut-throat' but I was definitely single-minded.

'We know you won't let emotions or sentiment get in the way of doing your job.'

Oh.

'You brought me here to close the magazine?' I said, as I worked it all out.

Lizzie had the grace to look slightly shame-faced.

'Well,' she said. 'Close it or make it work. Take back some of the sales we've lost to *Grace*.'

I looked at the budget again. With the figures she'd given me it was obvious which option she wanted. I could barely cover the staffing costs with this amount of money – and I had no chance of booking top photographers or paying for big-name writers. It was an impossible task.

'How long have I got?' I said. 'How long do I have to make *Mode* pay?'

Lizzie looked a bit confused. She'd clearly not considered this.

'Six months?'

I swallowed.

'Give me a year,' I said, wondering how on earth I managed to keep my voice steady when I was so terrified by the task that lay ahead. 'I need a year to have a proper go at this.'

Lizzie looked at something on the papers in front of her. She rubbed the bridge of her nose and sighed.

'Nine months?' she said.

I shrugged.

'Is that the best you can offer?' I said. She nodded.

'So if I can increase sales enough in that time, you'll let the magazine carry on?' I said.

Lizzie nodded again.

'If you can make it work on the new budget, then we'll reconsider,' she said, sounding incredulous that I was even thinking about it.

'Great,' I said, faking excitement when all I felt was despair. 'Nine months is more than enough.'

I gathered up my things and stood up, hoping she couldn't see my legs trembling. 'If you'll excuse me, I'm going to meet my team now.'

Dear Reader,

Thank you so much for taking the time to read this book – we hope you enjoyed it! If you did, we'd be so appreciative if you left a review.

Here at HQ Digital we are dedicated to publishing fiction that will keep you turning the pages into the early hours. We publish a variety of genres, from heartwarming romance, to thrilling crime and sweeping historical fiction.

To find out more about our books, enter competitions and discover exclusive content, please join our community of readers by following us at:

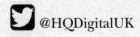 @HQDigitalUK

 facebook.com/HQDigitalUK

Are you a budding writer? We're also looking for authors to join the HQ Digital family! Please submit your manuscript to:

HQDigital@harpercollins.co.uk.

Hope to hear from you soon!

ONE PLACE. MANY STORIES